LIGHTHOUSE POINT

AJ BAILEY ADVENTURE SERIES - BOOK 15

NICHOLAS HARVEY

This book is dedicated to the memory of Daniel Wheldon.
Motor racing can still be a cruel sport.
Rest in peace my friend.
1978 - 2011

1

1968 – ANTWERP, BELGIUM

The narrow paved street of Hoveniersstraat was bustling with people, wandering from stand to stand as vendors did their best to peddle their goods, proffering fruits, vegetables, delicacies, and treats alongside clothes and essential household items. The tall stone and concrete buildings towered over the activities while diamond merchants, mostly dressed in traditional Jewish long black coats and wide-brimmed hats, bartered and traded as they roamed from door to door.

A man, using the codename Shepard and wearing the overalls of a Régie des Télégraphes et Téléphones technician, followed an elderly merchant through a door, unlocked by a security guard. The diamond merchant nodded politely to the guard and Shepard did the same, waiting for the man's eyes to flash recognition, before following half a flight of stairs behind the merchant to the third floor. The Jewish man entered an open door to his premises, into a small reception area, and nodded to the woman behind the desk. He then unlocked a security door using three keys before continuing to the back of the business. Shepard pretended to be focused on the telephone wires strung along the top of the wall as he watched from the corner of his eye until the security door was closed and he caught the sound of locks being turned. He continued following the lines, which dropped to a service box mounted on the wall of the square landing surrounding the stairwell. A closed door opposite led from the space into another business catering to the diamond trade, as did all the offices in the building.

Shepard dropped his soft-sided tool bag from his gloved hand to the tiled floor, unzipped the top and took out a walkie-talkie.

Keying the mic, he spoke quietly in Dutch, "Shepard to Glenn. I'm at the third floor box. Over."

After a moment, a man's crackly voice replied. "Glenn to Shepard. Roger. I'm at the main feed. Over."

"Okay. Do it now," Shepard ordered, then placed the radio back in the bag and unlocked the service box, revealing a nest of telephone wires.

Entering the door where he'd followed the merchant, Shepard forced the smile of a labourer in the midst of tackling a problem. "Phone service will be down for ten, maybe twenty minutes. Sorry," he said and turned to leave.

"No, no. You can't do that," the woman fussed from behind the desk. "Our security relies on the telephone."

"I'll let you know if I see any thief-like men coming your way. I'm just out here in the hall," Shepard replied, and moved to the door.

"No, no, please wait a moment," the woman urged. "Let me get Mr Gunzburg. He'll want to talk to you."

"I really don't have time for chatting with your boss," Shepard said impatiently. "After this, they have me on a job over by the river. You know how long it'll take me to get there in city traffic?"

"I'll get him right now," the woman replied, rushing to the inner door where she knocked three times, then pressed a button which sounded a buzzer on the other side of the concrete wall and steel door.

After a few moments with the woman standing in front of the

door so she could be seen through the security peephole, latches slid, locks turned, and the door opened.

"I think Mr Gunzburg should come out and speak with the telephone repair man," she explained to a person Shepard couldn't see. "He's about to shut off the service."

The voice from the other room replied in what Shepard assumed was Yiddish, as he didn't understand a word, but the door closed and the locks were reset.

"He'll be right out," the woman relayed before shuffling back behind the desk.

Shepard looked at his watch, huffed, then shrugged his shoulders and began looking at the framed pictures of diamonds in various settings adorning the walls. He didn't have long to wait. The secure door was unlocked and the man he'd followed earlier appeared, a pained look on his face.

"I'm Idel Gunzburg, the owner. What's going on?"

"Gotta take your line down for a bit," Shepard replied. "Mice."

"Mice?" Gunzburg questioned.

"Yeah. Little bastards have chewed through some wires in the box outside. Won't take us long. Twenty minutes, tops."

"Régie des Télégraphes et Téléphones didn't call to tell me. I have to make special arrangements for the phone lines to be down. Besides, my phone is working fine."

"I doubt it," Shepard countered. "Wire's half chewed through outside. Built quite the nest. We've been fixing lines for the past few days. Yours should be the last one."

Gunzburg turned to his receptionist. "Our telephone line is working, right?"

"Last call I had earlier this morning it was," she replied, and picked up the receiver. She quickly pulled it away from her ear. "It's all crackly now." She handed the receiver to Gunzburg.

He frowned at the sound through the earpiece. "It was fine this morning."

Shepard shrugged his shoulders. "Guess the little bastards

chewed on yours for breakfast. We got a call the other day from someone else in the building about their line. Found one hell of a mess downstairs in the service box. But I can leave yours if you like. Call the RTT office and schedule another time when you can organise your security or whatever you need to do. No skin off my nose."

He started towards the door once more.

"How do I call when the phone doesn't work!" Gunzburg exclaimed.

"Borrow next door's," Shepard suggested. "Theirs is fine, I believe."

Gunzburg waved his hand in the air. "He's a schmuck. We don't talk."

Shepard huffed. "You want it fixed or not, sir?"

"I want my daughter to marry a prince, but she's dating a moron with a fast car and a father who works for a man who sells fish. It doesn't seem to matter what I want," Gunzburg fumed. "So fix the telephone and pray I don't get robbed blind while the wretched thing is broken."

Shepard nodded.

"I'll get the security guard up here, just in case," the old man added.

Shepard realised Gunzburg was following him into the wide hallway surrounding the stairwell. The square opening in the centre allowed them to see all the way down to the ground floor.

"I'd tell him to stop anyone he doesn't know from coming in, and leave him down there," Shepard said disinterestedly. "Can't rob you if they can't come in the building."

Gunzburg thought for a moment. "He's not supposed to let anyone in who doesn't work here or have an appointment. If he's up here, no one without a key can come in."

"I came in without a key," Shepard pointed out.

Gunzburg frowned. "You followed me in," he said, as though he'd just solved an unsolvable mystery. "Are you planning on robbing me?"

"My wife prefers rubies," Shepard replied, keeping his left hand tucked in his pocket so his lack of wedding band wasn't visible. Although, he considered, his soon to be ex-girlfriend would gladly take any gemstone he brought home.

"I have rubies," Gunzburg claimed. "I'm known for the diamonds, but I could put a lovely ruby on your wife's finger."

"I think I would have to rob you," Shepard laughed. "I'm sure I couldn't afford to buy one."

"That's probably true." The merchant looked over the railing again and saw the security guard in the entry foyer, thought for another moment, then grunted and turned around. "Do me a favour. Let me know if you see any jewel thieves coming up the stairs."

"You'll be the first to know," Shepard assured him.

Gunzburg continued into his reception area and Shepard checked his watch as he fished the walkie-talkie from his bag.

"Shepard to Glenn. Two minutes until lunch. Stand by. Over."

"Glenn to Shepard. Copy."

Taking a few tools from his bag, he set them on the floor and pulled on a clump of telephone wires, letting a loop dangle from the service box, making it appear as though work was in progress. He thumbed through the lines until he found the one he was looking for, diligently labelled by the installer. He cut the wire.

A few minutes later, doors on different floors opened as employees left the businesses for their lunch breaks. Shepard waited until six people had left Gunzburg's office, then picked up the walkie-talkie once more.

"Shepard to Glenn. We're a go. Over."

"Copy," came the reply.

Shepard briskly walked into the reception carrying his tool bag, where the same woman was still at the desk.

"How many phones do you have inside?" he asked.

"Back there?" she countered, pointing over her shoulder.

"Yeah. We've located this line," he said, nodding to her desk, "And two more lines we think go back there."

"We have three," she replied.

"Then that's the three lines we found."

"No, we have three back there, plus this one," the woman corrected.

"Oh. Then we're missing one at the service box."

"No one has said their telephone isn't working," she replied.

"That's 'cos it probably is, but the idiots who installed them didn't label them all, so we can't check it on our end," he explained. "I just need to send a signal down the line and my co-worker will tag the line so we have them sorted."

"Mr Gunzburg won't like this," she said, shaking her head.

Shepard sighed. "Can't say I'm thrilled myself, ma'am. If they'd just labelled them properly, I'd be wrapping up by now. We'd connect the repaired wires downstairs and be off."

He looked at the woman, who was yet to move from her chair. Finally, she must have decided to face her boss one more time, as she stood and moved to the security door and knocked three times, paused, then hit the buzzer. After a few moments, the door opened a crack.

"What is it now?" Gunzburg asked, remaining out of Shepard's view.

"It's the telephone man," the woman explained. "He can't find one of our lines and says he has to come back there."

"Well, he can't," the merchant snapped.

"That's what I told him," she quickly replied.

"Then why are you bothering me?"

"Because I can't finish up until I track your last line," Shepard intervened. "Take me less than two minutes and I'll be out of your hair."

Silence followed, and the woman shifted uncomfortably from foot to foot.

"Two minutes?" Gunzburg finally asked.

"Or less," Shepard confirmed.

The door opened wider, and the receptionist stepped aside. Shepard walked through into a room with a long workbench down the centre. Three polishing stations adorned each side of the bench with circular polishing wheels and the various holders, tools, and magnifying lenses for viewing, shaping, and finishing the stones. All six stools were vacant, just as Shepard had hoped.

Gunzburg closed and locked the door. "I have a telephone in my office. There's one over here in the polishing room, and a third in my display room."

Shepard's eyes nonchalantly surveyed the area, pausing deliberately on the telephone for a moment, before taking in everything else. The work areas contained all the paraphernalia for working with diamonds, but not a single stone. As he'd learnt in his research, the merchants insisted every diamond, finished or not, be locked away when not being worked on or shown to a client.

He walked to the telephone and picked up the receiver, hearing a scratchy, crackling sound.

"Not that one," he said, and looked at Gunzburg. "Your office?"

The man led Shepard across the workshop to a door, which he unlocked and swung open. Inside, a cluttered desk overflowed with paperwork. Shepard found the telephone amongst the mess and picked up the receiver.

"Not this one either."

He stepped out of the office and the merchant locked the door behind him before pausing and scratching his chin.

"I'll bring the telephone out and you can test it on one of these lines," he said.

Shepard shook his head. "It's not the telephone I need, it's the line. Besides, they're all hard wired for security reasons."

"Then you stay out here and I'll hand you the telephone through the door."

"Sure. If it'll reach," Shepard replied.

The older man nodded and sorted through a ring of keys he pulled from his pocket. The door to the next room was steel with multiple locks. Gunzburg turned two keys in the locks, but paused before the third, key in hand.

"Wait over there a bit," he said, shooing Shepard farther from the door.

"No problem," the technician replied, holding up both hands and stepping backwards two steps. "This will only take a minute, I promise."

Gunzburg turned the third lock, twisted the handle, and before the door had opened more than a few inches, Shepard descended upon him. With a brutal shove, the diamond merchant was thrust into the room, bashing his head on the steel door and tumbling to the floor. Groaning, he turned on his side and looked up. Shepard stared down at him with a cruel grin.

"You didn't trust your instincts, old man. You knew something wasn't right all along, didn't you?"

Gunzburg groaned again and nodded. Shepard stepped over him and turned on the light switch. The small room was spotless. In the centre, black velvet covered a table, and at one end, a large safe was built into the wall.

"Get up," Shepard demanded. "Open it."

"I might as well die," Gunzburg murmured, wincing in pain. "My life is over if you take what's in there."

Shepard reached into his tool bag and raised a gun, aiming at the merchant's face. "I can make that happen, but you should know I'll be waiting for your workers to return, and if they can't, or won't, open the safe, I'll shoot them one by one. You have two sons working here, I believe. And a brother."

The merchant's eyes met Shepard's, searching for something in the gunman's face. If it was sympathy or compassion he hoped to find, Shepard offered nothing but disappointment.

"They don't know the combination," Gunzburg said.

"Then they'll all die for your stubbornness."

"You'll ruin me."

"I don't care," Shepard replied. "Open the safe."

Gunzburg moaned, but dragged himself across the floor to the safe. Shepard watched the old man haul himself to his feet, putting a hand on top of the six-foot-tall safe, steadying himself. His fingers fumbled around.

"I don't blame you for trying," Shepard said. "But I cut that wire. Your light in the reception is disconnected."

Gunzburg's shoulders slumped even further and his hand left the top of the safe. "They ran the wire outside my offices?"

"Pretty stupid, huh?" Shepard responded.

The diamond merchant shook his head and began turning the dial on the safe, entering his combination.

2

PRESENT DAY – BONAIRE

Annabelle Jayne Bailey jerked forward in her seat as the roar of jet engines startled her awake and her headphones tumbled to her lap. Her travel partner, friend, and mentor, Reg Moore, chuckled in his deep voice, sounding like a diesel generator chugging away.

"We there?" she mumbled, gathering up her headphones and wiping a little drool from the corner of her mouth.

"Nah," Reg replied in his London accent. "We landed on the Caribbean Sea to refuel and get more appetising snacks for you."

AJ rubbed her eyes and squinted out the window.

"Course we're here, you plonker," Reg added.

Sweeping her shoulder-length purple-streaked blonde hair from her face, AJ looked around as the plane shuddered to a crawl before turning around at the end of the runway.

"It's flat. Like Cayman," she commented.

"This end is," Reg replied. "North end is hilly."

AJ tried to stretch, but the seating area was too small, even for her five-foot-four frame. She was about to complain but looked at Reg, who was built like a six-foot bear, and decided to stay quiet. He'd been crushed into his seat for three and a half hours and was over twice her age.

The plane stopped on the tarmac and AJ read a sign in large blue letters along a pink wall, 'Flamingo Airport'. Beyond, the pink and white theme extended across the terminal building. She'd read a bit about the Dutch island of Bonaire, and knew of its reputation as a Mecca for scuba divers, but this would be her first visit. Running a dive operation in Grand Cayman offered little time for travel, and getting from one Caribbean Island to another wasn't as easy as it might seem. They'd had to fly north to Miami in order to turn around and fly a long way south to reach the ABC Islands just above Venezuela.

"Bloody hell, it's windy," she muttered, walking down the old style airstair, wrestling two overloaded carry-on bags.

"Blows like this most of the time here," Reg said, plodding down the steps behind her, managing his own bags with ease. "Partly why it's drier and less humid."

AJ lumbered towards the terminal, then dumped her bags on the ground when a lady in a uniform asked for her proof of entry tax. Fumbling with her mobile phone, she found the confirmation and showed the woman, who scanned the QR code before waving her on.

"Temperature's lovely," she said, waiting in line for the immigration booth under a covered outdoor entrance.

"About like home," Reg remarked, edging forward after each person ahead cleared the booth.

AJ handed over her UK passport.

"Purpose for your visit?" the officer asked in Dutch-accented English.

"Diving," AJ replied.

The stern, square-jawed young man looked from AJ to Reg. "Travelling together?"

"Yeah," AJ replied. "Brought my grandad along so he can sit on the beach with a hanky on his head like they do in Blackpool. Do you have bingo games here?"

The officer frowned at her.

"Don't listen to her," Reg growled. "She banged her head as a child. We work together, and I'm not her bloody grandad."

"So you're here to work?" the officer quickly responded, but didn't wait for an answer. Instead, he waved another officer over who he spoke to in Dutch before turning back to AJ and Reg.

"Go with this man."

An hour later, AJ and Reg left the office of Bonaire's immigration and customs service and stomped in silence to baggage claim where theirs was the only luggage next to a motionless carousel. With bags being rolled, carried, and slung across their bodies, the two were waved through the final customs check and they shuffled through the automatic doors to exit the airport. The moment the doors closed behind them, they broke their silence.

"You had to bring up work, you silly sod!" AJ started.

"Me? You started this by calling me grandad, you cheeky little cow!"

"Calling you a relative is a long way from telling the immigration bloke we're here on a job!" she rebutted. "We agreed it was best to say we're on holiday!"

"Well, you buggered that up," Reg growled.

"Me!"

The barbs and bickering continued as they walked to the kerb, then quickly stopped when a van rolled to a halt beside them. A debonair-looking older man opened the passenger door and stepped out.

"Reg Moore?" he asked in accented English.

Reg extended his hand. "Pleased to meet you, sir. Sorry we're late." He turned to AJ, who extended her hand. "This is AJ Bailey."

"John de Konig," the man replied, shaking their hands in turn. "I was beginning to worry."

"Slight delay in immigration, but all sorted now," Reg said, frowning at AJ.

"Hopefully you told them you were here on holiday," De Konig said with a wry grin. "Saves a lot of hassle."

AJ scoffed but didn't say anything.

"Right, let's get these loaded up," Reg grumbled, picking up a couple of their bags stuffed full of dive gear.

A second man, who'd come around from the driver's side, opened the rear doors, and Reg began loading their gear. AJ helped and offered her hand to the driver.

"AJ. Nice to meet you."

"Laurens," the man replied, shaking with a firm grip.

He wasn't a tall man, but he was stocky and muscular with the short cropped hair of the military. AJ guessed he was a little older than herself. Probably mid to late thirties. He eyed her colourful full-sleeve tattoos, but didn't comment or alter his stern expression.

"Laurens is the diver I mentioned," De Konig offered. "He'll be accompanying you."

Reg nodded to the younger man. "It'll be great to have someone along with local knowledge."

Laurens returned a hint of a smile, then continued loading bags in the back.

"Did you eat on the plane?" De Konig asked.

AJ scoffed again. "If you call the tiniest bag of pretzels known to man a meal, then we did," she said and laughed. "Air travel is to be endured rather than enjoyed these days."

"Very true," De Konig agreed. "We waited to eat, so we'll stop on the way to the apartment I rented for you."

After they'd all climbed into the van, Laurens drove them out of the airport to a two-lane road where he turned left. The surface was paved but patched and bumpy, the van jolting with every seam. Within a hundred yards, the road curved left and paralleled the bright blue ocean, which appeared to be tranquil and calm. The dusty landscape was unlike any Caribbean island AJ had been to. A few hardy looking trees lined the road, and the ground was sun-baked pale brown dirt which blended seamlessly into sand near the ocean's edge.

With the airport runway still on their left, Laurens pulled over to the side of the road and stopped near a small, brightly coloured trailer. As they hopped out, AJ noticed the sign read 'Cactus Blue'.

Through the open flaps at the rear and the side facing the ocean, she saw a pretty woman cooking food on a grill.

"Best lunch on the island," De Konig claimed, and the woman turned and smiled.

"*Hallo,* John," the lady greeted him.

"I brought some friends straight from the airport," De Konig said, using English. "They said they were hungry."

"*Goedendag,*" the lady greeted AJ and Reg. "I can take care of your hunger. You like burgers?"

"Do you have fish?" AJ asked. "I don't eat meat."

"I have fresh lionfish. It's our speciality."

AJ beamed. "Perfect. We hunt them at home."

"We'll have four, thank you, Tham," De Konig said cheerily, looking at Reg for his approval.

Reg nodded. "Good with me."

De Konig lifted the lid of a large cooler and handed each of them a glass bottle. "Fresh local fruit juice," he announced and pointed to a bottle opener on a string.

The group sat, sipping on their drinks while Tham worked away in the trailer and the ocean lapped gently against the shore just fifty feet away.

"How soon can you start diving?" De Konig asked, looking at Reg.

"Tomorrow I'd say, if we can get all the tanks we need," Reg replied. "I emailed with Technical Diving Services Bonaire and they say they have everything. We just need to decide on our schedule and dive plans, then I can have them fill tanks as needed."

"What do you need from me?" De Konig asked.

AJ looked over at Laurens, who didn't seem to say very much. "Have you dived the site?"

Laurens shook his head. "No. We don't believe anyone has."

AJ noticed his accent was stronger than the older man's and wondered if his quiet manner was simply a lack of confidence in his English. His general demeanour didn't appear to lack any confidence. Far from it. He moved with the purpose of a man who committed to everything he did, and his stern expression hadn't wavered yet.

"But you're sure this is the wreck you've been looking for?" Reg asked.

"Between the sonar scans and dropping a camera down, I'm confident enough to hire you two," De Konig responded with a reserved grin.

"Here you go," Tham called out from the trailer.

They all went to the counter and collected their lionfish burgers, which were garnished with jalapeños, cheese, green onions, and a honey mustard dressing. The meat eaters also had bacon, but Tham had left it off AJ's. Sitting back down, no one said a word for several minutes as they ate.

"This is amazing," AJ finally said, loudly enough for Tham to hear.

The chef smiled and gave her a thumbs-up.

"Bloody good," Reg agreed. "How confident are you on your depth readings?" he asked, turning back to the two men while wiping mustard from the corner of his mouth.

"Our soundings support what we see on the marine charts," De Konig replied. "The wreck is at 64 metres. Or 210 feet, if you'd prefer."

"The sea floor slopes away fairly quickly here, doesn't it?" Reg asked. "So 210 feet can't be that far from shore."

De Konig nodded. "It's off a headland and the underwater geography mimics the land, so there's a narrow shelf which extends shallower for farther than the sea floor surrounding it. It's almost half a kilometre from shore, so too far to access without a boat."

"When we spoke, you mentioned you had a suitable boat," Reg continued. "But no onboard compressor to fill tanks, correct?"

"It's a 36-foot catamaran with twin outboards and a full canopy for shade. I think you'll find it adequate," De Konig explained.

Reg looked over at AJ, who'd been enjoying her sandwich and listening in to the conversation.

"We can work up a dive plan for two dives tomorrow," she offered. "As long as they can fill tanks first thing in the morning."

Reg looked at Laurens. "Do you know the guys at TDS?"

He shook his head.

"Alright. I'll call them once we get to our digs," Reg responded.

AJ finished her lionfish burger and stood, looking around for a rubbish bin.

"Blimey. Someone's donkeys have got out," she said, seeing three of them wandering down the beach towards them.

"No, they're wild here," De Konig replied, not appearing surprised at all.

"They just saunter about all over the island?" AJ asked, as one donkey loped along in her direction.

"Yes. There's a donkey sanctuary and they round up the ones they can, but a large population still lives in the wild."

The donkey stopped three paces away from AJ and looked at her. His compatriots hung farther back.

"Sorry," she told the grey animal. "I didn't think to bring donkey treats with me, mate."

The donkey kept staring at her.

"You're not supposed to feed the wild donkeys," De Konig explained. "It makes them seek out people and vehicles, which gets them run over."

"I think this one has already figured out that people have tasty treats," AJ chuckled, easing a step closer.

"He's figured out the easy mark," Reg scoffed. "Picked you out from a hundred yards."

"Here," Tham called out. "Don't tell anyone."

She tossed an apple to AJ, who caught it, and by the time she'd turned back to the donkey, he'd covered the distance between them. She held the apple out and he didn't waste any time worrying about whether it was donkey diet friendly. He bit off half of it and crunched away contentedly while his buddies began crowding in. AJ outstretched her flattened palm and the first one on the scene took the second half.

"Snooze you lose," she told the third donkey, who looked at her disconsolately.

She turned to Tham, who shook her head. "I only had the one."

AJ reached over and stroked the third donkey's head. "Sorry mate, I'll bring you something tomorrow."

Reg shook his head as he stood. "Been here an hour and you're already breaking the bloody rules."

"It's probably a guideline more than a rule," she countered, wiping the donkey slobber on her leggings.

"No. It's a rule," De Konig said with a chuckle as he paid Tham.

Tham winked at AJ. "These three are on the sanctuary's list to pick up, so it'll make it easier for them if they come right up to them."

"See," AJ said, playfully thumping Reg on his beefy arm.

The donkeys watched them walk towards the van.

"So, you've been pretty cryptic about exactly where we're diving," Reg said before they got in. "Do we get to know now we're here?"

De Konig opened the passenger door, then paused. "My apologies for the secrecy, but you know how these things are."

"Sure," Reg agreed. "But you told me it's just an old barge with someone's possessions on board. Hardly the Nuestra Señora de Atocha treasure fleet."

De Konig smiled. "Indeed, it is not, but I must still insist upon the utmost discretion and security."

"Goes without saying, mate," Reg assured him. "Mum's the word."

De Konig nodded once more. "You'll be diving off Lighthouse Point."

3

1968 – ANTWERP, BELGIUM

Idel Gunzburg sat at the black velvet-covered table with his head in hands. Shepard pulled the remaining tools from his bag and placed them on the floor, then removed his work gloves, keeping on the thin, soft cotton gloves he wore beneath. Systematically, he pulled tray after tray of precious gems from the safe, placing them on the table. From the bottom shelf, he took stacks of cash, which he stuffed in the bottom of the bag.

Shepard glanced at his watch. It was 12:35pm. The workers would be back at 1:00pm, expecting Gunzburg to let them in. When he didn't, the alarm would be raised and Shepard knew he and Glenn needed to be long gone by then.

"No reputable cutter will accept those uncut diamonds," the old man muttered, looking up. "Once the word is out, you'll have nowhere to take them."

Shepard ignored the man, opening drawers instead until he found one filled with empty soft jewellery bags. He threw a handful onto the table and began filling them first with cut and polished stones, then with smaller uncut gems. He paused when he reached a tray containing rubies and emeralds.

"If I had a wife, no doubt she'd be pleased with these," he said, and shovelled them into a bag.

"My work is known worldwide," Gunzburg said, watching his life savings and current inventory being stolen before his eyes. "The best buyers who handle gems of this value will recognise my cut. You'll be caught as soon as you try to sell them."

"You seem to think I run in reputable circles, old man," Shepard replied, continuing sorting and filling bags, which he then dropped into his duffel. "I operate in a different market."

Gunzburg nodded in submissive agreement. "True, no doubt. But one day a stone will find its way back to a reputable jeweller, and they'll alert the authorities."

"I'm sure you're right," Shepard sneered, examining the gemstones he'd chosen to leave behind. "But by then, that'll be of little concern to me."

The diamond merchant followed Shepard's stare and looked over the trays, no doubt noting the thief had left the largest and most valuable cut and polished stones. He'd taken every uncut diamond and all the smaller finished gems.

"Your business will survive," Shepard said, seeing the man's surprise.

Gunzburg nodded again. "You've planned this well. And, perhaps, my business will remain, but what about me? I've seen your face."

Satisfied with his choices, Shepard zipped the tool bag closed and picked up a roll of duct tape he'd removed with the tools.

"So have many other people in and around the building over the past few days while I made sure they were used to me coming and going," Shepard replied. "Shooting them all would take too long and cause far too much of a commotion, so it's your lucky day. Put your hands together behind your back."

Gunzburg did so and twisted in the chair so Shepard could wrap the tape around his wrists. "I'd be lying if I said I felt lucky, but I'll accept your offer not to kill me."

Shepard stole another glance at his watch, noting it was now

12:42pm. He quickly tore off another strip and placed it over the diamond merchant's mouth. The old man snorted and huffed, verging on panic.

"Breathe through your nose. You'll be fine."

Picking up Gunzburg's keys and the tool bag, Shepard checked around for anything he didn't want to leave behind. The tools, stolen from a work site months before, had been carefully handled with gloves and held only the fingerprints of the original owners. He hoped leaving them would focus the authorities' attentions in the wrong place for a while. Noticing his work gloves on the table, he slipped them back on, then picked up the bag and keys once more.

Locking the door behind him, leaving the old man trapped in his own secure room, Shepard briskly moved across the workshop floor. Fiddling with the keys, he finally found the right one for each of the three locks and pushed the door open. The receptionist was looking his way as he stepped through the doorway.

"That was a lot longer than two minutes," she pointed out.

Shepard pantomimed saying goodbye to Gunzburg before turning to the woman. "Yeah, but we finally figured it out." He nodded towards the front door. "Would you mind seeing if my partner is down in the lobby? Just peek over the railing for me while I double-check your line."

The receptionist hesitated. "I just tried it again a few minutes ago and there's still no dial tone."

Shepard raised his tool bag, which weighed far more now that it was full of money and gems. "I have a testing device in here. Just have a quick look for me. The guard has probably kept him down there."

Still looking confused, the woman stood and walked out to the stairwell. Shepard quickly locked all three deadbolts, struggling with the last one as he heard her footsteps returning.

"I don't see anyone…"

"That's okay, he's still outside," Shepard said, cutting her off. "We'll finish up out there and you'll be all set."

"Okay," she stammered, taking her seat. "And Mr Gunzburg knows all this, I assume?"

"He's fully aware of what's going on," Shepard replied as he hurried from the reception, keeping the keys hidden in his pocket.

Moving directly to the stairs, he briskly scampered down, taking two at a time. Halfway down, he slowed to a more casual pace as he passed by two of Gunzburg's employees on their way up. He kept his head down and they ignored him, deep in their own conversation. Shepard knew they'd be knocking on the inner door to the workshop in no time, so he quickened his pace again, pausing for the security guard to open the lobby door.

"All done?" the man asked.

"Almost," Shepard replied, trying to sound casual.

Offering nothing more, he stepped to the street and pulled the walkie-talkie from the bag. "Shepard to Glenn. Operation complete. Pull the plug. Over."

"Copy," came the reply, and Shepard walked boldly on amongst the shoppers filling Hoveniersstraat.

At the end, the street turned sharply right, becoming Rijfstraat, which was still restricted to pedestrians and bicycles. Shepard kept walking, pausing at Vestingstraat, a one-way street with traffic coming from his left. Spotting the unmarked blue Renault Estafette van approaching, he waited for it to stop, then slid open the side door and hopped inside.

"Cut all the lines?" he asked the younger man behind the wheel.

"Hell, I snipped through everything I could lay my hands on," Glenn replied as he pulled away, then turned left onto Pelikaanstraat with shops lining the left side and the stunning iron and glass architecture of the train station dominating the right side.

Shepard quickly removed his overalls, revealing his jeans and casual brown shirt beneath. He placed a black beret on his head, pulling it down low on his forehead. Taking off his work boots, he replaced them with canvas athletic shoes, then set about moving all the cash bundles and gems from the tool bag to a nondescript suitcase. Glenn continued in the city traffic, turning left by the station's grand cathedral-like entrance on Der Keyserlei, before taking the first right on a narrow street between more tall buildings called Breydelstraat. They quickly came to an open triangular piazza, where he stopped the van.

Shepard finished by stuffing his overalls, boots, work gloves, and the empty tool bag into the suitcase. Glenn stepped out of the van, trading seats with another man, who began turning around.

"Don't," Shepard growled, before slipping out the side door with suitcase in hand.

The van pulled away, and the two thieves headed on foot towards the train station. Shepard took off the thin cotton gloves and shoved them in his pocket as he walked.

"You sure about that guy?" he asked in a low voice.

"He's solid," Glenn replied. "He's Polish. Barely speaks the language, and he's here illegally. He won't say a word."

Shepard knew it would be the fine details which tripped him up, and concerning himself with each step would keep him free of the authorities.

"He doesn't know our names, right?"

"Nope."

"Where's he dropping the van?"

"Near the German border like we talked about, and I told him someone would be checking the van was in the right place tonight. If it wasn't, we were coming after him," Glenn replied impatiently. "Quit worrying about the van. I handled it."

As satisfied as he could be, Shepard pressed on, pushing the door open to the magnificent train station and stepping into the massive entrance hall with its towering, ornately decorated ceiling and skylight windows. Damaged during the war, Antwerp's pride and joy had been lovingly patched back up, but the thieves didn't have time to stop and admire the architecture.

People milled across the marble tiled floor, moving from platform to platform or leaving the station. Shepard picked out several policemen, but none of them appeared to be urgently scanning the crowds.

"Split up. I'll meet you on the train," he said, and walked to his left, quickly leaving Glenn behind.

Weaving between passengers all consumed with their own business, Shepard lugged the heavy suitcase, following the route he'd pre-planned to the correct platform. Leaving the entrance hallway, he showed his ticket to a guard who allowed him to pass, then continued down the long building, using stairs to reach the correct level. Finally, he placed the suitcase on the ground, leaned against one of the enormous metal supports, and waited.

He'd left the diamond merchants a few minutes later than planned, but they'd made most of the time back up getting to the station efficiently, and after less than five minutes his train pulled in. Passengers began emerging from the carriages, and Shepard stood by, keeping an eye out for Glenn, who he'd not seen yet. The younger man followed instructions well, but he was easily distracted, which concerned the man who'd diligently planned every last detail of the job.

As the platform began clearing of exiting passengers, Shepard walked towards the train, then paused upon hearing a commotion near the stairs. Continuing, he stepped up into the doorway to see over the crowd, and spotted two policemen moving down the platform, questioning people as they went. Shepard knew the timing was about right if they'd got to Gunzburg faster than he'd anticipated. It would make sense that they'd have a second set of keys hidden somewhere, but in the days he'd been watching the business, no one but the owner had used any. *Perhaps the security guard had a set locked away?*

The two policemen rushed through the crowd, obviously searching for someone, and Shepard still hadn't seen Glenn. He moved into the train and sought out the private compartment he'd booked. Heaving the suitcase up, he slid it onto the overhead storage, then moved to the window to see what was happening outside. One policeman was still questioning people on the platform, but the other had disappeared. He swung around as the compartment door opened and Glenn came in.

"The coppers are all over the station," the young man hissed.

"I know," Shepard replied. "We shouldn't be seen together."

"Where can we hide?"

"Go to the bar," Shepard ordered. "It's two cars back by the diner. Wait there until we leave the station and make sure you have your ticket."

Glenn nodded and reached for the door handle, but before he made it there, the door flung open and the second policeman stared straight at Shepard.

"Are you two travelling together?" he demanded.

There was no point in lying. The policeman would see their tickets, and Shepard kicked himself for not booking separate seats. He'd been too worried about keeping an eye on Glenn.

"Yes. What's the problem?"

The policeman looked both men over. "Who else is with you?"

"No one," Shepard responded, seeing the man's eyes move to the suitcase.

He'd left the handgun in the case, but regardless, shooting the policeman wouldn't be an option. The noise would bring every train guard and copper running. But if he could pull the man into the compartment and subdue him without making a racket, maybe they could still figure a way out of this. Shepard began rising from his seat, and Glenn looked his way, clearly unsure what to do.

"We're looking for a woman and a six-year-old girl," the policeman said. "The kid's got blonde curly hair. Wearing a blue dress. If you see them, alert the guard or a policeman."

The man closed the door and moved on while Shepard dropped back into his seat.

"Shit," Glenn breathed in relief, dropping onto the bench next to him.

Five minutes later, a knock on the compartment door was the conductor, who checked their tickets and wished them a pleasant trip to Paris, reminding them to change trains in Brussels. After another ten minutes, the train finally pulled from Antwerp station and began rattling south down the tracks. Shepard stood, closed the blind on the compartment door window, and pulled the suitcase down.

"We only have a few minutes," he said, donning the thin cotton gloves and opening the case.

He pulled out the tool bag and began filling it with the overalls, boots, gloves and anything else which could be traced back to the robbery. He placed the gun on the bench.

"Open the window," he ordered, and Glenn undid the latch and slid the lower half of the frame up.

"I think I can see the bridge," the younger man said, with his head out the window, and as he ducked back inside, Shepard struck him with all his might across the base of the skull with the butt of the gun.

Slumped unconscious, with one hand still awkwardly draped out the window, Glenn was dead weight in Shepard's hands as he hauled his partner from the floor and shoved his upper body into the opening. The train rocked and rhythmically clattered along the tracks while Shepard poked his own head out the window. Up ahead, he could see the metal framework of the Nete river bridge. Hurriedly, he fumbled for the man's pulse in his neck but couldn't locate one.

With one hand gripping the back of Glenn's shirt, Shepard scooped up his legs, and as the ground alongside the train fell away to the banks of the river, he shovelled Glenn's body out the window. In a quick glance back, Shepard caught his partner's figure bouncing violently off the edge of the bridge before plummeting into the water with a large splash.

He waited by the window, watching for a pointing hand or a frantic cry from a nearby compartment, but he saw or heard nothing except the clickety-clack of the train continuing towards Brussels. At the river Dyle, Shepard tossed the tool bag and the gun from the window, dropped the cotton gloves to the tracks, then finally settled into his seat, letting out a long sigh of relief. He was leaving the life he'd had up until this moment behind. Everything, and everyone. For the briefest of moments he felt a tinge of regret in never seeing his girlfriend again, but like the trees of the western farmlands of Belgium, it too flew by, never to be seen again.

With a small fortune in cash, he could live comfortably for a good many years before needing to sell a single gemstone, and living well was his plan.

4

PRESENT DAY – BONAIRE

By the time AJ and Reg had settled into their apartment, the sun was low in the sky over the ocean. The view from the second floor unit was stunning. Sand Dollar was an older, two-storey condominium complex built in a zig-zag along the coastline at a time when waterfront land on the island allowed such a luxury. A stone wall lined the grounds, with steps leading into the ocean at several points along the property. Next to their building was a dive shop and a smaller condo building, which housed a restaurant on the ground floor. A gated pier stretched into the water with a stock of dive tanks readily available for the residents of both resorts.

"Bring your laptop," Reg said, slipping his flip-flops back on his feet. "I'm ready for a drink."

AJ did as instructed and the two wandered down to the restaurant, named Breeze 'n Bites. Large sliding wood and glass doors stood open, leaving two sides of the eatery catching the breeze, as the name suggested. They chose two stools at the long bar, and a man in a collared shirt greeted them in accented English.

"Do you have Seven Fathoms rum, mate?" Reg asked.

"I don't, but I have our local Cadushy rum."

"Is it good neat?"

The man raised one eyebrow, and Reg laughed.

"Better mix it with a Coke then."

"For you, miss?" the bartender asked.

"Same is fine, thanks," AJ replied, distracted with opening her laptop and firing up MultiDeco, the program they'd use to plan their technical dives.

"Here are a couple of menus," the man offered. "Still a few minutes left in happy hour if you want the bar snacks. My name is Dick. Let me know if you have any questions."

Dick turned around to make the drinks and AJ picked up a smaller specials menu.

"Is a flammkuchen something like a pizza, Dick?" she asked, looking at a picture.

"Similar," he replied. "Thinner crust. More like a flatbread, I think."

"You have one made with tuna!" she announced in surprise.

Dick placed their drinks on the bar. "It's popular."

"My friend Nora's from Norway. It sounds like something she'd like."

"Want to try it?" Dick asked.

"I'll have the caprese one," Reg said. "I'll trade if you don't like the tuna," he added.

AJ eyed him suspiciously. "You promise? I know you. You say that and then you'll just laugh and won't swap."

"Scout's honour," Reg replied with a big grin.

"If you don't like the tuna, I'll eat it for my supper and make you something else," Dick volunteered.

"Blimey. Can't turn that down then, can I? Thank you."

Dick walked back to the kitchen, and AJ returned her attention to the computer.

"Does De Konig know trimix fills are going to be pricey?" she asked, filling out the details for their proposed dive.

"He said yes in an email, but I have a feeling he'll choke when he sees how much it actually costs," Reg replied. "Especially here on an island."

"Laurens ought to have told him, right?"

Reg scoffed. "I'm not sure about that bloke. We need to ask him about his experience in the morning before we splash."

"I think he's just unsure of his English," AJ ventured, not completely convinced it was the reason for his standoffishness.

"Hmm," Reg grunted, then pointed at the screen. "Use my RMV rate for all the dives. You're a bloody fish."

"Tech divers?" Dick asked, sitting on a stool behind the bar.

Reg nodded. "Yeah. Salvage job for a local bloke. You dive?"

Dick shook his head. "Snorkel with the family, but the dive shop staff are always in here, so I hear some of the terms they use. Don't know what RVM is, though."

"RMV," Reg corrected. "It's the volume of gas a diver breathes per minute. When we dive, the deeper we go, the more pressure is exerted on our bodies because of the water mass above us. If gas was delivered to our lungs at atmospheric pressure like we're breathing now, sitting at your bar, our lungs would be squeezed to the size of a walnut. So the first stage of our regulators compensates and delivers more volume. We have to calculate how much we'll breathe, so we'll have enough gas for the dive."

"It wouldn't be good to run out," Dick commented with a smile.

"Yeah, that tends to end badly," Reg replied and took a sip of his drink.

AJ tapped away a little more on the keyboard, then sat back. "Two hundred and ten feet is a bugger of a depth."

"I can ask him to move the wreck closer to the beach if you like?" Reg jested. "Maybe he can arrange for a taco stand and an ice cream shop down there too."

AJ rolled her eyes. "We'll need big tanks if we want to stay on the wreck more than fifteen or twenty minutes is what I mean."

"I'm sure TDS will have 100s," Reg replied.

"That's fine for you, you big ox, but twin 100s weigh about the same as me when they're full."

"Don't be a big girl's blouse," Reg chuckled and took another sip of his drink, winking at Dick, who seemed to enjoy their banter.

"You'll only spend twenty minutes underwater for each dive?" he asked.

AJ shook her head. "No. We'll only spend twenty minutes at 210 feet. We'll spend the next forty-three minutes doing our decompression stops on the ascent."

"That's because of all the bubbles from the gases at depth, is it?" Dick asked.

"Exactly," Reg confirmed. "We'll be able to look up and see the surface above us, but we'll risk serious injury, or worse, if we come up before our deco obligation is complete."

"Trip to the recompression chamber," AJ added. "Never had to, and hope I never have to take a ride in the chamber."

"Kind of important to get those calculations right, then," Dick commented as a smiling waitress brought their food to the bar.

"Yup," AJ agreed. "But worse than an embolism or death would be the grief he'd give me," she said, nodding to Reg. "So I'll triple-check my numbers."

She picked up a piece of her flammkuchen and wrinkled her nose. "Smells a bit fishy."

Reg shook his head. "That'll be the fish in it, I'm guessing."

AJ took a bite. "Ooh. It's bloody good," she said as she chewed as best she could. "It's also bloody hot!"

Dick left to help another customer, grinning as he went.

AJ startled awake, and sat up in bed, blinking against the bright light.

"Get your arse up," came Reg's deep voice, although she could barely make him out as she squinted and pulled the covers up.

"What time is it?" she groaned.

"Time to get up," he repeated as he left her room, leaving the door open and the light on.

Despite the constant early hours which came with running a dive boat, AJ had never been a morning person. She considered laying her head back down for a few more minutes, but knew Reg would be back and she couldn't face another rude awakening. Dragging herself from the covers, she quickly threw an oversized Mermaid Divers T-shirt over her head, then plodded to the bathroom.

"Coffee?" she asked grumpily, when she finally made it to the living room, where a full kitchen occupied one end.

"We need to go by the supermarket later today," Reg replied. "Got filters, but no coffee or milk."

AJ grunted, and the two gathered up their bags of dive gear and lugged them out the door. Laurens was waiting in the car park with the van, and between them they quickly loaded the gear.

"I need coffee," AJ greeted the Dutchman, who nodded in return.

"I'm afraid she's about as much use as a chocolate teapot until the sun comes up," Reg said, climbing into the passenger seat.

"And had coffee," AJ added from the bench seat behind them.

Whether or not Laurens understood was hard to tell as he didn't respond, but he backed up the van then pulled away.

It was a short drive down the atrociously paved 'main road' to a large dive resort. Laurens drove through the open, unguarded entrance gate and past what appeared to be newly constructed two-storey condos on the right to a turnaround in front of the resort's reception building. Parking, he hopped out, so AJ and Reg followed. To the right was another building with the resort's gift shop, and they continued to the far side, where a small dive shop was located.

"This is the dive shop for the whole resort?" AJ asked.

"No. Just tech diving," Laurens replied before opening the door.

AJ looked up and saw the sign by the door read 'Technical Diving Services'.

"Morning," a tall, slim guy greeted them from behind a counter.

Laurens stayed quiet and stepped aside, so Reg responded. "Morning. I'm Reg Moore. I messaged with someone here about getting tanks filled."

"That was one of the owners, Zach, but he told me you were coming by. I'm Bryan."

The man had an American accent but spoke in a slow, deliberate way with a deeper, booming voice than his frame suggested.

"Tell me what you need and I'll get you set up."

"Do you have 100s?" Reg asked.

"Do you have coffee?" AJ interjected before Bryan could answer the first question.

"Yes, and yes," he said with a grin and pointed to a coffee maker on top of a file cabinet in the corner of the small room, which appeared to double as their retail shop and classroom, a table with bench seats filling the middle of the store.

AJ wasted no time abducting the first mug she found and popping a pod into the single-serve machine. While it began gurgling, she turned back to Bryan.

"Dive plan is 210 feet, so we need 18/45 trimix in 100s, then 50 percent and 100 percent O_2 40s for deco."

Bryan nodded. "All three of you diving?"

Reg and AJ looked at Laurens, who nodded.

"Side or back mount?" Bryan asked.

"Back," Reg replied.

Bryan looked at AJ. "That's quite the load you're planning."

"I know," AJ huffed, watching the coffee machine as though she could intimidate it into brewing faster. "If we do twenty minutes for bottom time on the first dive, we could use 80s, but to get thirty minutes at 210 we'll need the 100s to get a comfortable margin in reserve."

"Where are you diving?" Bryan asked.

"Not important," Laurens quickly responded, and the other three turned to him.

"Private salvage-type job," Reg added in a more amiable tone. "So we're not supposed to say."

"Fair enough," Bryan replied with a smile. "I need to see your cert cards for the fills, then we can get started."

The three showed Bryan their certification cards, proving they had the training and knowledge to dive with mixed gases on advanced technical decompression dives, then followed him around the next building to a small room where a wall of gauges, valves, and hoses awaited. AJ tried not to spill from her steaming mug as they walked, then keenly sipped while she stopped outside to watch a pair of small bright yellow and black birds flit about the trees. They disturbed a green parrot, who squawked before moving to the roof of another building. AJ smiled at the activity, then stepped inside the fill room where Bryan had begun gathering tanks.

"One thought," he said, carrying a 100-cubic-foot aluminium tank in each hand. "We have a few 85s I can cave fill for you, if you'd prefer?"

"I'll take them instead of 100s!" AJ blurted, spraying a little coffee.

Bryan laughed. "Thought you might."

Reg looked at Laurens. "Would you prefer them, or stick with 100s?"

The man stared blankly back.

"The 85s are steel tanks," Reg explained. "And a cave fill is pushing to the maximum pressure allowed, which is 3600psi. Gives us around 230 cubic feet of gas for the pair instead of 200 with twin 100s at 3000psi."

"The divers in Florida's cave country started using them for long cave penetrations. Hence the term." AJ added.

Laurens nodded. "I'll use whatever you do," he said, looking back at Reg.

"How many 85s you got?" Reg asked.

"I could get you six, so two each."

"Alright," Reg said, scratching his thick, scraggly beard. "We'll use 80s for the reconnaissance dive, then 85s for the longer, second dive."

"Then six 50 percent nitrox deco bottles and six 100 percent oxygen deco bottles," AJ threw in.

"Gotcha," Bryan replied, already filling their trimix blends. "I'll give you a couple of 80s with 50 percent for safety hang tanks too."

"Perfect," Reg responded, and gave Bryan a friendly slap on the shoulder. "Appreciate all the help."

An hour and a half later, the van pulled away, loaded with dive tanks of varying sizes, all labelled with their contents and the safely diveable depths for the gas. Amazed the little shop had been able to accommodate them so well, AJ tapped away on her laptop, working up dive plan options with the unexpected tank options. Meanwhile, Reg didn't waste any time grilling their new dive buddy.

"Where did you train?" he casually asked Laurens, as they turned right out of the resort.

"Military," came the short reply.

"Navy myself," Reg replied. "Been diving much here in Bonaire?"

Laurens shook his head. "A little recreational is all."

"So, when was your last tech dive?" Reg pressed.

"Six months ago," the man replied without taking his eyes off the road. "Maybe a few months more."

AJ caught Reg's glance over his shoulder and raised her eyebrows.

"I don't mean to sound like a prick, mate," Reg continued. "But we like to know who we're diving with when we go a few hundred feet down. Have you done this sort of diving much?"

Laurens finally turned his head and forced a grin. "Enough," he replied. "Mostly in the military, which I can't tell you about."

"Dutch Navy?"

Laurens nodded. "I have many decompression dives."

AJ leaned forward in her seat, feeling like the guy could be more forthcoming, but before she could ask anything more, he turned the van into a small marina and backed up to a boat slip.

"That's our boat?" Reg asked, looking out the rear window.

"Yes," Laurens replied, getting out.

"I thought he said a catamaran. Isn't that a bloody pontoon boat?" AJ muttered, reading the name on the stern, *Beste Leven.*

"Yup," Reg replied sullenly.

"That's a family outing on the lake kind of boat, isn't it?"

"Yup," Reg said again.

5

1970 (TWO YEARS LATER) – JARAMA, SPAIN

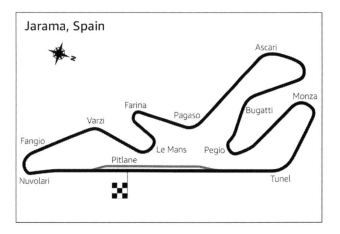

The smell of petrol, oil, and hot rubber wafted across the tarmac as the sun beat down on the Jarama racetrack, twenty miles north of Madrid. Loud voices barked orders and directions as the race organisers marched around the starting grid with policemen in tow. Race cars were being wheeled to and fro as chaos reigned just minutes before the start of the Spanish Grand Prix.

Lady Georgiana Ashford stood by the Lotus 49B she owned and entered under her team name, Ashford Motor Racing Team, or

AMRT for short. The car's royal blue paint scheme, with a single centre line red stripe bordered by thin white stripes to either side, gleamed in the bright sunshine.

"This is a bloody shambles," she shouted to Barney Morgan, the team manager.

Barney slipped his flat cap from his head and scratched his balding scalp. "It's a right mess, I'm afraid. But we should be fine," he yelled back, his London accent in contrast to her upper-class timbre.

Georgie wanted to believe him, but the look on his face left her doubtful. During the two days of practice and qualifying sessions leading up to race day, the track officials and Formula One's governing body, Commission Sportive Internationale, had wrangled with the teams over the number of starters allowed for the race. Teams and drivers had travelled thousands of miles expecting to compete, but the track wanted the grid limited to only sixteen of the twenty-two entries, stating safety concerns. Ten of the most successful drivers were guaranteed a starting spot, leaving the other dozen to fight it out for the remaining six positions.

AMRT's driver, Carlos Ramirez, had tied with another driver on lap time for the 16th spot, but was listed in the final starting position on the merit of having set his time first. Georgie hoped that her driver's Spanish nationality also weighed in their favour.

All appeared calm near the front of the grid, where Australian Jack Brabham, in a car built by his own team, had beaten the Kiwi, Denny Hulme, to pole position. Reigning world champion Jackie Stewart completed the front row in a March entered by Ken Tyrrell's team.

"Oh my goodness," Georgie exclaimed, turning around as men scuffled near the car behind her.

Phil Woodford, the team's lead mechanic, moved in front of her in case the fracas spilled their way. Barney's 19-year-old son, who went by the nickname Tina, joined him.

"Very gallant of you, lads," Georgie said, as she watched the police take over and force several teams to wheel their cars from the grid.

"We are good?" Carlos asked in heavily accented English.

"Good as gold, mate," Barney assured their driver, but he still looked concerned.

Georgie gave Carlos a smile, sweeping back her long curls of carefully coiffed hair. "I think you should get in the car and we'll carry on as though we're supposed to be here. Which, of course, we are."

Carlos nodded and handed her his aviator sunglasses. "I feel good today," he said, slipping his helmet on. "We make prize money."

"I do hope so," Georgie replied, and leaned in, giving her handsome driver a peck on the cheek as she always did before the start. "Good luck. Go fast. But please be careful."

Carlos grinned. "Fast, I can do. But careful not make fast, Lady Ashford."

He climbed into the narrow single-seater car while Phil held the seatbelts aside, allowing the driver to lower himself into the fibreglass seat, sliding his feet to the pedals at the front of the innovative aluminium monocoque chassis. The twenty-eight-year-old driver had preferred not to wear seatbelts in the past, but his new car owner this season had insisted.

"If Jackie Stewart thinks it's wise, then so do we," Georgie had told him at their only test session on a chilly February day at Brands Hatch in England, just before they'd shipped everything off to South Africa for the first race. He might have argued if driving for Georgie's brand new team wasn't his only option to keep his spotty Formula One career alive. Many still thought the better option, during a crash, was to be flung from the vehicle rather than becoming trapped inside the mangled wreckage while 45 gallons of petrol ignited around them.

Arms waved and people yelled from the front of the grid, and the Spanish voice over the public address system enthusiastically echoed from the grandstands and pit lane area. Tina hurriedly screwed the valve cap on the left front tyre he'd been double-checking the pressure of, and Phil finished snugly strapping Carlos's belts.

"Good luck, mate," he said, squeezing the driver's shoulder.

Carlos's eyes remained steadfast on the cars ahead as he lifted his goggles from his neck to his face, making sure the strap was in the correct position around his open-faced helmet.

"I must say," Georgia said to Barney as they rushed to the side of the track. "I do get frightfully excited before the start."

Barney wiped the sweat from his brow. "I wish they'd talk in bloody English," he moaned, huffing in the heat. "It's hard to know what's going on when they shout and carry on over the tannoy."

An official waved his hand in the air with a circular motion, and sixteen drivers hit the buttons on their dashboards to start their engines. All shouting, cheers, and verbal directions were lost to the raucous sound of thoroughbred race engines roaring to life. Barney quickly handed Georgie earplugs, which she rolled between her fingers before squeezing them into her ears.

As the lone car on the seventh row of the three-two-three style grid formation, Carlos had a clear view of his competition. His Lotus, without the latest updates, was no match for the Brabham, McLaren or March on the front row, but he felt good about his chances of moving forward on the opening laps. As a Spaniard, he knew the Jarama circuit well, and had posted a lap time that should have placed him on the third row. Mired in further controversy, the organisers had mistakenly omitted to time all the cars in Friday afternoon's session when Carlos had posted his best lap. They managed to time every lap on Saturday, when Phil had spent most of the two sessions troubleshooting and finally rectifying an ignition wiring problem. By the time the car was back up to speed, the chequered flag waved on the session and Carlos had barely slipped into the field.

A marshal waved a green flag in the air, and the engine notes soared as the field pulled away on the warm-up lap. Ahead, one car barely moved from its spot, and as Carlos shot by he noted it was the Kiwi Chris Amon in a works-entered March having problems.

Hanging back from the other cars, Carlos accelerated off turn two and shot through the kink, braking hard for the left-handed turn four. He turned in smoothly and the front tyres gripped the asphalt, gliding the Lotus to a late apex at the inside kerbing. Carlos waited a moment to see if the rear tyres would follow suit, and as soon as the chassis loaded the outside tyres, he began unwinding the steering wheel and accelerating off the turn, quickly catching the pack.

The car was back to feeling like it had on Friday afternoon. Well balanced, despite the heavy fuel load, and predictable. He followed the field around, brimming with confidence and certain if the car held together he'd make it into the top ten, or even better. Points were paid, along with money, for the top six, which would be a major task from the back of the grid, but anything felt possible.

Georgie stood on the low wall in front of the pit lane garages so she could see the grid as the cars came around for the start. Barney wobbled unsteadily next to her, stretching to see over the mechanics packed along the steel barrier dividing the pit lane from the circuit. The starter stood at the edge of the track with the Spanish flag in his hand. The spectators were all on their feet in the grandstands and packed across every embankment and viewing area around the circuit.

The roar of engines rose to a crescendo as the starter waved the flag and the cars spun their lightly grooved tyres as the drivers fought to put the horsepower to the road. Stewart took the lead on the run to the first corner, with the two Australians duelling for second behind him.

Georgie peered through the swirling dust and tyre smoke to

pick out her blue car at the rear of the field. She grabbed Barney's sleeve, shaking excitedly as she watched the Lotus make a marvellous start and accelerate past the row in front on the run to the first turn. As the cars disappeared into a haze down by the first corner, Georgie hopped down from the wall and ran to the back of the garages to catch a peek of the cars in the back section of the 2.1-mile circuit.

The American, Mario Andretti, struggled to find a gear on his upshift as they exited the first turn, and Carlos dived inside the March before turn two. With Amon sidelined, and Andretti behind him, along with Johnny Servoz-Gavin and Rolf Stommelen who he'd passed on the start, Carlos was already twelfth, with the legendary Graham Hill in a privately entered Lotus just ahead.

Although the car felt sluggish with the extra weight of full tanks, it was responding to Carlos's every command a little better than the cars around him. Determined to make the most of his home track knowledge, he stayed close to the gearbox of Hill's Lotus through the right-hand turn three kink, noticing the Englishman was struggling to keep the rear of his car under control.

They braked hard for the tight turn four, and Carlos pounced, diving to the inside of Hill before the turn-in point. Hill had little defence as his Lotus oversteered wide, leaving room for Carlos to hug the late apex and accelerate into eleventh place.

Turn five came quickly, and Carlos inched closer to the next two cars on the road, John Surtees and Henri Pescarolo in a French Matra, who were tussling for position. Through the turn six kink, the cars accelerated through the gears on the uphill back straight towards turn seven. After reaching fifth gear and a 155 mph, Carlos braked later than Surtees for the third gear right-hand turn, closing the gap to a few feet, and with a slightly better corner exit, he moved inside the McLaren as they braked for turn eight.

Surprised by the move with his attention on Pescarolo ahead, Surtees began turning in before he realised Carlos was arriving alongside him. They touched wheels as the Spaniard barged his way through to take the position, breathing a sigh of relief that they hadn't tangled harder and crashed. A glance in his mirror told Carlos that Surtees had tucked in behind him as they swept down-hill into the Bugatti esses, a fast left then right turn leading into the hard-braking zone for turn ten.

The moment Carlos steered into the second part of the esses and loaded the left front tyre, he knew something was terribly wrong. The contact with Surtees had knocked the valve stem askew in the rim, and as he turned right, the valve stem snapped, allowing the air to rapidly escape. Carlos eased into the brake, but the chassis bottomed out on the tarmac and the Lotus shot straight for the grass on the outside of the turn... which quickly became the inside of the left-hand turn ten.

Barely slowing at all, Carlos was a passenger as the car careened through the rough infield, shot back onto the track in the middle of turn ten, and speared into the side of Jacky Ickx's Ferrari. The impact launched Carlos forward into his seatbelts, causing his neck to whip as his chin bashed into his chest. Pain shot through his legs and as the crumpled Lotus came to a stop, the world around the Spaniard erupted into an inferno.

The Ferrari's side tank had been decimated by the collision, spewing petrol all over both cars, which instantly ignited from the hot exhausts. One of Carlos's fuel cells had also been punctured, leaking more fuel and adding to the blaze. He tried to clear his groggy head and fumbled for the seatbelt latch. Flames engulfed the Ferrari, and feeling like he was witnessing a miracle, Carlos watched a figure emerge from the pyre, staggering across the track with his fire-resistant Nomex overalls blackened in patches with flames still licking from his back.

Desperate to get out of the burning car, Carlos heaved himself up as the belts fell away, but his lower legs and ankles screamed in pain. Something was broken, or worse, but if he stayed in the wreckage, he'd be burnt alive. Yelling in agony, he wrenched his feet free of the twisted aluminium monocoque and tried to stand in the seat. His right foot held, but his left ankle twisted grotesquely, and Carlos fell from the cockpit, hitting the ground with a painful thud, his legs still awkwardly dangling over the side of the Lotus.

His cheek felt wet against the tarmac as the stifling odour of petrol overwhelmed him. The heat was unbearable and the pain from his legs made him nauseous, pushing him to the brink of passing out. His vision became hazy, but with a terrifying wave of despair, Carlos watched the flames ignite the stream of fuel running from the wreckage to where he lay slumped on the ground. Hopelessly watching the fire streak towards him, the last thing he recalled was a violent tug on his shoulders, just as he passed out.

6

PRESENT DAY – BONAIRE

The divers moved the tanks from the van to a series of racks mounted along the back of the bench seats running down each side of the pontoon boat's flat, rectangular deck. The helm station was centre console-style near the bow, a canopy shaded the whole boat, and two outboards hung off the back of the pontoons.

"This actually makes a decent dive platform," AJ noted as they began setting out their gear on the deck.

Reg grunted in response. "As long as it stays calm out there."

"Wherever it is we're going," AJ joked.

"I think it's time to share more details with you," came De Konig's voice from the dock. He smiled and stepped aboard the boat, carrying a laptop under his arm. "I'll show you the video we have."

"I thought nobody had dived the wreck," Reg pointed out.

"They haven't," De Konig replied. "We lowered a camera down to capture this. Laurens has seen it, so while he takes us out, I'll show you two."

AJ and Reg quickly finished assembling their Dive Rite rigs, fastening the twin 80 tanks to the backplates and high-capacity inflation bladders known as wings. Bryan had supplied all the 40-

cubic-foot deco bottles with straps and clips, so once their XT regulators were hooked up and checked, they tethered the rigs to the back of the benches and waited for Laurens to do the same.

The Dutchman moved a little slower, and AJ noticed his gear was all brand new. She exchanged another knowing look with Reg. Everyone had new gear at some time or another, no matter how much experience they had under their belt, but newbies almost always had shiny equipment. It was also from a brand she'd never heard of, who might well make solid gear, but technical diving was not an environment in which to cut corners or costs. She and Reg had used Dive Rite equipment for years and even been on a few dives with Lamar and his wife, Lee Ann, the owners from Florida, as well as their son, Jared. The family were at the forefront of the technical diving industry.

When Laurens was finished, he started the outboards and AJ and Reg handled the lines for him as he idled out of the slip. Once they were on their way, De Konig opened his laptop on the table behind the helm station and hit play on a video.

"We mounted a series of underwater video cameras on a weighted frame and lowered it on two lines," he explained. "One from this boat, and the other line from a small tender. We grappled to the wreck, so the tender acted as the steering system. As you can see, it wasn't perfect, but we got enough footage to be confident of what we'd found."

The video wasn't particularly steady, but the visibility was decent, so AJ could see a wreck of some description.

"It's inverted?" Reg asked, squinting at the laptop's screen.

"Yes," De Konig confirmed.

"Looks a bit like a landing barge," Reg added.

"Very perceptive of you," the older man replied. "I believe the vessel either started life as an LCM-8 landing craft or was a copy of the basic design. We don't know much about it."

"And you own the salvage rights to the wreck?" AJ asked, although she knew this had been discussed before she and Reg had agreed to take the job.

This sort of work wasn't usually of interest to them, as neither had the time, but AJ wanted to dive Bonaire as she'd never been, and it had sounded like a fun trip. Now, looking at an upside-down barge on a barren, sandy ocean floor, she felt less enthused.

"I indeed own the salvage rights," De Konig confirmed.

"So what's on this barge that's worth all this effort and money?" Reg asked. "Or under this barge, I should say."

"The personal goods of a man who was shipping his possessions from Aruba to Bonaire many years ago," De Konig explained.

"Someone you knew?" AJ asked.

The older man shook his head. "I just thought there might be something interesting aboard."

"If you're after his socks and shirts," Reg joked, "I'd say they're long gone by now."

De Konig laughed. "As you can see, the barge inverted on the way down, so our first concern is how to access the cargo."

"We'll shoot better video on the first dive," AJ commented. "And have a look for access points, but from your video here, I wouldn't get too excited. We might not have a way in."

"And there might not be anywhere to go if we do get past the gunwales," Reg added. "There's every chance the whole barge is packed with sand. That won't be a matter of a few lift bags and clearing a bit of debris. We're talking about raising the vessel off the sea floor, and that's a much bigger job than we're equipped for." He looked around the pontoon. "In the words of Roy Scheider, 'You're gonna need a bigger boat.'"

De Konig didn't laugh this time. "Then let's hope you find a way under the wreck."

AJ was dying to ask more questions but the man obviously wanted to play his hand close to his chest, and he was paying them handsomely to dive for him, so she let it go.

"Your gig, so your rules," Reg said, apparently sharing AJ's thoughts. "But I made it clear when we accepted this job, we won't be involved in anything illegal, so I'm taking you at your word on that. There's nothing toxic or explosive involved, right?"

"Absolutely none to my knowledge, Reg," De Konig replied. "And I promise I'll share more information as we move forward. I'd prefer not to reveal everything until we know you can gain access to the cargo."

"Fair enough," Reg said.

The pontoon cruised along a lot faster than AJ had expected, and she realised she'd not been paying close attention to their surroundings. She had noticed what appeared to be a town and a small port along the shore as they motored south, and an uninhabited island to the west, but now the coastline curved to a promontory, and De Konig must have seen her looking.

"That's Lighthouse Point," he said, pointing ahead. "The island we just passed off the starboard side is Klein Bonaire, which simply means Little Bonaire, in English."

"I don't see a lighthouse," AJ responded. "I noticed a yellow one in the town back there."

"The one we passed is at the old fort in Kralendijk, our main town. The one up here is not very tall, so it's shielded by the trees from our direction, but it is still active. Our largest lighthouse is Willemstoren. It's at the southernmost point and is quite prominent. You should take the van one day while you're here and drive around the island. We have lots to see."

As they neared the point, Laurens began slowing and AJ peered at the GPS plotter he was using to guide them to the wreck.

"Are we planning to grapple the wreck?" Reg asked.

"It's taken us a while in the past," De Konig replied, "but it's been the best way. We anchored in the sand one time to shoot video and never managed to find the barge. Laurens gets better at locating it each time."

"The hook is under the bow bench," Laurens added. "If one of you can get it, tie it to the centre cleat. I'll tell you when to release it."

AJ moved forward and found the grappling hook attached to a large spool of line. Finding the end, she fastened it to the cleat as directed.

"We should fix a line to the wreck while we're down there," AJ shouted back. "Make it easier next time."

"I don't want to mark the site with a buoy," De Konig quickly rebutted.

AJ grinned at him. "Don't worry, we'll show you a trick we've used before."

"Drop the hook," Laurens ordered, and AJ tossed the four-pronged grapnel into the water.

After idling stationary for a minute to allow the device to settle to the sea floor, Laurens selected reverse and began slowly backing towards shore. AJ moved to the helm, watching the GPS screen with the others. The pontoon passed over the recorded location for the wreck, and Laurens did a good job of keeping the pontoon on a straight track in reverse.

"How much line do we have?" Reg asked.

"Ninety metres," Lauren replied.

"Just under 300 feet," AJ converted aloud.

When the pontoon seemed like it had travelled too far from the dot on the GPS, the boat suddenly jerked to a stop and Laurens put the motors in neutral.

"First try!" De Konig exclaimed. "Well done. You're showing off in front of our new friends, Laurens."

The younger Dutchman didn't acknowledge the compliment, or the humour, but waited a little longer then shut down the twin outboards.

"Do you have another line?" AJ asked.

"We have a spare," De Konig replied.

"Have any carabiners or shackles?"

"I think we have a couple of options."

"How about a small buoy?"

De Konig frowned. "We can't mark the site with a buoy. It's bad enough people will see us out here each day. It's one of the reasons I chose this boat, as it looks like tourists out for a day on the water."

"Don't worry, there'll be nothing visible from the surface," AJ assured him. "Got a buoy?"

"We do," De Konig reluctantly confirmed.

"Good. We'll take the line and hardware with us," AJ told him.

For the next thirty minutes, the three divers ran through their final checks, went over the dive plan, and eventually geared up. Twin 80-cubic-foot tanks on their backs, plus two 40-cubic-foot deco tanks, and the rest of their equipment added up to over 120lbs of gear. That weight was irrelevant once submerged, but getting from the boat to the water was a chore. Reg let the other two divers splash in with their twin tanks, then handed them the smaller deco bottles one at a time.

"I apologise, but I'm not much use helping with your tanks," De Konig said, watching Reg deliver deco tanks. "Bad back, I'm afraid."

"No problem, mate," Reg replied, sweat rolling down his face. "We're used to lugging these things around."

Bobbing on the surface, AJ and Laurens clipped the extra tanks to D-rings on their harnesses, then moved aside for Reg to join them. Once in the water, the big man reached up and slid his deco bottles off the deck, clipped them in place, then grabbed one of the extra 80s Bryan had given them filled with 50 percent nitrox, which was now set up with a regulator. AJ helped him clip the fifth tank to his harness and laughed.

"You look like you just surfaced in the middle of a gang of scuba tanks."

Reg rolled his eyes. "Ready?" he asked the pair, who both returned an okay sign. "Alright. I'll pause on the way to drop the spare nitrox, then we'll head down asap. Leaving the bottom at twenty minutes, okay?"

AJ and Laurens both returned an okay sign in response, so Reg pointed his thumb at the water, indicating they were ready to descend.

The line grappled to the wreck ran at an angle, as the pontoon had taken up the slack in the 90-metre rope. There didn't seem to be much current, but they all still used the line as a descent guide, trying not to pull too hard in case they dislodged the hook. In the lead position, AJ reached 70 feet, then paused, allowing enough room for Laurens to wait above her and Reg to fasten the nitrox tank at 60 feet as planned. With all the air crushed from their wetsuits by the increasing water pressure, they all used their inflators to blow gas into their wings just to hold their position.

Using a 12-inch strap with loops on each end, Reg attached one end to the ring on the tank band, then tightly wrapped the strap around the grapple line before attaching the other end to the same ring. Doing the same for the second tank band, he secured the tank to the line where they'd retrieve it on ascent after the last dive of the day.

With an okay signal from Reg, AJ continued down the line, her descent rate picking up speed as she went deeper, requiring little bursts of gas into her wing to steady her pace. Constantly pinching her nose, she equalised her ears and sinuses and exhaled through her nose to keep her mask from squeezing her face. Behind her, Laurens appeared to be doing fine, and Reg was following closely behind the Dutchman as they'd quietly discussed on the boat. Until Laurens had proven his competency, they planned on keeping a close eye on the man.

At 150 feet, AJ felt the slight chill of the water temperature dropping from the balmy 80s of the surface. Below, she could see nothing except the deep blue ocean turning to a blackness. Checking her Shearwater Perdix 2 wrist-mounted computer, she noted they'd already been down for four minutes, which was their planned total descent time. The stop for the bail-out tank accounted for the delay, but she'd still be leaving the bottom at twenty minutes, adding in another layer of conservancy to the dive.

Seeing 165 feet on the screen, she looked below her once more, and instead of the dark endless murk of the depths, she made out a shadow amongst lighter surroundings. With more gas into her wing, she slowed her descent, and as she approached 185 feet, the details became clearer and she could make out the rectangular shape of the barge.

Descending through the open water, AJ had seen almost no fish at all, but on the wreck, which appeared to be resting in the sand at 210 feet precisely as they'd been told, a plethora of life flitted about. With the lens effect of viewing through a mask underwater, the landing barge appeared far bigger than its 80 feet, but as she levelled off next to the flat-bottomed hull, one thing was abundantly clear. The top side of the vessel was buried in the sandy ocean floor.

7

1970 – JARAMA, SPAIN

Georgie watched in horror as a thick plume of smoke billowed into the air from beyond the fencing and the crowd near turn ten. She clutched her chest and ran back past the race transporters to the pit lane garages. Cars roared by on the front straight at full speed as she grabbed Barney.

"There's been an accident!" Georgie shouted. "Did Carlos come by?"

Barney looked dumbfounded, turning back to the circuit and craning his neck to see the cars pass by. ·

Phil leaned down from the wall. "I didn't see him!" He waved at Tina to be ready for their car coming into the pits, but Georgie caught his sleeve.

"It's awful! There's a huge fire. It must be Carlos," she stammered in shock.

Word of an accident had now reached the pit lane, and people were shouting and pointing at the smoke rising into the blue skies over the Jarama circuit. Several Ferrari mechanics in red overalls also dashed out of sight.

"Bloody hell," Phil swore and took off at a run with Tina in tow.

Not knowing what she should do, Georgie followed, although

her stylish knee-high platform boots left her well behind the two mechanics. Barney reached her side.

"Did you see the crash?" he asked, already winded.

"No, no. I saw the cars over there," she said, pointing to the back straight in view from the paddock. "Then I heard them closer and all of a sudden this terrible cloud of smoke."

They ran between cars parked near the fence at the side of the paddock and pushed through the crowd huddled against the wire. Georgie couldn't believe her eyes. An inferno raged from the outer part of the slightly banked turn, two crumpled race cars barely visible amongst the flames. Marshals frantically sprayed the fire with extinguishers while the remaining competitors slipped and slid by the scene. Unbelievably, the race was continuing, with nothing more than yellow caution flags slowing the drivers at turn ten.

An ambulance with sirens wailing above the screaming race engines bounced and jolted across the grass on the infield to where a crowd of corner workers surrounded two figures lying on the ground. Georgie spotted Phil and Tina near the blazing wreckage, waiting for the last car to go by before they ran across the circuit and joined the people attending to the two drivers.

"I can't bear it, Barney," she gasped, clutching the wire fence. "This is simply too terrible."

Her team manager placed a hand on his boss's shoulder. "Let's see. We must hope for the best, ma'am. But I'm afraid the car's going to be a total write-off."

"Bugger the car, Barney," Georgie replied. "We can buy more cars."

Barney sighed. "Of course, ma'am," he mumbled, but was saved by Phil, who looked their way, finding their faces against the fence, and gave them a thumbs-up.

"Thank goodness!" Georgie exclaimed, and hugged Barney, who wasn't sure what to do at the sudden outburst, so he hugged her back.

The hospital was old and shabby, although sanitary as best Georgie could tell as she and Barney walked down a hallway in the well-used building. The place reeked of disinfectant and musty furnishings. They found Carlos in the room number the front desk had given them, propped up on several pillows with his eyes closed. The bedclothes hid his legs and whatever bandages or cast which covered his shattered left ankle, reassembled during his long overnight surgery.

"How are you?" Georgie asked softly as Carlos's eyes blinked open.

Her driver managed a weak smile. "I am... what is it the rock stars say? Stoned?"

Georgie laughed, relieved that any tension had immediately been broken. She'd barely slept after waiting at the hospital for hours until the staff had sent them home.

"I dare say you are. Hopefully you're not in too much pain."

Carlos gently shook his head. "Not yet." His brow creased. "Is Jacky okay?"

"Minor burns," Barney said. "He was treated and released last night."

"I need to tell him I'm sorry," Carlos responded, his voice low and strained as though he might succumb to sleep at any moment.

Georgie wanted to ask him what happened, but couldn't assemble the right words. Every different way she could fathom to phrase the question felt more like an accusation than genuine concern.

"So what happened, mate?" Barney asked, negating her dilemma.

Carlos closed his eyes and after a few moments, Georgie began wondering if he had yielded to the morphine and drifted off, but he opened them again.

"The car was perfect," he whispered, his groggy blue eyes

lighting up for a moment as he looked over at his team owner. "I make many places on the first lap."

Georgie and Barney glanced at each other as Carlos appeared to lose his train of thought.

"I touch wheels with Surtees," he unsteadily continued, "and next corner, the tyre goes down. I have no control."

"So nothing broke on the car?" Barney blurted, a little too eagerly. "It was definitely the tyre?"

"Si," Carlos confirmed. "The chassis hit the ground, the grass, then the Ferrari." He raised his hand towards Georgie. "I'm so sorry about your beautiful race car."

Georgie gently took his hand in hers, conscious of the angry red blotches from the minor burns he'd suffered.

"They can make another car, but there's only one Carlos," she responded. "I'm so happy you're going to be okay. I've been beside myself with worry."

Carlos's lips curled into a brief smile before he finally drifted into a drug-induced restless slumber.

"We must get to the airport," Barney whispered, "or we'll miss our flight."

Georgie looked at her driver, lying forlornly in the hospital bed. Yesterday, he'd been a gladiator of the racetrack, proud to compete before his home crowd, and now a wounded warrior who'd likely never drive again. Because of an accident in a car she'd provided for him.

After a pair of seasons in the Formula Two category, Barney had presented Georgie with an opportunity for their fledgling team to step up to the most prestigious racing series in the world. The Formula One Grand Prix championship. Carlos had approached Barney, who he'd known for several years, and promised to bring a sponsor to help with running costs if Lady Georgiana Ashford would purchase the car, engine, and equipment to run for the season.

With their Formula Two driver retiring from racing, Georgie didn't take much persuading, and was beyond excited to rub shoulders with the sport's elite. Colin Chapman, who owned Lotus, sold them a two-year-old former works chassis and introduced them to Cosworth, the engine designer who built the DFV V8 motors badged as Fords. Money quickly flew out the door, as cheques needed to be written at every step, and when they finally stood on the grid at Kyalami in South Africa for round one of the championship, only one thing was missing. Carlos's elusive sponsor.

Georgie had paid for everything, and despite the Spanish driver's insistence that his backer was coming through, not a penny appeared, even when they'd arrived in Jarama. The difficult decision she'd been facing after leaving Spain had now been made for her. The car was destroyed beyond all repair, engine included, and her driver and his promise of sponsorship support lay before her in a hospital bed.

Barney was right, she decided; they might as well make their flight home. Carlos was in good hands and would be moved to his family home in Barcelona when he was well enough to travel, so there was little more they could do in Spain.

Despondently, she followed Barney down the hallway.

"How can we let the lads know it wasn't a problem with the car?" she asked, as they stepped aside for a nurse wheeling a patient on a gurney.

"We can leave a message at the hotel," Barney replied. "The officials weren't releasing what's left of the Lotus until this afternoon, so I booked them in the hotel for another night. No rush getting home at this point."

"Right," Georgie agreed as they continued to the hospital entrance. "No rush at all, I suppose."

"We could run the F2 car again," Barney suggested as they stepped from the building into the brilliant sunshine and waved to a taxi driver. "We couldn't make the next round as it's next week, but round three at Rouen in France is over a month away."

They got in the back of the taxi, and Barney leaned forward between the front seats. "*Aeropuerto, por favor,*" he said awkwardly in his London accent.

The driver nodded, used the rear view mirror to check out the beautiful woman in the back of his cab, then pulled away, heading for the airport.

"I had thought about that," Georgie said, "but it seems so disappointing to step back down, doesn't it?"

Barney nodded. "It does at that. But I'd hate to lay off the lads at this time of year when everyone has their teams together. Be hard for them to find anything. Me included."

Georgie's shoulders slumped. "The idea of it makes me positively ill, Barney, but I'm afraid we've exhausted well over half the budget I have for the entire season, and we've only just begun. I've already cancelled several trips and events so I'd have enough for the team. There are simply not enough funds available to start over."

Barney nodded once again, this time even more despondently. "I understand, your ladyship. You've been more than kind to all of us. Just a shame, that's all."

"Don't ladyship me, Barney, especially now," she said, cuffing him on the arm. "I think we've officially been through enough together to drop the formalities."

Barney gave her a smile before they fell into silence for the rest of the ride to the airport. Once there, Barney paid the taxi driver, and they walked inside. Their suitcases would return in the race car transporter, so all Georgie carried was a large purse and Barney a briefcase as they breezed through the airport, pausing briefly to check their flight number on the board.

Their gate was bustling with what appeared to be the whole Formula One paddock, from team owners and drivers, to press and a few series officials. All the Formula One teams were based in England, apart from Ferrari and Matra, so Monday's first flight to London was jam packed. One or two people wandered by and enquired after Carlos, as Georgie and Barney stood on the periphery of the crowd.

Georgie already felt like an outsider. A former and very brief Grand Prix team owner. Her family didn't mind how she spent her yearly allowance, as long as it didn't embarrass them or bring them bad press, but they didn't understand her obsession with motor racing. Horses were far more in keeping with their heritage.

She could hear her father's highbrow comment. "Oh well, best rid of all that nonsense, my dear," he'd say, unintentionally slapping her in the face with his patronising tone, before he'd blabber on about her brother and his business success with the family's shipping company.

"Have a minute?" a man said. A voice she recognised.

Looking up, she saw Colin Chapman peering at her from beneath his flat cap, which he ceremoniously threw in the air anytime his cars won a Grand Prix.

"Of course," she replied, and they stepped away from the crowd to an empty waiting area for another gate.

Barney hurried over to join them, having slipped away to call the hotel and leave a message for Phil and Tina.

"How can we help you?" Georgie asked.

"Can I ask what your plans are now?" Chapman responded, never one for beating around the bush.

Georgie sighed. "We've been discussing that very subject. I'm really not sure, to be honest. We find ourselves short of a car, engine, and driver, so that may relegate us to dusting off the Formula Two chassis for the rest of the year."

"Do you have operating expenses covered to compete in any more Formula One races?" Chapman asked boldly.

"Yes, but that doesn't do us much good without anything to run, or someone to drive it."

Chapman waved a hand in the air. "Drivers are easy to find. It's the good ones that are trickier to get your hands on. Leave that to me. What if I loaned you a chassis to run? Could you afford a DFV to go in the back?"

Georgie was speechless.

"What chassis would this be, sir?" Barney asked.

Chapman brushed his neatly trimmed moustache with his fingers. "We're having a few teething issues with the new Lotus 72.

It's going to be bloody fast, but needs the anti-squat and anti-dive geometry sorted out. I need to put Rindt back in a 49 so he can focus on championship points, which leaves his 72 chassis available. I don't have enough people and what-have-you to run a third car, so if you can put an engine in it and cover the running costs, I'll loan you the chassis and provide help with the chassis set-up. What do you think?"

Barney's eyes lit up in anticipation, and Georgie couldn't contain the butterflies in her stomach. Not only could they keep racing in Formula One, but they'd be operating as a works-assisted team in their first season.

Georgie held out her hand. "We'd be delighted to help, sir."

Chapman shook her hand. "Good. Have your lads come to the factory as soon as they're back."

With that, he walked back to the crowd, who were boarding the plane.

"Stone the crows," Georgie muttered, staring at her team manager.

"Can we afford another engine?" Barney asked with an anxious smile. "They're 7,500 quid. And when I say we, I mean you, of course."

"Not really," Georgie replied, "but I could hardly say no, could I?"

8

BONAIRE

Dividing the tasks, AJ handed the shackles and line she'd brought down to Reg, then took out a GoPro underwater camera from her thigh pocket. It was rated to 196 feet, but she was hoping they'd manufactured the housing with a healthy safety margin. Signalling for Laurens to follow her, she left Reg to figure out a way to safely harness the line to the barge.

Slowly circling the wreck, she carefully filmed where the gunwales met the sea floor, handing Laurens one of her dive lights to brighten the picture. The barge had settled with the bow facing the shore as though it had wandered to the bottom on its way towards the island. Whatever cabin structure had existed was either buried deep into the sand or crushed as the vessel inverted. The gunwales appeared to make a perfect seal all the way around, with sand heaped against the open ocean side of the wreck at the stern. On first inspection, AJ was sure they could verify what they'd assumed from the crude video De Konig had already shot. There was no easy access to the cargo.

After two laps of filming, AJ moved to the starboard side, where a cloud of debris wafted into the water column. She found Reg on his knees, shovelling sand aside, with the line he'd affixed.coiled beside him. He looked up through the hazy cloud and she held up three fingers, indicating they had three minutes until they should be ascending. Reg gave her an okay signal, then returned to his digging.

Moving to the bow, AJ investigated an odd-shaped sand pile she'd noticed a few yards from the wreck. Sweeping sand aside, she soon made a thick cloud of her own as the tiny grains and particulate scattered into the water around her. After a minute of foraging, her gloved hand finally scraped along something solid. Brushing more sand away, she hoped to have exposed whatever was buried there, but the water was far too cloudy to tell. Rising from the sea floor, she checked her Perdix, then finned towards Reg, who was already on his way. With a subtle nod, they headed for the line, making sure Laurens was following.

Reg played out the rope he'd tied to the stern as they began their ascent, swimming next to the grapple line. With almost no current, they didn't even need to hold on. AJ had been pleased that Laurens appeared to be okay with his buoyancy and control at the wreck. Tech diving with the extra gear and tanks was a far cry from recreational diving with a single tank and minimal equipment. Maintaining neutral buoyancy took a lot more work, and it was easy to overinflate the wing or not keep up and lose control. The Dutchman had seemed competent, and she'd only noticed him bumping into the sand or the hull a few times.

Looking up from 175 feet, the surface was nothing more than a slightly lighter blue overhead, bringing home how far underwater they really were. The line to the pontoon vanished into the distance above them. A steady ascent was critical to avoid bubbles of gas expanding in their bodies and causing what's commonly known as the bends. The biggest challenge was controlling the venting of their wings. Let out too much gas, and they wouldn't go up. Too little and they'd take off in an uncontrolled ascent and win a trip to the recompression chamber. AJ and Reg made sure to keep Laurens slightly below them so he could judge the rate of ascent from them, and to his credit, she noted he was doing just that. He bumped into her a few times, but otherwise maintained control.

AJ double-checked the dive plan on her wrist slate. The Perdix guided her through each deco stop based on the gases they'd programmed into the dive computer and the actual time spent at each depth. The slate had their theoretical stops based on the dive plan they'd programmed in the laptop software. Comparing the two let her know how they were doing and made an issue easier to flag. Their dive had been more conservative than planned as they'd reached the bottom later than scheduled, so the computer sent them past the 90 feet and 80 feet stops on her slate. At 70, they levelled off and after AJ exchanged confirmation hand signals with the other two divers, they began switching from the trimix in the back tanks to the 50 percent nitrox in their first deco bottle.

AJ and Reg had both opened the valves on their nitrox tanks as they'd ascended in anticipation of the exchange, but Laurens fumbled with his, initially opening the valve on the 100 percent oxygen tank. AJ reached over and quickly stopped him. Pure oxygen is toxic to the human body below a depth of 20 feet. The switch to 50 percent nitrox at 70 feet was just above the maximum depth for that mix, so selecting the correct bottle and maintaining depth control were both vital.

Laurens glared at her through his mask, but she pointed to the nitrox deco tank and waved her hand back and forth over the oxygen tank. She watched his eyes flash recognition. After a moment, he blinked a few times and held up an okay sign before switching to the correct bottle and putting the correct regulator in his mouth. AJ and Reg then changed the gas selection on their dive computers so they'd be calculating from the correct blend. When she was done, AJ held up her hand and tapped her Perdix, reminding Laurens to do the same. He didn't acknowledge, but she watched him work the buttons on his own computer, so she figured he'd taken the hint.

From there, the team moved in 10-foot increments, spending progressively longer at each shallower depth as their dive computers directed. They ignored the emergency tank Reg had positioned, leaving it in place for the second dive. After six minutes at 30 feet, they ascended to 20 and AJ exchanged confirmation signals with the other two before stowing her nitrox reg and breathing from the second deco tank filled with pure oxygen. Once again, she carefully observed Lauren's switch, which he did correctly this time, then made sure he adjusted his computer for the new gas.

Now, clearly floating above them, tantalisingly close, the pontoon boat was only a few fin strokes away, yet still out of reach. Unless they remained underwater with increased pressure exerted on their bodies until their systems had safely processed the excess nitrogen they'd absorbed through the compressed gases at depth, they'd risk serious injury or even death by surfacing. The ocean between them and the boat may well have been beautifully clear, with gorgeous sun rays dancing through the blue water, but it was akin to being pinned down by deadly crossfire. Divers referred to the concept as the soft ceiling.

After twenty more minutes, the three divers finally surfaced to be greeted by the excitedly curious stare of John De Konig. Reg unclipped his deco tanks and heaved them one by one to the deck, where De Konig tried his best to slide them out of the way with his foot, wincing each time. The big man then scaled the ladder and tied the second line to the railing before ditching his rig. He then took the deco tanks from the other two so they could come back aboard.

"Well?" De Konig asked impatiently. "Is it accessible?"

Reg gave AJ a steadying arm, helping her across the deck to the bench where she began unfastening her backplate harness.

"About as your video showed, I'd say," Reg replied, returning to the step to assist Laurens. "Not very promising, I'm afraid, but we'll study the video AJ shot."

Laurens shook off Reg's help as he moved to the bench and sat down. "I know what I'm doing," he said, glaring at AJ. "You shouldn't interfere. You screwed me up."

"You were about to breathe 100 percent oxygen at over 20 metres," she quickly retorted, doing the conversion for him. "You would have gone into convulsions and drowned. Bloody right I stopped you. That's not interfering, mate."

Laurens growled something in Dutch and waved his hand at her. "I was preparing the oxygen tank for the next stop. I knew which was which."

AJ wanted to call bullshit on the guy, but she knew it was a battle she wouldn't win. Instead she turned to Reg and subtly shook her head. He blinked his acknowledgement in return, affirming they were seeing the situation the same way.

"Let's look at the video and see what we're dealing with," Reg said. "Then we'll discuss the plan for the second dive."

De Konig opened up his laptop and AJ retrieved the memory card from her GoPro, handing it to the man before unzipping her wetsuit and pulling it down around her waist. Towelling off, she put a long-sleeved sun-shirt over her bathing suit and a baseball cap on her head to keep her hair from her eyes. De Konig brought up the first video and the three of them crowded around to watch. Laurens remained at the bench, switching out his tanks.

"I did some digging in this area," Reg pointed out as the footage moved around the wreck. "The water was too clouded up to film afterwards, but we'll check it out on the second dive."

"Did you find the top of the gunwale?" AJ asked.

Reg shrugged his shoulders. "I don't think so, but it was hard to tell. Get down a bit and the sand is hard packed."

"Do you need tools?" De Konig asked.

"We'll take the small shovels you brought along next time," Reg replied. "If this was shallow water, we'd use mailbox blowers to clear the sand, but this deep we'd have to use a vacuum system, and they ain't cheap."

"Not to mention we don't have one available," AJ added, "and I doubt there's any lying around on the island."

De Konig scratched his head and continued watching the video.

"I did mention we might need specialised equipment once we saw what we were up against," Reg pointed out.

"You did," the older man replied, turning away from the screen and thinking for a moment. "Take a more thorough look on the second dive, and we'll decide after that. Obviously, I'm very keen to make this work here and now, if at all possible. A second attempt with more equipment at a later date would be a last resort."

"Understandable," Reg acknowledged. "We'll give it our best effort. It would be a lot easier if we had a schematic of the barge. You said it's either an LCM-8 or a copy of one?"

De Konig paused the video. "I haven't been able to find any records of the vessel, who owned it, or who chartered it. All I had to go on was the report of a boat lost in a violent storm that took everyone by surprise in this area. Supposedly, two crew members miraculously made it ashore and reported they were the only ones aboard but left the island shortly afterwards. The event drew my attention as it matched the time frame I was looking for."

"Which was?" AJ asked.

"Unimportant," De Konig replied. "But based on what we've both videoed, I think it's safe to assume that the vessel was an LCM-8 or similar."

He switched over to the internet and searched LCM-8, selecting images. An array of pictures of the basic, rectangular landing barge appeared, going back to its first launching in 1959, to modern day adaptations and modified uses.

"There's a lot of variations of cabin layout on those things," Reg pointed out. "But they all have the same open cargo area and swing down ramp at the bow."

"With the bow facing shore," AJ said, pointing to one of the pictures of a military version carrying Jeeps, "I think our best bet will be the gunwales just rearward from the ramp. The stern has far more sand build-up."

"It would be helpful to know what the cargo was," Reg urged. "Was it strapped to the deck? Did it scatter across the sea floor as the vessel sank, or is it trapped underneath?"

"Based on the sonar scans," De Konig replied cautiously, "what we're looking for doesn't appear to be within a few hundred metres' radius of the wreck site. I believe the cargo would have been strapped down and most likely remained in the hold, despite being inverted. Once we gain access to the cargo, I'll explain exactly what we're after. Until then, it's an unimportant detail."

Reg sighed. "Fair enough." He then lowered his voice. "It'll just be AJ and me going down on this next dive, Mr De Konig. An extra pair of hands would be great, but your boy doesn't have the experience for this kind of diving."

"You need all the hands you can get to manually remove all this sand," the older man replied. "I suggest you make use of him."

"It's a safety issue," AJ added. "There's no room for mistakes at these depths."

"He'll be fine," De Konig replied. "He's just knocking off a little rust."

"While we're having to worry about him, it's taking away from finding your cargo, sir," Reg pressed. "You hired us to do the diving, so we're responsible for all the divers. I'm telling you, he's not ready for this. If we were doing training dives, we'd be happy to work with him and coach him, but this is dangerous salvage work. He's a distraction, not a help."

De Konig took a moment, and AJ noticed Laurens was looking their way. Either he'd overheard the conversation or sensed what was being discussed. He stared at her blankly, making her feel uncomfortable, which she'd figured was his intention.

"It's important to me he's with you," De Konig finally said. "Please take him on the second dive and give him whatever guidance you can before going in. I'll talk to him about following your instructions, and I'm sorry he was short with you, AJ. That won't happen again. If he has any further issues, we'll revisit the issue, but for this next dive, I'd ask you to please include him and put him to work."

AJ and Reg looked at each other, mirroring the other's concerns. They'd worked together so many times that they operated as one, so adding another diver was always tricky. If the guy was more likeable, it wouldn't change the situation, but she'd feel a little more empathy for the bloke. Bullheadedness and ego could be killers 35 fathoms below the surface.

"If he'll cut out this he-man, silent, military bullshit and pay attention to our directions," Reg conceded, "then we'll try this again. But if we both feel he's not up to the task after this one, he's staying on the boat."

De Konig squeezed Reg's arm. "I appreciate your concerns and your willingness to help the project. He'll be fine, you'll see."

9

1970 – HETHEL, ENGLAND

The drive from Ashford Motor Racing Team's modest workshop in Finchley, North London to Lotus's expansive factory and test facility in Hethel, Norfolk was over a hundred miles. Georgie insisted on driving her Aston Martin DB6 Mark II Volante with the top down, which meant Barney hung gamely on the door handle the entire trip and his hair looked like a bird's nest by the time they arrived.

"I didn't spend all this money on a car to drive the thing slowly," she'd explained after Barney's first experience as a passenger shortly after Georgie had upgraded from her Triumph Spitfire to the Aston.

"You see, that didn't take long," she said, stepping from the car once she'd parked outside Colin Chapman's impressive facility.

Barney felt like kissing the ground, having survived her ladyship's breakneck dash across the English countryside.

"I can't believe we're racing against a team who have all these resources at their disposal," Georgie said as they walked to the front doors. "I feel like David facing nothing but Goliaths."

She paused and stared for a moment at the long two-storey building where Lotus road cars were built. A much smaller workshop was dedicated to the racing team, but it was still daunting to imagine the design, engineering, and manpower available when needed. They walked inside to be greeted by a polite young woman who reminded Georgie of the singer Lulu, which she assumed was not an accident. Told they were better off driving around to the race shop as it was a long walk, they returned to the Aston Martin and this time Georgie drove slowly around the facility, following the directions she'd been given.

Inside the race shop, a very tired-looking Phil came over and greeted them.

"It's coming along quite well," he explained, leading them to the Lotus 72 on chassis stands where Tina wiped his hands on a rag and said hello.

With the bodywork removed, Georgie always thought the race cars looked so complicated and days away from being race ready, yet the mechanics seemed to magically bolt them together in time whenever needed.

"The engine arrived, I see," she commented, noting the DFV attached to the back of the monocoque.

"Yesterday," Phil replied. "We stayed late last night to finish the plumbing for the radiators and oil cooler."

"I thought this chassis had already run," Georgie said in surprise. "Where are all the hoses and whatnot they used?"

Phil and Tina exchanged a glance. "They keep changing the specs on bits and pieces, ma'am, so we had to redo everything." He pointed to the front suspension, which appeared to be only partially assembled. "We're waiting on lower wishbones to match the new geometry. We had the front end built, but then Mr Chapman came up with a different pick-up point position, and we had to take it all apart so they could weld the chassis again."

"Gosh," Georgie muttered. "Well, I'm sorry for all the trouble, lads, but she looks magnificent. Where's all the bodywork?"

"Being painted, ma'am," Phil replied.

"I gave them the correct colours," Barney offered.

Georgie grinned, imagining the sleek, modern, wedge-shaped

Lotus 72 in her racing paint scheme. The Ferraris were red, so she chose royal blue as the primary colour, and then the red stripe with white borders completed the Union Jack theme.

"Ah, glad you could make it," Colin Chapman's voice came from across the workshop as he strode their way.

Georgie noticed the man was always impeccably dressed when and wherever she saw him, which had been in his office when she'd purchased the Lotus 49, and at the racetrack in the heat and grime of a race weekend.

"Thank you for making space available for the lads to work," she replied. "It appears to be coming along..." she added, but trailed off, feeling stuck in the middle.

She wanted to defend her mechanics and ask why they were having to do everything twice, but didn't want to question Chapman's organisation. In the end, if it made the car go faster, no one would remember the headaches, so she left the point alone.

"It'll be ready for Monaco," Chapman replied, while he looked towards the large sliding doors leading outside. "I asked you here today to meet someone. He should be back anytime soon," he said, turning back to her. "Let's walk outside."

Georgie and Barney fell in behind the forty-two-year-old man many believed to be an automotive design genius, and followed him to the courtyard behind the workshop. The sound of a distant engine being run to its limit echoed off the buildings in the cool, spring air. Crisp blips of the rpm followed as the driver down-shifted for a corner, before the engine note rose quickly again as the car accelerated from the turn.

Chapman stood there listening intently while one of his cars was driven at speed around the test track he'd created on the old World War II airfield where he'd chosen to build his factory specifically for that very reason. After a few minutes, Georgie heard the car slow and a moment later, a Lotus Cortina saloon car appeared around the corner of a building and rolled to a stop in front of them.

The driver's door opened, and a man stepped out in racing

overalls and an open-face helmet, his face hidden behind a fire-resistant balaclava. He left the engine running at idle for a few moments longer before leaning inside and turning it off. The hot car made tinging noises as the brakes and engine began quickly cooling after being stressed to the limit on the track.

To Georgie's surprise, when the driver slipped off his helmet and balaclava, she was looking at a much younger fellow than she'd expected. He had sandy blonde hair, bright blue eyes, and a boyish grin. He could have been seventeen, but she guessed he was a little older or Chapman wouldn't be entrusting one of his cars to the lad.

"Miles, I'd like you to meet Lady Ashford and her team manager, Barney Morgan," Chapman said, waving him over. "Lady Ashford, this is Miles Preston, who I'd like you to consider as your driver while you're using one of my chassis."

Georgie extended a hand and felt decidedly old as she considered the nice-looking kid before her. Who could have been her son. If her husband hadn't been killed in action within a few months of their marriage, and she hadn't miscarried their baby.

"It's a pleasure to meet you, your ladyship," the young man said in an accent hinting at a West Country upbringing.

"Pleasure's mine, and Georgie will do just fine or you'll make me feel older than I already do."

"Been racing saloon cars, haven't you, lad?" Barney asked, nodding to the Cortina.

"Yes, sir, I have a Ford Escort my father and I built, and now Mr Chapman has been kind enough to let me drive this development Cortina. We've entered it in the next round at Silverstone this weekend."

"Have you raced any formula cars?" Barney asked.

Miles's smile was captivating, and his eyes sparkled as he spoke. "No, sir. But I've driven Formula One and Formula Two cars here at the testing facility over the past year or so. A few hundred laps I'd say."

"Hmm," Barney grunted, looking at Chapman.

Georgie caught a wry grin on the Lotus boss's face. "Rob Walker called me this morning. I'd approached him first about the idea of running a second car to Graham Hill, but he declined. Apparently, he's changed his mind, but I told him I had another arrangement sorted. I dare say I can call him back."

Barney's face turned ashen. "I wasn't saying we had a problem, sir..." he bumbled.

"I'm assuming this is what you meant when you said 'Leave that to me?'" Georgie interjected, refusing to be intimidated by Chapman's forthright manner.

The man nodded. "Miles has proven himself to be an excellent test driver, and he doesn't tear up equipment. Unless you have a better option you're proposing, I suggest you utilise the young man. I'm already paying him a salary, so you just cover his expenses and give him a cut of prize money."

Miles's face froze. From his reaction, Georgie figured this news was as unexpected to the driver as it was to her. Barney had spoken to a couple of potential drivers with experience, but none were very exciting in her eyes.

Chapman pointed to the Lotus Cortina. "This one has a passenger seat and seatbelts. Take her ladyship for a few laps, Miles. She can let me know her decision when you come back."

"That's not necessary," Georgie began, unsure whether she was willing to put her life in the hands of an eager young racer.

"Nonsense," Chapman said with a wave of his hand. "Come and see me when you get back."

As he walked away, the other three stood still and looked at each other.

"Shall we?" Miles finally said, breaking the silence and walking around the Cortina to open the passenger door.

Georgie thrust her handbag into Barney's arms. "If I don't come back alive, my father will almost certainly blame you for this, Mr Morgan. He'll insist on a head rolling, and he already thinks you've conned me into this racing malarkey."

"Good to know," Barney stammered. "I think we'd all prefer you survive this experience."

Georgie slid into the form-fitting racing seat and Miles helped her fasten the four-point harness, nervously trying not to touch her inappropriately while securing her in place. Barney ran into the building and returned a few moments later with a crash helmet, which he handed to her.

"Probably need one of these, ma'am."

"I bloody well hope I don't *need* one," she replied, "but I'd like it all the same."

Barney closed the door as Miles situated himself in the driver's seat and fired up the twin cam engine, which emanated a low growl. He buckled himself in, strapped on his helmet, and turned the Cortina around.

"I promise this will be okay," he shouted over the noise of the engine. "I can take it easy if you'd prefer?"

Georgie looked over at the young man, returning his enthusiastic gaze. Despite his boyish features and eager smile, his eyes held the maturity and caring of someone much older.

"In for a penny, in for a pound, as they say," she responded. "I believe Mr Chapman intended for you to impress me, so I'll leave it up to you as to how you think you'll accomplish that."

He looked thoughtful as he absorbed her words, then nodded and pulled away.

Georgie's feet shivered in anticipation, feeling the vibration through the steel floor of the bare interior. With all the road car rubber insulated joints removed from the suspension in favour of rose joints and spherical bearings, every bump and undulation jolted through the chassis and into the seat.

Miles pulled between two buildings to a large, open expanse of grass, concrete, and tarmac. The two wide runways of the former RAF Hethel bomber station were clear to see, with a series of smaller roadways linking them to form the test track. He drove onto the course and smoothly accelerated into third gear, where he levelled off the speed at an rpm level where he could shout and still be heard.

For one complete lap, he drove well below the car's capability and explained the idiosyncrasies of the circuit, the gear he would use for each corner, and mentioned details about certain braking techniques and racing line adjustments he'd be making to optimise speed. When he completed the lap, he turned to Georgie.

"Looking well ahead will help, your ladyship."

She nodded in return, and before she could remind him to address her more casually, Miles pushed the throttle to the floor and the engine note made conversation impossible.

For the next five minutes, Georgie marvelled at the precision and skill with which the young driver placed the car on the racing line while all four tyres slid through the corners. His hands urged the steering wheel with smooth and deliberate inputs as he caressed the throttle pedal, keeping the Cortina at its absolute limit of adhesion at all times.

After three laps were complete, he slowed and exited the track, winding his way between the buildings until he came to rest outside the Formula One workshop. Unbuckling, he got out and came around to the passenger side, helping Georgie unstrap and climb out. They removed their helmets and Miles turned off the engine, having let it idle for a minute or so.

"I hope that was okay, your ladyship," he said with a look of concern.

Barney and Colin Chapman slid the workshop door open and stepped outside to join them. Georgie ignored them both, stepping closer to the young driver. She smiled and held out her hand.

"Welcome to the Ashford Motor Racing Team, Miles Preston. I hope you have a passport. You're going to be racing in Monaco in two and a half weeks."

10

BONAIRE

Laurens wasn't what AJ would describe as amiable, but he did pay attention throughout Reg's dive briefing and responded when questioned. The plan for the second dive was simple: find a way beyond the gunwales of the wreck within thirty minutes. The technical details involved in achieving that were even more critical than the first dive. The extra ten minutes of bottom time bought them an additional thirty-seven minutes of decompression obligation.

Part of the standard procedure for technical diving was to clearly mark each tank with the gas mix and MOD – maximum operating depth – on two pieces of tape – one visible to the diver when the tank was clipped in place and the other visible to another diver. On the first dive, AJ could read the labels on the sides of Laurens' tanks, which was why she'd been confident he was about to breathe from the wrong one. But looking at his other labels, it was obvious he hadn't been able to see them clearly himself. She was pleased to see he corrected that issue on the fresh tanks.

"Got that buoy?" AJ asked De Konig.

The older man nodded and handed her a small, round, white buoy with a ring on the bottom. "I'm still not sure about this," he grumbled.

AJ grinned and fastened a carabiner to the end of the line Reg had secured to the wreck. She then clipped it to the ring on the buoy and tossed the ball overboard.

"It'll be fine," she said, returning to the bench to gear up. "You'll see."

De Konig didn't look convinced.

The gentle chop rocked the deck as AJ waddled to the bow of the pontoon, dwarfed by the heavy tanks on her back. Taking a giant stride, she splashed in, then took the deco tanks Reg handed down to her. Once they were clipped in place, he passed her a short, metal shovel, which she strapped to one of the deco tanks with a pair of bungees. Laurens followed suit, then Reg, who brought a stout metal pole with him for levering things or poking at the packed sand to break it up.

Once everyone was ready, Reg gave the thumbs-down signal, and the three divers submerged for what would be a hundred-minute dive, if all went to plan.

Without the stop on the descent, AJ led the way again and didn't waste any time, lightly adding gas to her wing as they dropped through the water column, clearing her ears as she went. A mild current had picked up, and she found herself finning against it to stay in contact with the line. Every twenty feet or so, she'd grab the line and pull herself forward to save a little finning effort. If the current picked up any more, they'd have to use the line to descend, which would take a little longer.

This time, they reached the wreck shortly after three minutes, which was the planned descent time. AJ released gas into her wing to arrest her descent and levelled off, moving quickly to the pile of sand she'd worked on clearing. In the three hours since they'd left, the haze had settled and she could see a dark object amongst the pale yellow sand. Gently brushing more aside, she took out her camera and filmed the object. It was still difficult to identify and wouldn't budge when she shoved against it, but she had an idea what it might be, and checking the film would be better use of her time than digging around further.

Moving to the starboard side, she joined Reg, who had settled on his knees next to where he'd been digging before. A shallow scallop from the seabed revealed more of the gunwale, but they still hadn't reached the top of it. Or bottom, given the boat was upside down.

Reg pointed to the corner of the vessel only six feet away and indicated they should dig along the side in that direction. He then pointed to the stern, tapped himself on the chest, and signalled a hand over hand motion. AJ returned an okay sign and watched him fin towards the stern where he would pull the line they'd affixed until the buoy was submerged above them. Judging that point would be guesswork, as he couldn't see the surface and the current would drag the line and buoy, so reeling in a hundred feet of line would probably pull the buoy underwater by more than they wanted. AJ stopped watching Reg and decided he would figure it out, and she had her own work to do.

Unstrapping the shovel, she pointed for Laurens to position himself closer to the bow. She would move sand his way, and then he'd shovel it beyond the wreck. For once, the current was actually a help as it carried some of the haze and sediment away from them. AJ began digging, and kept an eye on Laurens as he tried to do the same, scooping the sand along the channel they were making.

Working with four tanks strapped to her body and a wing trying to tip her forward all the time was not an easy task. AJ dumped some of the gas from her wing, as she didn't need or want to be neutrally buoyant while kneeling on the sea floor. Next to her, Laurens kept rolling to his side and having to reach out to push himself upright again. She tapped him on the arm and signalled for him to vent some gas from his wing. He frowned at her through his mask, but did as she suggested and they went back to work.

If he hadn't been with them, AJ would have unclipped her deco bottles and set them aside to make life easier, but she didn't want him doing that. If somehow a diver lost contact with their deco gases, they'd be in big trouble. Without the higher oxygen rich mixes, the gas on their backs, which actually contained only 18 percent oxygen instead of the 21 percent present in air, would have a far longer decompression obligation. They could literally run out of gas to breathe while still being stuck under a soft ceiling. Which was one of the reasons Reg had placed the bottle at 60 feet, but she hoped they wouldn't need to use it.

Stirring up the sand brought with it a crowd of inquisitive fish, hoping for tasty molluscs to be churned up. AJ was worried she'd accidentally hit one of them with the shovel, but they seemed to dodge out the way just in time. Not that she could tell particularly well, as a hazy cloud now enshrouded them.

AJ reached through the murk and tapped Laurens on the arm. He leaned closer, and she used hand signals to tell him to sit back for a minute and let the water settle. He shrugged his shoulders, but stopped digging and shuffled backwards a few feet. AJ reached into the trough they'd made and felt along the metal of the side of the barge. It still disappeared into the sand below. They'd dug down a foot or more, but the soft top sand kept rolling down and refilling a lot of what progress they'd made.

Moving towards the bow, she felt the ridge where the gunwale met the full-width front ramp. Sliding her hand down into their trough, she finally felt the underside of the gunwale, a foot behind the ramp. She felt a surge of excitement, which was quickly tempered by the task they now faced. Tunnelling under the gunwale would require some form of shoring, otherwise half of every dive would be wasted clearing out the sand which caved in, or shifted into their trough every time they left. If the current picked up even more, it could easily negate all their progress.

Taking her shovel, AJ placed the blade vertically into the base of the trough three feet aft of the ramp. She wiggled and pressed it in until the shovel stayed in place, forming a meagre temporary fence. She reached for Laurens' shovel, which he held in one hand, frowning at her through his mask. AJ tried to figure out how to explain what she was thinking to him in sign language or pantomiming, but realised it was too complicated. She had a slate she could write on, but they had so little time, she just beckoned at the shovel. Laurens didn't move, so she reached over and took hold of the handle, thinking he must surely understand by now that she needed it. The man stubbornly held on like a kid clinging to his favourite toy.

She tried again, pointing to the tool and then at herself. This time, Laurens threw his hands up and tossed the shovel at her.

"What a prick," she mumbled into her regulator, dumbfounded at why the man was being difficult over nothing.

Surely he wasn't so Neanderthal to have an issue taking instructions from a woman? AJ glanced at her Perdix. Their run time was already at fourteen minutes and she needed to get to work. Spinning around, she returned to shovelling sand, carefully scooping it from the trough and pushing it away from the bow. The hole was deep enough that it needed to be widened under where she was kneeling to stop the wall collapsing, but without shoring materials, she didn't have any options.

She reached into the trough again and could now feel the rough, corroded top of the gunwale along an eight-inch section. AJ used the tip of the blade to scrape back more sand in that area, but most of it slid down again. Setting the shovel aside, she cupped her hands and removed the sand instead, then went back and forth between scraping and scooping. After a while, she paused and wriggled her hand under the gunwale. The gap didn't seem to have increased, but the water was too silted out to see what was going on. Then it dawned on her. The sand under the barge was now falling through the hole she'd made. Reg could be right: the wide open cargo area of the barge was probably packed full of sand.

Frustrated and disappointed, she sat back and felt a hand on her shoulder. At first she flinched, thinking it was Laurens and the idea of him touching her, however innocently it might be, made her skin crawl. But then she realised it was Reg as he settled in the sand next to her. He held up an okay sign in the hazy water. She nodded and responded with the same signal. Sure, she was okay, but bloody annoyed.

Reg then held up a one finger from both hands and tapped them together. It was the diver's signal asking where her buddy was. AJ turned and looked behind her, pointing to where Laurens had been moments before. But he was no longer there. Swinging around the other way, she stared into the cloudy water, but couldn't make out another form.

"What an idiot," she grunted into her reg, but instantly felt bad.

She'd sort of brushed him aside and taken over, but a useful buddy would have moved downstream and continued clearing the sand away. She wondered if that's where he was and she just couldn't see him through the haze. Signalling to Reg that she was ascending above the mess to look around, she blew gas into her wing until she felt herself hovering over the sea floor. Another soft burst and she rose ten feet to look down, seeing the underside of the hull and nothing but sand all around it. Reg joined her and they looked at each other in puzzlement.

Laurens had vanished.

11

1970 – MONACO

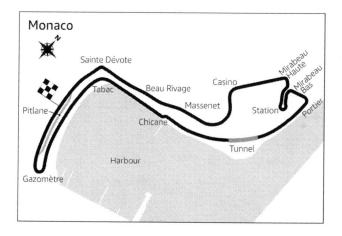

The drizzly rain had stopped, but thick clouds shrouded the Principality of Monaco, the tiny Mediterranean hillside country. Miles paused briefly at the start line, then began walking another lap of the circuit. It would be his third of the morning around the two-mile layout. Most of the streets were yet to be closed to local traffic, so he stayed by the newly installed guard rails edging the racing surface. He'd never seen anything quite like it.

Everything about the Grand Prix street circuit was unforgiving.

A minor mistake at most racetracks would mean riding the concrete kerb or dropping a wheel off the side of the tarmac. But at Monaco, an inch wide of the perfect racing line meant heavy contact with the curved steel Armco barrier and an end to your day. A similar error in the harbour-front section had landed a few unfortunate drivers in the water. The rainy conditions made the task of precision exponentially harder.

At each curve and turn, Miles studied the crown of the road, spotted holes, ruts, and surface changes, and estimated the gear he would need to be in, jotting everything down in a small notebook. Colin Chapman had told him he'd have the factory drivers, Jochen Rindt and John Miles, give him some pointers, but he hadn't seen either one yet. Although it was still only eight o'clock in the morning and practice wasn't for hours. Monaco had a unique tradition of holding first practice on Thursday, making a four-day event of the Grand Prix instead of the usual three.

After the first turn named Sainte Dévote, Miles strolled up the steep hill through Beau Rivage, a series of slight curves taken flat out, to the left-handed Massenet. A sharper right called Casino led into a short run with an awkward camber shift before hard braking for Mirabeau, a right-hand turn which exited downhill to Station Hairpin, the tightest corner on the track.

As Miles stood by the edge of the road looking at the impossibly tight 180-degree turn, a little Fiat 500 stopped alongside, blocking his view.

"Hop in," the driver said in an upper-class English accent. Miles leaned down to see who it was.

He'd briefly met Graham Hill, the double world champion and five-time Monaco Grand Prix winner, at Hethel, but couldn't believe the man had remembered the young test driver. Miles quickly hopped into the passenger seat.

"Good morning, sir."

"Colin told me you were driving here," Hill said, pulling away slowly in the Fiat. "Fed you to the bloody lions, I'd say, old chap. Monaco isn't the ideal track to make your first Grand Prix start."

"Undoubtedly true, sir, but I could hardly say no," Miles replied.

"Too right," Hill answered with a chuckle. "Well, pay attention and I'll tell you a few things I've learnt over the years."

For the next twenty minutes, the former champion drove around the soon to be closed-off streets of Monaco, and pointed out useful markers, hazardous spots, and any other tidbits which came to his mind. By the time Hill dropped him by the pit lane, Miles' notebook was packed with scribblings and sketches, and he thanked the man profusely.

Georgie watched nervously from the narrow pit lane as the youngster, Miles Preston, took his first few laps around the Monaco street circuit. Barney stood alongside as they both leaned over the barrier, watching the Formula One cars scream past at well over a hundred miles an hour, the raucous sound deafeningly bouncing between the tall buildings.

She hit the lever on her timing clipboard as Miles sped across the start/finish line, triggering the three stopwatches mounted across the top of the board. One stopped timing the current lap, one started timing the current lap, and the final stopwatch reset in preparation for the following lap. Georgie held the board up for Barney to see the lap time: 1:29.3 – 1 minute, 29 seconds, and 3 tenths. The top drivers were lapping in the 1:25 range from what they were seeing on the pit boards being hung over the barrier for the drivers to see.

Four seconds seemed like nothing to Georgie, but she knew the whole grid was sometimes covered by under one second from fastest to slowest. Still, it was Miles's first time on the circuit, and he was still learning the rhythm of the difficult layout... without hitting those treacherous steel barriers, lining the track like sword-wielding centurions.

As she peered over the barrier, watching for the blue Lotus 72 to appear, Barney tapped her arm and nodded to the pit lane entrance. Miles had brought the car in. They made sure no one else was coming, then trotted across the road to where Phil and Tina greeted their driver.

"Stiffen the rear roll bar one inch, please," Georgie overheard the young driver shout to Phil. "And send me out behind one of the faster cars."

She waited to see what her veteran mechanic would do. Usually, the driver would relay the handling characteristics of the car to the lead mechanic, who would then decide which adjustments to make. For a first-time driver to be calling the shots was strange to say the least, but Phil and Tina immediately moved to the rear of the car and adjusted the clamps on the antiroll bar.

Tina then ran to the entry of the pit lane and frantically waved when he saw Jackie Stewart approaching the final turn. Phil pointed to the pit road exit and Miles accelerated away with the tyres spinning, re-joining the racetrack before Sainte Dévote, where he pulled to the right and let the Scotsman fly by on the racing line. The Lotus then disappeared from view up the hill in hot pursuit of Stewart's March, which happened to be the fastest car on the track.

Just under a minute and a half later, back at the barrier with clipboard in hand, Georgie eagerly clicked the lever as Miles flew by, not too far behind the blue March.

"He's keeping up terribly well!" she yelled, but Barney was pointing at the official just beyond where they stood.

He was waving the chequered flag indicating the practice session was over.

"Blast! I'm sure he was about to go much faster," she complained.

"We still have three more sessions to improve," Barney reminded her. "He has to be faster than five other cars to make the field this week. If he drives like that out lap, I'm sure we'll be in."

But the next day, persistent rain drowned their hopes, slowing the times dramatically so that no one improved. Miles swore he was being cautious in the treacherous conditions, but Barney and

Phil still brought him in after twenty minutes, not wanting to risk a weekend-ending incident. Most teams chose the same path, electing to allow their drivers only a handful of laps to acclimatise to the wet track in case it rained for the race on Sunday. Jackie Stewart set the fastest time for the session, several seconds clear of Pedro Rodríguez in the BRM, and Miles ended up ranked sixth, which made everyone in the team smile.

Saturday became an incredibly tense and important day, with only one more session for all the cars, then a shorter second session for the non-seeded drivers to fight it out a little longer for the final six grid spots. Each entry's fastest time from any of the sessions counted towards their final starting position or, for five drivers, an early trip home.

Georgie made her way to the pit lane before the start of the session, where the clouds had finally moved on and the track was dry after more rain earlier in the morning. Barney, Phil, and Miles huddled in deep conversation, but they paused to greet their team owner.

"Please, don't let me interrupt you," she said. "Whatever you're talking about seemed very important."

"We're coming up with a strategy for the session," Barney responded. "And when I say we, I mean these two. I just happened to be here."

"That sounds very professional," Georgie said with a broad smile. "I thought we just went out and tried to go fast."

"That's generally what we've always done," Barney admitted. "But Miles told us a few things about how Chapman goes about it, so we're trying it out."

"It's not complicated, ma'am," Miles added. "We just discuss the options for adjustments based on whether the car is understeering or oversteering, and in what type of corner."

Georgie smiled once more, impressed at her team's willingness to improve and learn, especially on the input of their new young driver. She also reminded herself of the technical terms she'd been taught over the past few years. She was pretty sure understeer was when the front tyres slid too much and oversteer was when the rear did instead, but she didn't want to sound foolish and ask again.

"All right," Phil concluded. "For oversteer, we'll start by lowering the rear ride height, and understeer we'll soften the front antiroll bar as we can't lower the front any more."

Miles nodded. "There's more speed in me than there is in the car, so I think laps behind one or two of the faster drivers will help the most, but as my confidence grows, I think I'll be looking for more front grip."

Barney looked at his watch. "Better get ready chaps, only five minutes until the session."

"Be careful and go fast," Georgie chimed in, excited, apprehensive, and nervous all at the same time, but she couldn't believe how calm her driver appeared to be.

Miles seemed to be taking it all in his stride despite being thrust into the world's greatest motor racing arena at its most iconic venue.

Lowering himself into the Lotus 72, Miles took long, slow breaths to keep himself calm. He felt far more comfortable with his balaclava and helmet on, when no one could see his face. He was sure everyone could tell he was terrified.

As the engine warmed up, Phil helped strap him in. Miles made sure to organise his manly bits before the crotch straps were tightened around his upper thighs, connecting to the lap belts. Some drivers hated the feeling of being tied to the race car, but with the ever-increasing cornering forces from the wings the designers had added to the front and rear of the cars, Miles liked the sensation of being one with the race car. He could feel every nuance of the handling and anticipate the car's reaction in most situations.

A flag waved at the end of the pit lane and the engine notes all rose as a line of Formula One race cars streamed towards the guardrail-lined tight and twisty streets of Monaco. Miles couldn't believe he was following the likes of Jackie Stewart, Jack Brabham, Bruce McLaren, and Graham Hill onto the track for the most important qualifying session of his relatively short career. Little more than a year ago, he'd been slaving away on his Ford Escort, struggling to afford tyres and petrol for the next race, and here he was, driving a factory-supplied Lotus Grand Prix car at Monaco.

Pushing those exciting but daunting thoughts aside, Miles focused on the road ahead as he chased the lone Ferrari entered for Jacky Ickx up the hill through Beau Rivage.

The grooved tyres would take several laps to warm up to work at their optimum, leaving all the drivers slipping and sliding around for a bit. Miles was used to the Firestones from the test track at Hethel, and patiently waited for the grip to increase, while keeping Ickx in his sights ahead.

Finding the limits of braking and cornering was a constantly evolving process as the tyres' adhesion increased and the track surface gained grip as the dust was thrown aside and rubber laid down. The new aerofoils, or wings, had added another complication as the downforce increased exponentially with speed, meaning the car was being pressed harder into the ground the faster it went. The braking power that could be used at 150 mph was a lot more than at 50 mph, so the driver had to compensate by decreasing his pressure on the brake pedal as he slowed at a neck-snapping rate for the tighter corners.

The suspension changes applied at the factory had made the Lotus 72 far more predictable to drive, and Miles's confidence soared with each lap around Monaco. After ten laps, the Lotus had been separated from the Ferrari, who'd pitted, and Miles's times had levelled off according to his pit board, with a best of 1:27.0, so he too came to the pit lane.

"Pretty bloody good, mate," Phil shouted over the scream of racing engines on the track. "Stewart's in the 24s, but he's the only one. I think a time in the mid 26s should lock us in the field."

Miles knew that was a guess on Phil's part as no one knew the official lap times being recorded by the stopwatches in the control room, but all the mechanics looked at each other's pit boards, so they had a general idea. The added complication were the guaranteed starters. If some of those ten had troubles and set slower times, it meant faster drivers from the other eleven may still not qualify.

"How's the balance?" Phil asked.

"It's not bad," Miles reported. "I'm worried if we take out the little bit of understeer I still have, I might struggle with power oversteer off the corners."

"Can you go faster the way it is?" Phil asked. "Your times have evened out."

"I think so," Miles responded, looking up at his mechanic. "Leave the car and send me out behind one of the top six."

Phil gave him a thumbs-up. "Tina's already at the pit entry. We have ten minutes left. Give it your best, mate."

With a flurry of hand signals, Miles fired the engine back up and shot down the pit lane, re-joining the track behind the young Kiwi, Chris Amon, in the factory-entered March. If they hadn't encountered a slow-moving car at the hairpin, Miles wouldn't have been able to stay with the swift New Zealander, but the traffic allowed him to close to a car length behind as Amon got back up to speed through the tunnel and along the harbour side straight.

Miles's mind and pulse were both racing as he tried his best to stay with the faster car while paying attention to Amon's line as well as his braking and turn-in points. While driving his own car at the limit. At the start/finish line he was still three car lengths behind, and he knew he needed to put a perfect lap together.

Through Sainte Dévote he gained slightly on the March, only for Amon to pull farther away at the corner exit leading up the steep hill towards Massenet. Miles made a mental note to back up his entry speed for a better exit. The Kiwi took another car length with a beautiful four-wheel drift through the left-hander, before smoothly braking for the tighter right-hand turn, Casino. Miles registered he had time to gain in Massenet.

Through Mirabeau and Station Hairpin, the two remained the same distance apart, but at Portier, leading onto the longest flat-out section of track, Amon once again entered slightly slower to improve his exit speed. The gain paid dividends for the whole run to the chicane, the tight jog designed to slow the cars down, where Miles thought he may have gained a little back. The March was now six car lengths ahead as they held station through Tabec, and Miles paid close attention to Amon's braking point for the last turn, the hairpin called Gazomètre.

Initially braking earlier than Miles thought he would, the Kiwi's car appeared far more settled in the awkwardly curving braking zone, which meant his turn-in for the hairpin was on a wider line, opening up the corner as much as possible.

They crossed the line, now eight car lengths apart, but Miles had learnt a lot. He shifted his focus away from what Amon was doing, now that the March was well ahead, and concentrated on applying everything he'd seen. As soon as he shifted away from chasing the other car, Miles recognised his hands had relaxed on the steering wheel and his inputs to the controls softened, smoothing out his driving.

Backing up his entry meant 100 more rpm at the exit of Sainte Dévote, and gentler, earlier release of the brakes for Massenet set up a controlled slide through the corner, with every tyre at its optimum slip angle. By the time he exited Portier and roared into the tunnel, he realised Amon had barely increased the gap, so he knew he'd improved. *But would it be fast enough to qualify?*

Surely, this would be his first and last Formula One race if he failed to get the car in the field. The steel barriers were a blur as he topped 175 mph before braking hard for the chicane. In the split second it took Miles to realise he'd braked six feet later than his mark, he cursed himself for losing focus. By trailing off the brake more slowly as he turned in, he managed to bleed off the extra speed and urged the car left, then quickly right, threading the needle between the concrete barriers placed at both apexes. But he knew he'd given up lap time with the small mistake.

Adrenaline and grit brought his concentration back, and he remembered to adjust his braking for Gazomètre. Instead of initially hitting the pedal hard, Miles squeezed on the brakes and immediately noticed how stable the car became as he was able to then brake with full force and line it up better for the right-hand hairpin.

As he sped by the line, he caught a glimpse of his pit board, which read 26-something, but he missed the last number. That was the lap time for his prior lap, so he had no idea if the one he'd just completed was better or not. It had felt like an improvement, but he had to push for more.

The top few fuelled for a handful of laps to keep the race car as nimble as possible, but Phil had put enough petrol in for Miles to run the whole session, knowing he needed the experience. With each lap, his fuel level was burning down, which meant the car was lighter and, in theory, a little faster.

Braking for Sainte Dévote, Miles blipped the throttle as he downshifted during the braking zone and eased the steering wheel into the corner, every ripple and undulation in the road humming through his hands as he fought the wheel. A better exit again showed another 100 rpm gain, and he was off to a great start for the lap.

Certain he still had more speed to find in Massenet, Miles lightened his braking again as he crested the hill and turned into the sweeping left-hand corner. The front responded a touch lazily to the extra speed, and he wished he'd made the adjustment to lessen the understeer after all. With more steering input than he would have liked, the front tyres finally found their grip, and the rear rotated into a slide. Miles quickly corrected with the steering, but instead of the balanced four-wheel drift he'd been seeking, he was now fighting an oversteer as he reached the braking zone for Casino.

Easing off the throttle, the rear tyres fell in line just before he applied the brakes, but he was already a few feet wider than ideal. Down two gears, he eased off the brake and turned into Casino, but his compromised entry line meant he apexed too early and the car drifted towards the Armco barrier at the exit. Determined not to lose too much lap time, he squeezed into the throttle and nudged at the steering wheel, inducing a power oversteer to redirect his trajectory. It almost worked.

The Lotus's left rear tyre clipped the guardrail, leaving a black mark for ten yards along the rounded steel barrier, but the impact was hard enough to bend the toe link. Immediately, Miles knew something was wrong and backed off, gathering the car back under control and cursing himself underneath his balaclava.

Limping the wounded car back to the pits with his arm raised as a warning to other drivers, he pulled up to Phil, who looked strangely excited. Miles undid his belts and stepping from the cockpit, inspecting the left rear.

"I'm so sorry," he began as Phil joined him. "I thought I could pull it off, but I should have given up the lap."

He noticed the engines had quietened around the track and cars idled past them in the pit lane.

"Is the session over?" he asked.

"No," Phil replied, as Barney and Georgie joined them. "Hill just hit the barrier so they've stopped the session. There won't be enough time left to start it again."

"I really screwed up..." Miles began, but Phil cut him off.

"We're in lad!"

"We are?" Miles responded in surprise, slipping off his helmet and balaclava. "Are you sure?"

"You did a 26.2, mate!" Phil raved, and Barney slapped him on the back.

"No more pointers for you, young man," a voice said, and Miles turned around.

Graham Hill kept on walking, helmet in hand, but glanced back and gave the kid a quick wink.

12

BONAIRE

At 190 feet, AJ and Reg exchanged a flurry of hand signals, formulating a plan. They'd already taken a lap above the wreck and verified Laurens wasn't anywhere to be seen. Above them, the two lines disappeared into the blue water with no diver in sight. In AJ's mind, that left two alternatives. The Dutchman had either swum away from the barge for some inexplicable reason, or he'd gone up and was already out of their range of visibility. Searching the vast area around the wreck wasn't feasible and held a low percentage chance of a result. Their best hope was going up.

Shortening their bottom time reduced their decompression obligation, which left more gas and time to either help Laurens if they found him on the line, or surface and begin a lost diver search. Which they both knew would become a body recovery in short order. Diving deep was an unforgiving endeavour.

Ascending as fast as they could safely go, AJ and Reg kept a hand in contact with the grapple line as the current had increased a little more. Reg's buoy line disappeared behind them as the pontoon pulled the grapple line farther towards the coastline than the air-filled buoy fighting to get back to the surface. AJ hoped

Laurens hadn't chosen the wrong line, if indeed he had decided to head up.

Her Perdix showed a brief pause at 80 feet, which they ignored to reach 70, where they switched to the 50 percent nitrox deco gas. The computer held them there for one minute, but their switch and double-check of each other's procedure took a minute and a half, which they knew made up for the lower pause they'd blown through.

Looking up, the boat was a blurry shadow, and AJ pointed to a second darker spot she thought might be Laurens. It was impossible to tell if it was contrast formed by the surface swells as they rose and fell, or possibly a diver on the line. If it was Laurens, he was too shallow too soon, even if he'd left the sea floor several minutes before they'd realised he was gone.

They moved up to 60 feet where the bail-out bottle hung. Reg checked the valve, which was still closed. AJ stared at what she'd thought might be Laurens above, but the darker apparition had gone. She looked down as they moved again to 50 feet, where they'd spend two minutes. No one was following from below. AJ felt sick to her stomach. Laurens had been with her. Her responsibility. Sure, especially in tech diving, everyone is responsible for themselves, but they'd noted the man seemed out of practice or simply inexperienced, and she should have watched him more diligently.

Reg nudged her. It was time to move up to 40 feet for three minutes. Once they levelled off, AJ stared at the round twin hulls, now clearly visible. Her emotions shifted to anger. They'd told De Konig that Laurens shouldn't go on the dive, but he'd insisted. They never should have caved to his whim. Why was he diving with them, anyway? The guy brought nothing to the table. An extra pair of hands? That was easily negated by the distraction of babysitting an inexperienced diver. AJ loved teaching diving and had all the patience in the world doing it, but this job wasn't a recreational cruise on the reef. It was hardcore, deep, technical, and dangerous diving.

Muttering into her regulator, she checked her dive computer. It was time to move up again. Thirty feet for four minutes. Maybe Laurens had become confused? The back gas they were breathing for the bulk of the dive was a trimix blend of oxygen, nitrogen, and helium. For divers, nitrogen was the enemy. The human body had evolved to breathe air and to dispose of the nitrogen making up 79 percent of the gas mixture. But breathing compressed gas equalised to the surrounding pressure at depth underwater inundated the body's systems with a massive increase in nitrogen molecules.

Aside from the need to decompress, a second issue with nitrogen is the narcotic effect it has on the human brain at depth. Often referred to as the 'rapture of the deep', the effects of nitrogen narcosis increase the deeper a diver goes, becoming noticeable as shallow as 60 feet and seriously affecting judgement below 130 feet. Hence recreational diving is limited to a maximum of 130 feet and considered technical below that depth. The cure is to ascend, as divers regain their faculties when returning to shallower water.

The helium content in the breathing mixture was to combat both those issues. Helium is harmless and easily disposed of through the body's systems. Nitrox used an increase in oxygen content to replace some of the nitrogen, but as oxygen becomes toxic at greater depths, trimix introduces helium to do the job instead. They were diving a blend of 18 percent oxygen – less than in air to keep them from oxygen toxicity – and 45 percent helium, leaving only 37 percent of nitrogen. The equivalent narcotic depth, or END, of the reduced nitrogen content was the same as diving to 101 feet on regular air. Not a depth from which an experienced diver usually felt anything more than slightly slower processing times.

They moved up to 20 feet and switched to their second deco bottle with pure oxygen. AJ made sure to change her computer to the new gas and watched Reg do the same. Looking up, she now saw a figure leaning over the bow of the pontoon boat, their profile wavy and blurred through the water. It could be De Konig, but she couldn't tell. It could just as easily have been Laurens, but they wouldn't know for another frustratingly agonising seventeen minutes. Surfacing sooner would be foolish. A rule in diving is never break your own decompression profile to help someone else who already had. One person in the chamber is always better than two. AJ knew the rule and would stick to it, but it didn't make the situation any less frustrating.

Finally, after what felt more like hours at 20, then 10 feet, they surfaced and called out to De Konig.

"Has Laurens come up?"

The older man appeared at the bow. His face was pale, and he looked either annoyed or on the verge of panic. She couldn't tell which.

"Yes, yes," he blathered. "Get aboard, quickly. He's not well."

"Damn it," Reg growled, scaling the awkwardly narrow ladder with all his bottles still attached.

AJ unclipped her deco bottles and handed them to Reg, who reappeared a moment later having ditched his gear. He kneeled down and hauled the bottles to the deck and AJ clambered up the ladder, feeling the full weight of gravity trying to drag her back into the water.

Laurens lay on the deck, curled in the foetal position, groaning. De Konig had had the presence of mind to put him on emergency oxygen, which Reg had forewarned him to have aboard for the project.

"Have you called the chamber?" AJ asked as she ditched her gear and hastily secured it.

"I didn't know who to call," De Konig replied, starting the outboards.

"Reg, drive the boat," AJ instructed, kneeling beside Laurens and making sure there was still oxygen in the small green tank and that it was flowing. "John, call emergency services and have an ambulance meet us at the closest dock we can reach."

De Konig looked at the coastline, then back at his man on the deck.

"Move," Reg told him, taking over the helm, and De Konig wisely stepped aside.

"Hope we don't snag the other line," AJ said to Reg in passing as she moved to the bow.

"I'll curve around some," Reg replied, easing the pontoon forward.

"Make the bloody call, mate," AJ barked at De Konig, who seemed shocked into paralysis or unwilling to help.

He looked back at her then nodded and began dialling a number on his mobile.

"Once we're unhooked from the wreck, I'll need a dock to head for," Reg added.

"Sod this," AJ muttered and with slack now in the grappling line, she unlooped it from the cleat and tossed it into the water.

"We're unhooked from the wreck!" Reg announced, turning the pontoon to port so he didn't run over the line with the outboards. "I need a heading!"

Angling slightly towards shore, he pushed the throttles forward, and the pontoon ran surprisingly smoothly through the light afternoon chop.

De Konig ended his call and pointed north-west. "See the airport?"

Reg nodded. "I think so. I see a tower."

"Aim for that," De Konig shouted over the wind and engine noise. "There's a dock where the ships bring propane to the island. It's just along from where we ate lunch yesterday."

From two miles away, that didn't mean much to AJ, as the details of the coastline were impossible to make out, but Reg had the throttles pinned and seemed to be heading in the right general direction.

"What happened?" De Konig asked as they gathered either side of Reg.

"One minute he was with me by the wreck," AJ replied, "and the next, he was nowhere to be seen. I've no idea why he surfaced."

Reg looked over at Laurens' gear laying under one of the benches where either he or De Konig must have shoved it.

"On it," AJ said, reading his mind.

She dropped to the deck and pulled the rig out, checking the valves on the manifold for the twin back tanks. Three large knobs turned the valves, two of which closed off each tank individually and the third shut one tank off from the other. Each tank had its own regulator. With the three valves open, the diver could breathe gas through either regulator, and the bottles remained equalised as the gas was used. This stopped one tank emptying first and causing the diver to be unbalanced as the mass changed. All three valves should be accessible by the diver reaching behind their head – it was usually awkward, but something every tech diver figures out how to do.

The valve controlling the tank on the right side was closed. The long line to what Laurens had been using as his primary regulator came from that first stage. The other two valves were open, meaning he would have been breathing from his back-up regulator on the short hose from the left-side tank. She checked the pressure gauge. It showed empty.

"Something was hissing like crazy for a while when he came up," De Konig shouted.

AJ thought for a moment, then cracked the valve open on the right-side tank. Gas immediately escaped from the back-up regulator and the pressure gauge shot up to 1300psi. She closed the valve and held the reg in her hand. It was leaking badly from a swivel joint by the second stage. It continued spewing gas until it drained the manifold and line while AJ checked the deco tanks. The pure oxygen tank was full, and the valve closed. The 50 percent nitrox valve was open, and from the pressure it appeared Laurens had breathed from it for at least some of his ascent. She stood and moved over to the man who was still lying in the same place on the deck.

"We're getting you to the chamber, mate," she told him, but he didn't appear to hear her.

He rocked back and forth, moaning softly, and had vomited over the deck. She undid his dive computer from his wrist and returned to the helm, scrolling through the menu to find where the last dive was recorded. As she thought, he hadn't switched gases on the computer during ascent, so it computed the dive based on using the trimix back gas the whole time. It was also flashing an alert saying he'd surfaced before his decompression obligation was complete.

"No shit," she told the computer.

"Learn anything?" Reg asked, his eyes focused on the dock they could now make out ahead.

"Best I can tell, the swivel on one of those recreational regulators he was using blew a seal, probably at the wreck when he was sitting behind me where I couldn't see. He closed the tank valve, but he closed the primary, not the back-up, which was the one leaking."

"He shut the gas off to the reg he was using?" Reg questioned.

"Looks that way," AJ replied. "And then at some point, he switched over to the nitrox mix on his ascent."

Reg shook his head. "Bugger. This is bad. How long was he down for?" he asked De Konig, who was supposed to keep an eye on their dive time from the surface in case they were overdue.

"I couldn't be sure," De Konig replied. "He was mumbling and moaning when he came aboard and I had no idea what was happening. He took his gear off, and I was looking over the bow for you two when he collapsed. I'd say he was down less time than it took for you two to come up after him."

"I don't think he even stopped on the way up, Reg," AJ said despondently, checking the computer again. "Eighteen-minute dive time," she read from the screen.

"I bet you he turned off the wrong valve, panicked, then switched to the nitrox and bolted," Reg responded, easing back the throttles as they approached the dock.

On the shore, an ambulance waited with lights flashing and two EMTs wheeled a gurney down the dock.

"Why would he panic like that?" De Konig muttered as AJ moved to the bow, ready to throw a line to the dock.

"Because he shouldn't have bloody well been down there in the first place," Reg snapped. "Like we told you."

13

1970 – MONACO

Georgie was simply too excited. At 43 years old, having experienced the London Blitz, a brief marriage and loss of her husband, and the challenge of being an independent woman in the 50s and 60s, not much got her pulse racing anymore, but standing on the grid for the Grand Prix of Monaco as a team owner certainly did.

Looking down from the royal box, Prince Rainier III and his beautiful wife, the academy award-winning actress Grace Kelly, surveyed the proceedings with their three children alongside. Media and television were everywhere, although only the hardcore motor racing press paid attention to the English kid making his first Formula One start from twelfth on the grid. Georgie couldn't believe Miles had outqualified the second factory-entered Lotus as well as nine other drivers.

Everyone stopped milling about as a brass band played 'A Marcia de Muneghu', Monaco's national anthem, and Georgie stood proudly to attention alongside the Lotus. Phil and Tina shuffled from one foot to the other, impatiently waiting for the song to be over so they could continue fussing with the race car.

At the front of the grid amongst a sea of people, Jackie Stewart's

March sat in pole position with Amon and Hulme alongside. Brabham and Ickx held the second row, with the Belgian driving the team's spare Ferrari after his was burnt to a cinder in Jarama. The Frenchmen Jean-Pierre Beltoise and Henri Pescarolo in their Matras sat alongside Jochen Rindt in the updated factory Lotus 49C on the third row, with Courage and McLaren behind them. Miles was starting from the middle of the fifth row with veteran Swiss driver Jo Siffert to his inside and fellow first-time starter, Ronnie Peterson, on his outside. Hill had outqualified the Swedish rookie, but having damaged his primary car beyond repair, was starting in the rear in his spare. No one had gone faster in the extra practice session the day before, which Miles had missed while the car had been repaired and realigned.

When the music stopped and the applause died down, Georgie walked around the car to where Miles was about to strap his helmet on. To her, he appeared to be cool as a cucumber once again.

"I have a tradition before every race," she said, feeling slightly awkward as she looked at the youngest driver who'd driven one of her entries. "A good luck kiss."

Miles smiled, and she swore he blushed as she leaned in and kissed him on the cheek.

"Go fast, and be careful," she said, then stepped back.

He'd peed just before coming to the grid, but Miles was busting to go again already. He'd been drinking water all morning to stay hydrated in what would be the most physical race of his life, but he knew it was nerves irritating his bladder. And now the beautiful team owner had kissed him and made him turn red. He quickly donned his fire-resistant balaclava then slipped on his helmet, cinching the buckle snuggly under his chin.

When he'd first starting racing cars, his father had shared a secret with him. His dad had been an infantryman in the war, and told him they'd all been terrified in the trenches, right before they were ordered to climb out of the mucky ditches and charge. He'd found that if he focused really hard on what he planned to do in the coming moments, the nerves wouldn't go away, but they'd take a back seat to the impending task. Ever since then, Miles had used his inner terror to sharpen his concentration, but apparently his bladder hadn't got the message.

Climbing into the Lotus, he prayed he wouldn't wet himself before they rolled from the grid, when he knew the nerves would instantly vanish.

"Remember, the tanks are chock-a-block full, mate," Phil said as he buckled him in. "Even more than in practice. She'll feel sluggish to start and you'll need to adjust your braking points."

"Yes, sir," Miles said automatically, his mind focused on running the opening laps with a pack of snarling competitors all trying to pass each other.

Phil had already been over this and every other detail a hundred times, but Miles knew Phil was as nervous as he was. Because he cared. The man took his job and responsibility very seriously, and had seen his precious car and driver in a ball of fire just weeks ago. Miles grabbed Phil's hand and held it tight.

"Thank you. For everything. You've given me a great race car. I promise I'll do my very best."

Phil squeezed his hand in return. "I know you will, son. Be safe," he replied, and he let go as his voice cracked a little.

With shrill whistles and lots of shouting, the grid cleared and a flag waved, sending the cars around the two-mile track on their warm-up lap. Miles didn't need to use the loo anymore, and his thoughts were consumed with generating heat into his tyres and brakes, and looking for any details which may have changed on the track. Oil dry from an earlier incident. An added or adjusted hay bale or barrier which compromised the ideal racing line.

The DFV engine had more power than anything he'd driven in the past, and while he'd become accustomed to its lively performance while testing at Hethel, he was suddenly aware of how easily it spun the tyres and accelerated amongst the other cars. But with steel barriers lining the track. If he didn't pay close attention, it would be easy to hit any one of them during the warm-up lap. He took a deep breath as he imagined how hectic it would be with sixteen Grand Prix machines all hurtling towards turn one at the start.

On the long, curving start/finish stretch, the cars formed up, each pulling up to their assigned stripe painted on the tarmac. From the low-slung perspective of the Lotus, Miles found himself peering out of the cockpit, searching for his mark, ultimately stopping when he was even with Siffert, figuring the veteran knew what he was doing.

The starter, 50 yards away beyond the front of the field, surveyed the cars to make sure everyone was ready. Satisfied, he raised the green flag and Miles put the Hewland gearbox into first, then picked up the engine rpm in step with all the other cars around him. As the starter's flag fell, the engines roared and Miles dropped the clutch. His Firestone tyres ripped at the tarmac, struggling for grip as the ferocious DFV pumped power through the driveshafts.

In clouds of tyre and engine smoke, the field lurched forward, gathering speed as the drivers found traction and began shifting gears each time their tachometers reached redline. Everything seemed to happen at once, as Miles's senses were overloaded with the chaos all around him. He fought for grip with his rear tyres, then had to flick his eyes down at the tachometer so he didn't over-rev the engine before shifting. Siffert moved ahead by half a car's length with a better launch, while Miles eased slightly ahead of Peterson to his left.

From the row in front, Courage made a good start, but Bruce McLaren spun his tyres too much, allowing Miles and Siffert to both challenge him in the approach to Sainte Dévote. Inches apart, the drivers stormed ahead and Miles made his shift from second gear to third based on the sound of his engine as he dare not take his eyes off the cars ahead and either side of him.

Pure instinct sent him to the brake pedal a moment earlier than the other two, sensing the three cars couldn't make it through the first turn side by side. He tucked in behind McLaren, blocking any attempt from Peterson, and let the two veterans duke it out through Sainte Dévote before finally falling in line nose to tail on the run up Beau Rivage.

At the front of the field, Stewart took the lead and began stretching away from Chris Amon and Jack Brabham. Ickx, Beltoise, Hulme, Rindt, and Pescarolo were next before Courage, Siffert, McLaren, and Miles. A snaking line of screaming race cars wound their way around the streets of the principality, inches from the Armco barriers and walls.

Ahead of Miles, Bruce McLaren was wrestling his car through the tight corners, oversteering the moment he tried applying power from the apex on, but the pace was furious and Miles told himself to be patient. A lunging move under braking could take them both out of the race, which was the last thing he could afford to do in his first Formula One race.

All of Miles's actual racing had been in saloon cars, with his experience behind the wheel of single-seaters alone on the Hethel test track, so he quickly realised the sight lines from the cockpit of the Lotus were vastly different and restricted. Instead of being able to look way ahead to accurately pick out his markers, he found his view blocked by the rear end and broad racing tyres of McLaren's car. Constantly reminding himself, he shifted his focus beyond the New Zealander, grabbing whatever glimpses he could of the road beyond instead of target-fixating on McLaren's gearbox.

The Formula One car was also far more physical to drive. The wide Firestones combined with the downforce generated by the wings in the faster corners and curving straights took a great deal of effort to steer the car. His head was thrust forward in the hard braking and the cornering G-force had his neck muscles begging for mercy. Usually, he'd only do five or six laps at a time around Hethel, so by ten laps into the eighty-lap race, he was already aware of the stress his body was about to be subjected to.

On lap twelve, Miles shot past Ickx's slowing Ferrari, which had broken a driveshaft, and he noticed over the following few laps that McLaren was struggling more and more with the handling of his car. Along the harbour, Miles braked a little early for the chicane, preparing for a great exit run to the final hairpin. It was lucky he did, as Bruce McLaren clipped the second apex barrier in the chicane and slid sideways directly in front of the Lotus. With light-ning-fast reactions, Miles nudged the steering wheel to the right and slipped by the stricken McLaren.

With a gap ahead, and no pressure from behind, Miles was finally able to settle in and find a rhythm around the challenging circuit. On the harbour straight he could see Siffert in the distance ahead, chasing several others, and lap by lap he was slowly closing on them. In his mirrors was nothing but an empty racetrack, having steadily pulled away from Peterson. According to his pit board which Tina hung over the barrier each lap, he was running in tenth.

At twenty-three laps into the race, he couldn't believe his eyes when he saw P8 on the board, Piers Courage having parked his De Tomaso with rack and pinion steering issues and Jean-Pierre Beltoise falling victim to a broken gearbox. A few laps later, Miles moved up to seventh when Stewart suffered ignition trouble, forcing him to the pits from the lead. The tough, unforgiving Monaco street circuit was already taking its toll on the field, and Miles doubled his efforts to be careful with his gear shifts and perfect on his racing line.

On one lap through Tabec, the left-hand corner after the chicane, he turned in a few feet too late and ran slightly wide of the apex, drifting off the perfect line towards the Armco. He corrected by steering into the slide and lessening his acceleration, but the car seemed to lose all grip and he cringed as the right rear tyre rubbed along the barrier. He held his breath all the way to Gazomètre, and only after he'd rounded the hairpin and acceler-ated along the start/finish straight without issue did he let himself believe he'd got away with one. As the race wore on, more and more dust, debris, and rubber from the racing tyres accumulated just off the racing line, making it treacherous to venture outside the narrow groove. Passing would become ever more hazardous.

At the halfway mark, Miles was still running seventh and the gap to Siffert had levelled off at six seconds, the two matching lap times. The driving was physical and the heat stifling. He dreaded to think how bad it must be in the cars with radiators in the front nose, as all the exiting hot air streamed over the driver's cockpit as well as cooking their feet in the front of the chassis. Chapman and his lead designer, Maurice Phillippe, had come up with many radical innovations on the Lotus 72, one of them being the placement of the radiators and oil coolers either side of the chassis, for which Miles was very grateful on the warm sunny day in Monaco.

Up ahead, Miles noticed it was no longer Siffert he was chasing. The Swiss had passed Pescarolo, who soon also moved up a spot, passing Hulme, who'd lost first gear. All the drivers were turning faster laps as their fuel loads burned down and the cars became more nimble, but the wounded Hulme was slowly inching back to Miles. The young Englishman was running on youthful stamina and adrenaline, begging the race to be over before fatigue forced him into an error.

On lap sixty-one, a car was swerving its way towards the Gazomètre hairpin, giving Miles another scare as he was forced offline to pass him. The luckless Chris Amon had lost a bolt in the rear suspension, and miraculously limped his March to the pit lane without crashing. Miles couldn't believe he was now running sixth in his first Grand Prix.

With ten laps to go, he was steadily reeling in Hulme, and instead of wishing for the race to be over, he was begging for enough laps to catch the New Zealander, no matter how knackered he felt. At two to go, Denny Hulme and Miles swept past Jo Siffert, whose throttle was sticking closed, and on the final lap, Miles had the Lotus within striking distance of the Kiwi as they approached Gazomètre for the last time.

For a moment, his youthful exuberance and determination urged him to pull out and attempt to outbrake the McLaren into the hairpin, but a surge of apprehension held him back. Following Hulme through the last turn, he was able to gain considerably as he still had the use of first gear, and the two drag-raced to the line, with Hulme staying ahead by a nose.

Miles was spent. Every muscle in his body ached as he slowed and shared a thumbs-up with one of his idols, the great Denny Hulme, on the cool-down lap. But he also wanted to kick himself. He'd chosen not to attack and gain another position at the final corner, and was sure he'd be criticised for chickening out. His elation at not just finishing his first Formula One race, but coming home fifth, was short lived. By the time he reached the pit lane, Miles was convinced the team, and especially Colin Chapman, who'd stuck his neck out to give him this opportunity, would be disappointed in him.

The pit lane was pure chaos. People were everywhere. The crowd had somehow found their way down from the grandstands, and officials and crew were doing their best to maintain some sense of order. When Miles finally came to a stop after finding Phil and Tina, the two mechanics practically dragged him from the race car, they were so overjoyed.

Amid the backslapping and congratulations, Miles managed to tell them. "I should have taken him at the last corner. I cost us a place."

"Are you bloody nuts, mate?" Phil enthused. "Rindt just won the race because Brabham tried going offline in Gazomètre, locked his brakes in all the marbles, and hit the hay bales!"

A flood of relief washed through Miles and he plonked himself down on a hot, sticky rear tyre. Pouring a bottle of cool water over his head, he finally allowed himself a broad smile.

Georgie fought through the crowd who'd somehow funnelled into the pit lane and were streaming onto the front straight where the top three cars had stopped by the podium. Letting Barney clear the way ahead, they finally reached the race car where their driver looked thoroughly spent, chugging water from a bottle.

"Bloody brilliant, Miles," she said, wanting to give him a hug, but he was covered in dirt and sweat. "That was brilliant!"

"Thank you, ma'am," he said, wiping his mouth and taking a towel from Barney. "The car was fantastic."

"The next one is Spa," Phil said, scratching his head and looking the car over. "Completely different racetrack altogether, ain't it? We'll have to change the set-up around a lot."

"Let's enjoy this moment first, Phil," Georgie said, punching her mechanic playfully on the arm. "I think this warrants a team dinner on the town."

"Looked good," a voice came from behind them, and they turned to see Colin Chapman emerging from the crowd with another man.

"Congratulations on the win," Georgie said excitedly. "Rindt was really coming on strong at the end."

"With a little luck thrown in," Chapman admitted. "But we'll take it." He turned to Miles. "The updates were better, I assume?"

"Yes, sir," Miles replied. "The car was far more predictable to drive, and I'm sure Jochen would get more speed out of it."

Chapman smirked. "You had the second fastest lap of the race, so don't sell yourself short, son."

A thought hit Georgie, and she caught her breath. "You want the chassis back for Spa, don't you?"

"I do," Chapman replied without hesitating. "I think we've sorted out the worst of the bugs, and proven its worth in a race. Rindt will drive this chassis in Belgium."

"Even with the prize money from here, I don't think I have the funds to buy another chassis from you," Georgie said, devastated.

"And I don't have a chassis I can sell you," Chapman replied.

Georgie's mouth fell open, and she saw the disappointment on the faces of every member of her team. Everyone talked about the highs and lows of motor racing, and she was living it sooner than she'd hoped.

"But let me introduce you to Martin van der Meer," Chapman continued, indicating the man standing next to him. "He ordered a 72 eight weeks ago, and his chassis will be finished next week. He doesn't have his team put together yet. I suggest you two work something out."

With that, Colin Chapman nodded, and disappeared into the throngs of people on the pit lane.

Georgie held out her hand to the well-dressed, handsome man. "Georgie Ashford. We were just discussing a celebratory dinner tonight. Perhaps you'd like to join us?"

Van der Meer firmly shook her hand. "I'd like that very much."

14

BONAIRE

AJ and Reg waited in the reception area of the building housing Bonaire's recompression chamber in the little capital town of Kralendijk. It had been two hours, they'd long since finished the coffee they'd bought over the road at Sweeti Bakery, which was now closed, and they were both famished. Finally, the door opened and De Konig joined them.

"They think initial signs are promising," he announced, clearly relieved. "He doesn't feel great, but he's talking with the doctor and appears to be alert and functioning. They said he has to stay in the chamber for several more hours as they slowly reduce the pressure."

"That's good to hear," AJ said, letting out a long sigh.

"Did he say what happened?" Reg asked.

De Konig sat down in a chair across from them. He looked weary. "You know I don't completely understand the diving stuff, and he was somewhat vague, but it sounded like something along the lines of what you'd figured out," he said, looking at AJ. "It started with an equipment failure while he was with you at the wreck."

"Did the doctor press him for details?" Reg asked. "The more they know, the more they can customise the recompression plan."

"He did. Laurens kept saying he knew he had to go up."

"He needed to close off the right bloody valve," Reg responded. "I don't mean to bang on about it, but we should never have let you talk us into taking him down again."

De Konig nodded. "You're right, of course. And I apologise. When I hired Laurens, he told me he was experienced and qualified."

"I'd say you were lied to," AJ commented. "Did you find him here on Bonaire?"

De Konig's brow creased in thought. "Yes, but he sort of found me, to be honest. He happened to be in the records office when I researched the barge. He was looking for some other wreck, or so he told me."

AJ leaned forward in her chair. "And why did you hire him?" she asked, the thought having come to her mind and struck her as strange. "You hire us to perform the dive, yet you also hire him to come with us. I don't get it. What was the point? You could have asked us to bring a third person if you thought the job needed more hands."

De Konig tensed. "I just thought he'd be useful, and clearly I was wrong."

"Is it about the money?" Reg pressed. "Was he cheap help?"

"No, no," De Konig snapped back, before swiftly calming himself. "Look, it's been a difficult day. Why don't we all get something to eat, a good night's sleep, and we'll pick things up tomorrow? Get the tanks refilled, and we'll meet at the boat at ten."

AJ looked at Reg, who raised one eyebrow. She responded with an almost imperceptible nod.

"Dinner and sleep sound good, Mr De Konig," Reg replied. "But we'll take the tanks back to TDS in the morning, then we're heading home. This isn't what we talked about. You told me you'd found a small uncharted wreck you'd like explored and possibly have us retrieve some of its cargo. You told me it was all above board. We get here and you saddle us with a minder who doesn't know his arse from a hole in the ground. And on top of that, you won't tell us anything about what we're truly looking for. Sure doesn't feel very legit to me, mate."

"Wait, wait, wait," De Konig reacted, getting to his feet and wincing, one hand going to his lower back. "You can't leave. We had a deal."

"You changed the deal," Reg retorted. "And we'll be on a plane tomorrow. The money you paid us upfront will cover the two dives we did for you."

De Konig flushed red, but didn't say anything right away, sitting back down and wincing again.

"Okay. You're right, I haven't been completely transparent with all the details. But secrecy is paramount."

"That horse has bolted," AJ said. "You don't put a diver in the chamber on a small island without everyone knowing about it pretty sharpish. Your little venture will be the talk of the Bonaire dive community by breakfast."

De Konig let out a long breath and nodded slowly. "I expect you're right. Which is more reason for us to press on with the project."

"It's more reason for *you* to press on," Reg corrected. "Whatever dodgy business you've got going on here isn't for us, I'm afraid."

The older man held up his hand. "Please. Let's get back on the right track. We all need a good meal and a decent night's sleep, plus I still have to move the boat and it's getting dark. I'll come by and pick you up at seven in the morning. We'll grab the tanks from the boat, and by the time we get to TDS, if I haven't answered all your questions to your satisfaction, we'll return the tanks and you'll be on your way. If you're happy with my explanation as to why I've been overly secretive about this, then we'll fill the tanks and go diving. Can you work with that?"

AJ thought it over. They didn't have anything to lose except for a lie-in, which shouldn't be underestimated in her opinion, but probably wasn't a good enough reason to turn the man down. She gave Reg another subtle nod.

"Fine," Reg replied. "We'll be ready at seven."

An hour later, after a taxi ride and a shower, AJ and Reg sat at the bar in Breeze 'n Bites.

"You two look ready for a drink," Dick greeted them.

"Too bloody right," Reg said. "Rum and Coke for me, please."

"Same," AJ said, "and a couple of waters please."

"Something to eat?" Dick asked.

"As fast as your chef can make it," Reg replied.

Dick chuckled. "Vely here will take your order and we'll put a rush on it."

A dark-skinned woman with an infectious smile handed them both a menu. "Let me know when you're ready to order," she said with a local accent quite unlike any AJ had heard before.

"What have you got that's local fresh catch?" Reg asked.

"We have snapper," Vely replied.

"That's me then," Reg replied, handing back the menu.

While the waitress quizzed Reg on the sides, AJ looked over the menu, but her head was too full of the day's events to process what she was reading.

"You know what? I'll have that flammer-whatsit I had last night. It was really good."

Vely laughed. "Flammkuchen."

"That's the one," AJ grinned. "And can I have a side of chips with it? It's been one of those days."

"Chips, like English chips? Or chips like American chips?" Vely asked, smiling mischievously.

"The original English chips please," AJ confirmed. "If you don't mind me asking, how many languages do you speak? I heard you talking to Dick in what I'm pretty sure was Dutch, and then to your friend back there in what I'm guessing is Papiamentu. That's the local language, right?"

Vely nodded. "I can get by in Spanish, too."

"That's four then, with English," AJ counted. "That's impressive."

The woman shrugged her shoulders. "We're always switching between languages all day, so we pick it up from a young age."

"Are you done giving this poor girl the Spanish inquisition?" Reg asked, frowning at AJ. "I bet she'll put our order in if you'll leave her alone."

AJ rolled her eyes. "Sorry about grumps," she said to Vely. "He's had a bad day, too."

The waitress just laughed and walked back to the kitchen as Dick placed their drinks on the counter.

"Proost. I hope tomorrow is a better day for you both," he said, and took a seat on a stool.

"Cheers," AJ and Reg said together, clinking their glasses.

"This should improve the situation," Reg added, nodding to Dick before taking a long sip. "Hey, what was it you found just clear of the wreck?" Reg asked in a low voice, leaning towards AJ. "I saw you digging away."

AJ laughed. "I forgot to check the film, but I'm pretty sure I uncovered a genuine antique recliner chair."

Reg chuckled. "Sounds like a winner for *Antiques Roadshow*."

"Yeah, pretty sure it's not what the old man is after," AJ said, shaking her head. "But it does support his personal possessions claim," she added in a whisper.

Reg nodded.

"Did you do your technical dives today?" Dick asked.

"We did a couple," AJ replied. "All did not go to plan."

"That's too bad. Everyone is okay though, I hope?"

AJ looked at Reg. She knew they shouldn't be discussing it, but the restaurant owner was only being polite.

"We're fine, thanks," Reg replied, carefully choosing his words. "Not sure we'll do any more dives though. We might be off home."

"You guys weren't anything to do with the guy they put in the chamber today, were you?" a woman said from a few stools down the bar.

She was a pretty American, older than AJ, but very fit. She wore a dive-related tank top and running shorts.

"What did you hear?" AJ asked.

The woman shrugged her shoulders. "That someone got bent down south and was taken to the chamber. Brought him in at the gas pier, I think. Word travels fast on a small island."

"That it does," AJ replied with a grin. "Well, hopefully the bloke's alright."

"I didn't mean to be rude," the woman said. "I heard Dick asking about your tech dives, which is why I asked. My name's Jo, by the way. I'm here for a few months working as a dive guide."

"I'm AJ, and this is Reg."

Jo looked her over carefully, studying AJ's tattooed arms, then reading the Mermaid Divers logo on her baseball cap. "AJ Bailey?"

"Have we met before?" AJ asked. "I apologise if we have. I'm not recalling where."

The woman laughed. "No, we haven't, but I read about your U-boat discovery in Grand Cayman, and I follow your Mermaid Divers social media."

Reg laughed from behind AJ, and nudged her. "Bloody celebrity now, ain't you? Be signing autographs next."

AJ blushed and elbowed him. "Nice to meet you, Jo."

"Are you here working, or on vacation?" Jo asked.

"Bit of both," AJ replied, staying noncommittal without lying. She had hoped to sneak in a few fun dives while they were there. Although their chances seemed to be dwindling as they were possibly leaving early.

"Your timing is good for the ostrocods," Jo said. "Have you seen them before?"

"Ostrocods?" AJ questioned. "I don't think I've ever heard of them."

Jo leaned closer, her eyes lighting up. "It's one of the most magical experiences underwater. You have to do it."

AJ looked at Reg. "You know about these ostrocods?"

The big man shook his head, then slid his empty glass in Dick's direction, giving him a nod. Dick took the glass and went to refill it.

"It's a night dive, just after dusk when the sky turns completely dark, a few days after a full moon," Jo explained.

"Sounds a bit Druid-like," AJ joked.

"I could explain the whole thing," Jo continued, "but honestly, it's better if you have no idea what's coming."

"Still sounding like a sacrifice might be involved," AJ chuckled.

Jo laughed. "Trust me, no creatures are harmed, and you'll be amazed. I'm diving Weber's Joy tomorrow night if you'd like to join me?"

"Sounds intriguing," AJ replied. "I'll have to look up Weber's Joy in the Reef Smart Bonaire guidebook in the apartment. But our plans have gone a bit wonky, so I'm not sure if we'll still be here. We're also diving deep during the day, so we have to be careful."

"It's a shallow dive," Jo said. "Don't have to go below 20 feet." She slid a card across the table. "Here's my number. WhatsApp me if you can make it. I'm taking two clients out there, but obviously you guys don't need a guide. It would just be a friendly tag along thing."

AJ picked up the card. "Thanks, Jo. I'll give you a shout if we're up for it."

"Good to meet you both," Jo said, and waved goodnight to the staff as she slid off her stool and left.

AJ tapped the card against her other hand. "That sounds intriguing."

"I tell you what's absolutely fascinating," Reg commented. "I reckon those two plates Vely has in her hands are for us."

The waitress placed the food in front of them, then handed them cutlery and napkins.

"Vely, I have a question," AJ said, but Reg interrupted before she could say any more.

"Here she bloody goes again. Just walk away, trust me, young lady. It'll make both our lives easier."

AJ cuffed him on the arm.

"Ignore him, my dear," AJ continued. "Teach me something in Papiamentu."

"What do you want to say?" Vely asked.

"How about you teach her how to say, 'Hush up and eat your bloody dinner'?" Reg offered.

Vely chuckled, and AJ hit him again.

"How about, 'Good morning'?" AJ suggested.

"*Bon dia*," Vely replied. "Then in the afternoon, it's *bon tardi*."

"*Bon dia* and *bon tardi*," AJ repeated. "I might be able to remember those two. How about goodbye?"

"*Ayo*," Vely replied.

"*Ayo*," AJ repeated.

"And I bet you can't wait to say *ayo* to this one," Reg threw in, grinning from ear to ear.

AJ smacked him again, which only made him laugh harder.

15

1970 – MONACO

The restaurant was packed. With a combination of explaining they had a Grand Prix driver in their group and a 250 Monégasque franc bribe, Barney pulled off a miracle and found them a table for six in La Rascasse. It wasn't the most glamorous spot, but they'd have a view of the Mediterranean, fine seafood on the menu, and more importantly, a place to sit.

Leaving Georgie and Miles to claim the table, Barney scurried off towards the hotel to collect Phil and Tina, and once they were left alone, Georgie sensed a discomfort from her new young driver. For a moment she wondered if he was embarrassed to be seen with an older woman, in case people had the wrong impression, but quickly realised he was simply shy. They ordered drinks and she contemplated how best to put the lad at ease.

"How did you first get into racing?" she asked, figuring cars were his favourite subject.

"My father," Miles replied. "He always fancied himself as a race car driver but never had the opportunities. He built me a go-kart when I was twelve."

"What does your father do?"

"He has a repair garage. Just him and his partner, who's an old army mate."

"Do you work at the garage too?" she asked.

"Every summer holiday," Miles responded with a smile. "Half terms too. Long hours, but I got to work on my go-kart in the evenings, and once I turned seventeen he bought a Ford Escort which we stripped and rebuilt from the ground up."

"That's how Colin Chapman spotted you?" Georgie asked, intrigued by the lad's dedication.

"Eventually, yes," Miles replied. "I had a good run at Snetterton in the wet. Gave one of his Lotus Cortinas a run for their money. He saw me after the race and told me I was a pain in the you know what."

Georgie laughed. "He really said that to you?"

Miles nodded, his boyish face and infectious smile making her smile too.

"He was kidding with me, but my dad was ready to give him a piece of his mind. I had to calm him down and get him to a pub on the way home. Couple of pints and he soon forgot about Mr Chapman and talked about all his ideas how to make the Escort better so we could beat 'em in the dry too."

"That's great your father is so behind your racing."

"Couldn't have done it without him," Miles said, beaming. "Or Mr Chapman, and now you, ma'am. I've been incredibly fortunate."

Georgie held up her wine glass. "I'd say you've earned the help. Chapman knew what he was doing when he put us together."

"I can't thank you enough for this opportunity, ma'am. It truly is a dream come true."

"I should be thanking you for taking a risk with an unknown team," Georgie replied, then thought for a moment. "How does your mother feel about your racing?"

Miles didn't reply right away, shifting in his seat. "She's supportive and excited for me, but she worries."

Georgie nodded. "I bet she does. I do too. Motor racing isn't the safest sport in the world."

Miles looked down at the table and fiddled with his glass of water. "She was fine with it until Paul Hawkins' accident at Oulton Park. I was in that race and she was there too. It all changed for her after that. She knew racing was dangerous, but this was a bad crash with a big fire. I think it brought the reality home. Now she does her best to hide how worried she gets."

Georgie swallowed. The thought of standing on Mrs Preston's doorstep informing her that Miles wasn't coming home almost brought her to tears, and she hid behind her wine glass, pretending to take an extended sip. She realised being surrounded by glamour and competition, and the challenge of fielding a Grand Prix car, could easily lapse her into complacency over the risks. Carlos's accident in Spain had been an eye-opener, but statistics reminded her it was unlikely to be the last violent accident of the Formula One season.

"What brought you into racing, ma'am?" Georgie realised she was being asked, and she snapped back to the moment.

"I like things that go fast," she replied, and was glad to see Barney return with the two mechanics.

While she wanted to know everything about Miles, she felt like she'd made a pig's ear of their first earnest conversation.

"That's him, isn't it?" Georgie said, nudging Barney just as he sat down, pointing across the restaurant to the good-looking man they'd briefly met earlier.

Barney stood and waved Martin over. Georgie guessed the man was in his thirties, and certainly younger than her, but he carried himself with the maturity of someone older.

"Good evening," he said, taking the open seat at the table, opposite Georgie. "Thank you again for inviting me."

She noticed he spoke perfect English with a slight accent she presumed was Dutch, judging by his name. His hair was perfectly groomed and a five-o'clock shadow adorned his tanned face, adding to his movie star appearance.

"Our pleasure," she responded. "Let me introduce you to everyone. Barney is our team manager and performer of extraordinary tasks, like getting us seated at a table on Sunday evening in Monaco."

She paused while the two shook hands across the table.

"Miles of course, who made his Formula One debut today in fine fashion."

"Very impressive drive," Martin said as the two shook.

"Thank you, sir," Miles replied with a hint of a blush. "I had a really good car."

"Which brings me to Phil, our wonderful lead mechanic," Georgie continued. "And our second mechanic, Tina. These two prepared the Lotus 72 in a matter of days before they had to leave in the transporter for this race. I think it's pretty amazing what they were able to do."

Martin smiled and shook both their hands. His attention remained on the younger mechanic. "Tina is an interesting name, no?"

The rest of the team laughed as Tina rolled his eyes. Phil ruffled the kid's hair playfully.

"His proper name is Ben," Barney explained. "And he happens to be my son. But he has a Ford Cortina at home that he's been rebuilding for... let's just say it's been an extended period of time, so his friends shortened it to 'Tina' and the nickname has stuck."

The poor youngster turned bright red while the others laughed.

"I've wondered for two weeks but didn't have the nerve to ask," Miles said, then once they'd all settled down, he asked Tina about his project at home.

Georgie turned to Martin. "Wine?" she offered, holding up one of the bottles she'd ordered for the table.

"Certainly," he responded and held out the wine glass from his place setting.

"What's your line of business, Mr Van der Meer?" she asked as she poured.

"Martin, please," he replied. "I have a few different revenue streams, so I'm fortunate to be able to travel and maintain a flexible schedule."

Georgie topped several other glasses off around the table before putting the bottle down, feeling like she'd learnt nothing from his answer. Of course, her own response to the same question would be equally vague. Born into wealth wasn't really an occupation, and was only in vogue amongst similarly fortuitous individuals these days. She shifted subjects.

"How did you become involved with Mr Chapman?"

"I'm a racing enthusiast," he replied, "and I drive a Lotus Elan on the road. So when I decided I'd like to be more involved, I called Colin."

Georgie wondered how their guest had simply *called Colin Chapman* and been put through to the company owner. That didn't usually happen for someone who'd done nothing more than purchase a road car.

"Have you raced yourself, or owned a team before?" she enquired.

Martin shook his head. "This is my first venture into motor racing, and I must say there appears to be far more to it than meets the eye."

Georgie smiled. "If you've seen the Lotus factory and test track, then I'm sure you have an idea of the momentous effort behind these race cars."

"I visited a few months back when I paid my deposit for the chassis," Martin replied. "It's impressive. Not quite like Ferrari's facility in Maranello, but it's difficult to compare to that kind of history."

"You tried to buy a Ferrari Formula One car?" Georgie asked in surprise.

Martin laughed. "I did. That's how little I knew about the inner workings of racing."

Ferrari were renowned for only producing their Grand Prix cars for the factory-run team and destroyed the old chassis so no one would ever see their designs up close. It surprised her he hadn't researched that before travelling to Italy. Anybody in European racing could have saved him a trip.

"And what are your plans for the 72 you've bought?" she asked, moving on.

He raised his eyebrows. "That's a good question. I presume Colin feels we should come to some kind of arrangement."

"I have a team and unfortunately no race car, as Mr Chapman plans to run the 72 he loaned us. Our Lotus 49 was destroyed at Jarama. If you don't have a team to prepare and run your chassis for you, then perhaps we can help each other out."

The Dutchman nodded thoughtfully. "If I let you use my chassis, what happens if it's damaged or destroyed?"

Georgie hesitated and was glad Barney leaned closer and joined the conversation he'd obviously been listening to.

"That would depend, sir. Are you looking to sponsor the entry? Do you have a company you'd like to advertise?"

"I'm a man of... independent means," he said hesitantly. "I don't have a company as such."

"Then I suppose the key question is, what do you want to get out of the relationship?" Barney asked.

Martin looked at Georgie and smiled. A warm shiver ran through her, unlike any feeling she'd experienced in many years. Maybe he looked at all women that way, but for a moment she felt like the most special and desired person in the world.

"Business-wise," Barney quickly added.

"As I said, I'm an enthusiast," Martin replied, turning his attention to the team manager. "My goal is to be involved in some way with a Formula One team. I'd planned to start one myself, but I'll admit I did a poor job of researching what that would take. So here we are."

"Then may I suggest that you make your chassis available to the team for the rest of the season," Barney responded. "In exchange, you'll be included in the team with pit lane passes for you and your guests and a hotel room where we stay, and be mentioned as a team supporter in interviews and press announcements."

Martin gave him a reserved smile. "What about the entry form?"

"How do you mean?" Barney asked, his face awash with concern.

"The car is entered under AMRT now, correct?"

"Yes," Barney replied. "Ashford Motor Racing Team, to be precise."

"Right," Martin said, his expression turning serious. "So we could enter it as AMRT with Van der Meer, couldn't we?"

"We could..." Barney stammered, looking at Georgie for her opinion.

"I'm not sure it will fit on the form," she said, her face breaking into a smile.

Martin laughed, and winked at her before turning to Barney. "I'm pulling your leg. I actually prefer not to be mentioned at all, and I'd rather choose my own hotels."

Barney looked like he would melt into his chair. Georgie patted his leg reassuringly.

"Surely you want something more than a few pit passes?" she asked, catching the man's alluring stare once more.

Martin shrugged his shoulders. "I really don't. But there are two points we should cover."

"What would they be?" Barney asked, recovering from the scare Martin had given him.

"The question of driver," the Dutchman said, and Georgie frowned.

"We have our driver," she quickly replied.

"Contracted?" Martin asked.

"Well, not to us," she admitted.

"Miles?" Martin said, getting the young driver's attention. "Do you have a contract with Lotus, or anyone else?"

"A contract?" Miles repeated, looking confused. "I'm employed by Lotus Cars, if that's what you mean."

Martin returned his attention to Georgie. "I'd say your driver is just like your chassis. He could be recalled at any time, Lady Ashford."

Georgie wanted to argue the point, but knew the man was right. Miles had just shown the world what he was capable of, and without a contract of some description, she was merely borrowing the youngster until Chapman, or another team owner or manufacturer, came calling with a nice offer.

"I want to drive for AMRT for as long as they'll have me," Miles chimed in, which made Georgie smile.

"And if Mr Chapman tells you to drive for Rob Walker's team at Spa, what will you say?" Martin asked.

Miles's mouth opened but no words came out as he thought through the hypothetical problem. Georgie answered instead.

"You raise a good point, and I assume you'd like to see Miles stay in our car for the season?"

Martin nodded. "The lad certainly had an impressive debut, so I'd say we… or, I should say you at this point, would be well advised to hang on to Miles if you can."

"Point well taken," Georgie replied. "If it's okay with you, Miles, I'll talk to Mr Chapman and see if we can come to a more formal arrangement."

"Whatever keeps me in your car, ma'am," Miles said.

"And your second point?" Barney asked.

"My other concern is about the chassis itself," Martin said. "As I brought up earlier, what if it's damaged or destroyed?"

Once again, Barney looked to his team owner for her thoughts on the matter.

"With a sponsor putting cash into the team in return for exposure, we would be responsible for making sure a car runs in their colours at each race we'd agreed to. So the chassis would be our responsibility. This situation would be somewhat the same, don't you think? It's on us to maintain and repair your chassis as needed to make the races."

"So you'll repair or replace it as necessary until the end of the season?" Martin asked.

"In which case, your contribution to the team is simply the depreciation of the value of the chassis," Barney pointed out.

Martin smiled once more. "That's true, and of course you're welcome to purchase your own chassis, but I believe you'll miss the race at Spa and probably Zandvoort as well."

"Which would be an awful shame, don't you agree?" Georgie countered in good humour, hoping Barney would now back down and let her decide what she was willing to compromise on.

"I do," Martin replied.

"I suggest we do this," Georgie continued. "Let's put our DFV in the back of your chassis and go to the race in Belgium. We'll try this out for one race and see how it goes. If everyone's happy after Spa, we'll agree to compete in the rest of the season. Meanwhile, I'll talk to Mr Chapman about securing Miles as our driver."

"And the damage issue?" Martin asked.

"We split the risk down the middle," Georgie replied. "I'll pay for maintenance items and anything which breaks on the car, and we split the cost of damage to the chassis. Parts cost only. The labour is again down to me as I employ the mechanics. How does that sound?"

Martin glanced over at Miles, then back to Georgie, her heart skipping once again as his sterling grey eyes seemed to pull her closer to him.

"It sounds like we have a deal, Lady Ashford," he said, reaching his hand across the table.

"My friends call me Georgie," she responded, shaking his hand and feeling the warmth of his touch in his firm but respectful grip.

"Then Georgie it is," he said with a smile. "As I do hope we will be good friends."

16

BONAIRE

AJ let Reg take the front passenger seat in the van, clambering onto the bench seat behind him and sliding the door closed.

"Good morning," De Konig greeted them.

"*Bon dia*," AJ replied sleepily.

They still hadn't made it to a market for coffee.

"Morning," Reg grunted. "We're ready to hear what's really going on whenever you're ready to tell us."

De Konig drove them out of the Sand Dollar complex and turned right on the main road.

"Straight to the point," he commented. "I like that."

"Don't see much use in being any other way," Reg replied.

De Konig slowed for the roundabout ahead, then kept moving slowly along. The sun was just rising to their left, giving AJ enough illumination combined with the van's headlights to see the herd of goats grazing on the thin-looking shrubs and grass.

"Who do these belong to?" she asked, smiling at the goats casually moving aside for the vehicle.

"No one," De Konig replied. "They're wild."

AJ laughed. "That's brilliant. People don't mind them wandering around in town."

"Varies," he replied. "Mostly they keep to the open land, but at night they often come around when it's quiet. Saves on mowing."

He cleared the small herd and continued towards Kralendijk, passing a large new-looking resort on the right, and then driving past the marina where they'd met him before. Reg looked over at the man expectantly.

"Coffee?" De Konig asked.

"Bloody right," AJ immediately replied.

The road curved right, then shortly after turned back to the left. De Konig pulled over by a café called Between 2 Buns. He'd barely stopped before AJ had the door open and was heading for the entrance. Ten minutes later, loaded with coffees and breakfast pastries and sandwiches, they were back on the bumpy two-lane road, heading the way they'd come.

De Konig took a swig of coffee, placed the cup in a holder, then fidgeted in his seat for a few moments.

"The truth is, there's no way to know for sure what's under that barge," he began. "There's no manifest from the vessel or official paperwork I've been able to find. But if it belonged to who I believe it belonged to, then there is something quite valuable trapped underneath."

"Which is?" Reg prompted when De Konig didn't continue.

"A Formula One race car."

AJ sat forward. "Seriously? You mean like a Lewis Hamilton type race car?"

De Konig glanced over his shoulder at her. "Much older."

"A vintage race car?" Reg asked.

"Yes," De Konig responded, and AJ noticed he didn't seem keen on expanding.

"You know things rust, rot, and decay underwater, right?" Reg said. "Chances are there's bugger all left of a car made of metal."

"Aren't they mostly carbon fibre?" AJ asked.

"Depends," Reg answered. "How old is this one? I think they began using carbon fibre sometime in the 80s."

"It's older than that," De Konig offered.

"Okay, so what is it? Who owned it? Who drove it?" Reg pressed. "Give us more details."

De Konig sighed and shook his head. "I can tell you the barge sank in 1970, and the whereabouts of the car has remained a mystery since that time period. It vanished from the racing scene and was never seen again."

"So, you're surmising that the car was on this barge which sank?" Reg asked.

De Konig shrugged his shoulders. "My research has led me to believe that, yes."

"Still feels like you're not telling us more than you are," AJ said between bites of her pastry.

De Konig raised a hand from the steering wheel. "And that's probably true, but look at this from my perspective. I've invested an enormous amount of time, money, and effort into tracking down the location of the barge. If word gets out before we recover what we can of the race car, I'll be inundated with requests, offers, enquiries, not to mention poachers who'll try to raid the site."

"We signed your non-disclosure agreement, mate," Reg pointed out. "So, we're legally obligated not to say a word. Not that we would have anyway if you'd simply asked us not to."

"I get that, and I'm probably being overly cautious for no reason," De Konig admitted. "But I've kept this thing a secret for so long, I can't risk any kind of leak when I'm this close."

"So Laurens was simply to keep an eye on us?" AJ asked pointedly.

De Konig sighed again as he turned into the marina and parked by the boat slip. "I suppose you could see it that way. In my mind, he was a layer of security. Clearly it was a mistake on my part."

"Have you heard from the doctor this morning?" AJ asked.

"I haven't," the older man replied. "But in this situation, I believe no news is good news."

"Okay," Reg said, scratching his beard. "What about my earlier point? I hope you're not expecting to pluck a shiny race car out from under that barge?"

"Of course not," De Konig replied. "But the most valuable part is the serial number plate, which is riveted to the chassis. If we can bring up that plate and a handful of original parts, no matter how small or seemingly insignificant, then it may be considered a ground-up restoration. But without the plate, which proves the provenance, its value is drastically diminished and it would simply be considered a replica."

Reg opened his door.

"Have I satisfied your curiosity enough to continue?" De Konig asked.

Reg stepped out, then turned back to face the man. "I don't know, to be honest. We'll need to talk about it. But either way, these tanks have to get loaded."

———

Twenty minutes later, with the tanks moved and Laurens' gear in the back of the van, De Konig drove them to the dive resort where TDS had their shop. On the way, they passed through the round-about again, but the goats had moved on as morning traffic picked up. Bryan brought a cart around, and they wheeled the tanks to the compressor room in several loads.

"Top them all off with the same fills?" he asked.

"Give us just a minute," Reg said, and steered AJ back to the van.

De Konig had walked down to the resort's pier and was making a phone call, so they sat in the van to talk.

"Well, what do you think?" Reg asked.

AJ chewed the situation over some more, airing her thoughts aloud.

"He's still not being completely straight with us, but I suppose that's understandable if this race car is worth a bunch of money. Still, makes me feel like hired help instead of part of the team."

"Agreed," Reg responded. "But that's what we are. Hired help. He didn't employ us as part of a research team, or bring us in for an entire project. He hired us to dive the wreck and see about salvaging what we could."

"True."

"The question is," Reg continued, "whether we feel comfortable continuing with him or not. I mean, strictly speaking, I know I had a pretty good go at the bloke yesterday, but really, we're doing exactly what we agreed to do. If anything, it's my fault for not asking more questions before taking on the gig. I fancied the trip, and you were keen to see Bonaire, so I probably should have done a better job of due diligence. It feels like it would be us reneging if we went home now. I certainly think we'd need to give him some of his deposit back."

"That's fair, Reg, but neither of us will starve if we bung him a few quid back and put this behind us. We shouldn't dive if we're not comfortable with the dive itself, or the bloke we're working for."

Reg nodded. "I think the diving's alright. I'm a bit curious to see what kinda nick this car's in after over fifty years upside down in the sand."

"Petrol's probably all drained out if you were thinking of putting it in your Land Rover," AJ replied with a grin.

Reg laughed. "Sod it. Let's give it another go today. If his nibs gives us reason to get worried again, we'll call it, but for now we'll keep going."

"Good," AJ replied, getting out of the van. "I fancy seeing what these ostrocod things are all about."

"You didn't google it to see?" Reg asked, following her.

"No! That lady, Jo, said it's best to be surprised."

"Blimey," Reg scoffed, which turned into a chuckle. "I bet little Miss Goody Two-Shoes never rattled her Christmas pressies to see what was in them, either."

"Oh, I still do that," AJ confessed.

"I was wondering if I'd see you this morning," Bryan commented when they gave him the go-ahead. "I heard the chamber had a visitor yesterday. Scuttlebutt said it was a tech diver, so I hoped it wasn't you guys."

AJ wrinkled her nose at him, and Bryan looked back and forth between the two of them.

"You're missing one, huh?"

AJ slowly nodded.

"Sorry to hear that. He gonna be okay?"

"Doc said he thought so, but you know how it is. They won't really know for a while."

"He still in there?" Bryan asked.

"Should have come out in the night sometime," AJ replied. "But they planned to keep him under observation today. He'll probably take a few more rides before they're done with him."

"He cork?" Bryan asked.

AJ nodded, acknowledging the diver's term for popping to the surface.

"From how deep?"

"Deep," AJ said, then realised she was being just like De Konig had treated them earlier. "I'm not trying to be awkward, Bryan, but we're under an NDA, so we're not supposed to disclose anything about this project."

Bryan grinned. "Sounds even more intriguing."

AJ laughed. "Yeah, as a techie, you'd dig what we're doing."

"But if you told me," Bryan joked, "you'd have to kill me."

"Something like that," AJ chuckled.

"Hey, Bryan," Reg began. "The guy that was with us yesterday, Laurens. Have you seen him before? Has he had tanks filled, or done any dives with you?"

Bryan shook his head. "Not with me. I can't swear he's never been in our shop as I'm not always here, but I see most folks who come through."

"What about the bloke we're with today?"

Bryan shook his head. "Never seen him either. Is he a diver?"

"No, but he has a boat, the *Beste Leven*," Reg said. "A pontoon set up for diving."

"I know the boat, but unless he sold it recently, the *Beste Leven* belongs to a customer of ours," Bryan replied. "Maybe he rented it to your friend."

Reg lifted a set of refilled tanks onto the cart. "That's a possibility."

"Don't make a fuss over it," AJ said thoughtfully. "But if you happen to speak to the owner, maybe you could ask him?"

Bryan nodded. "I'll text him and see. It's actually a decent dive boat for a small group with all that deck space."

"Works surprisingly well for what we're doing," AJ replied.

Reg came back with the empty cart. "Needless to say, Bryan, you don't have to worry about the third set of tanks. Laurens won't be needing them."

Bryan grinned. "Copy. What about the extra nitrox 80s? Did you use them?"

AJ and Reg looked at each other, and AJ's eyes got wider.

"Bollocks," she muttered.

"No, we didn't use them, so they're still full, mate," Reg said.

"There's something more to that story," Bryan guessed. "Going by the look on your face," he said, glancing at AJ.

"No worries," she replied, trying not to laugh. "One's on the boat and the other's still tied to the mooring line."

"And tell him where the bloody mooring line is, Annabelle Jayne," Reg said in an amused tone.

"Safely tethered to our dive site," she replied defensively.

"But?" Bryan queried.

De Konig stuck his head in the door before AJ could reply.

"I see you are filling tanks, so can I take that as good news?"

"Figured we'd go take another look," AJ responded.

"And pick up Bryan's tank AJ left lying around at 210 feet," Reg added.

17

1970 – SPA, BELGIUM

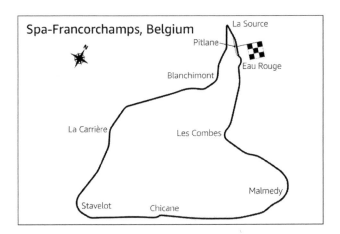

With first practice being in the afternoon, Georgie was in no hurry to get to the racetrack on Friday morning. The little town of Stavelot, which was actually closer to the circuit than Spa for which it was named after, was delightful, and once the sun drove away the morning chill typical of the Ardennes mountains, she enjoyed a leisurely breakfast followed by a stroll around the local shops.

By the time she took a taxi to the track, Georgie was in a wonderful mood and looking forward to the race weekend. And seeing Martin Van der Meer again. They'd spoken several times over the phone since Monaco, and she'd enjoyed telling him that Chapman had formally loaned Miles to the team for the rest of the season, with first option on him for the following year if Lotus didn't put him in one of their own entries. Georgie hadn't questioned the Lotus boss about what contract existed with Miles Preston that allowed him to make such stipulations, but she planned on asking the driver at an opportune moment. Maybe something had changed since Monaco.

Spotting her team's Leyland Tiger transporter in the paddock, she wandered over to be greeted by a group of sullen faces. Thinking they were likely worn out from the long hours they'd spent preparing another new chassis for the race, she began with a compliment.

"The car looks magnificent, chaps. You've done a bang-up job once again."

Phil and Tina both nodded their thanks and muttered a greeting. Barney quickly steered Georgie aside.

"I'm guessing you haven't heard?" he asked.

"Heard what?" she replied, slightly annoyed that her enjoyable morning was being spoiled by their sour mood.

"Bruce McLaren," Barney said, as though mentioning the Kiwi's name would jog her memory.

"What about him?" she replied impatiently.

"He was killed on Tuesday," Barney said with a pained expression. "Testing at Goodwood in one of his Can-Am sports cars."

Georgie felt the breath leave her lungs, and she stood motionless in shock. McLaren, at only 32 years old, was a cornerstone of the Formula One community and a pioneer. He was one of the few drivers to ever compete in a chassis built by his own company.

"Poor Patty," she finally whispered, thinking of Bruce's wife. "And don't they have a young daughter?"

Barney nodded. "Amanda. She's only four."

"What happened?" she asked, immediately wondering if she really wanted to know. The man was dead, leaving behind a widow and a little girl who'd barely remember her own father. Dead was dead, regardless of whether he'd slipped in the shower or crashed on the track.

"I was told the rear bodywork came loose, causing the car to spin at a very high speed section of the track. He hit an old bunker that was used as a marshal's post."

"I thought Goodwood was closed for racing because it was too dangerous?" Georgie asked.

"It was, back in 1966," Barney explained. "But it's still available for testing."

They stood in silence for a while, Georgie unsure what she should do next. Or say. To anyone. Part of the glamour of motor racing was the inherent danger... until it happened close to home. Carlos's accident with Ickx had been terrifying, but fortunately they'd both survived and would be okay. This was different. Bruce McLaren wasn't coming back.

"Are the team here?" Georgie asked.

Barney shook his head. "They withdrew. I don't think they even left England. Goodness knows what they'll do down the road."

"Will the race be cancelled?" she asked.

"Not likely," Barney replied, as though she'd asked a strange question. "As they say in West End theatre... and the circus, 'The show must go on.'"

The Spa-Francorchamps circuit was daunting. Almost nine miles per lap with very long, winding, flat-out sections and fast corners, resulting in average lap speeds well over 150 mph. Safety was on everyone's minds with the passing of Bruce McLaren, and the drivers now faced one of the most dangerous tracks of the season. Upon the drivers' insistence after last year's race, a chicane had been added to the circuit in the back section to reduce speeds, but with the incredible acceleration of the Formula One cars, they were soon back up to a terrifying pace.

For Miles, it was unlike any circuit he'd ever raced at, in a car he'd only driven around Hethel and Monaco. Two relatively short, twisting, and lower speed venues. First practice was spent simply learning the course and becoming acclimatised to the Belgian countryside flying by him as he topped 175 mph for much of the lap. It was no surprise to anyone when he finished the first session in eighteenth place, which was last of the cars which ran.

With the track being so long and the McLaren team missing from the entry, the organisers had decided to allow all eighteen entries present to compete, so at least he didn't have the pressure of having to qualify to race. The new Lotus also had the latest suspension geometry, similar to the specification Miles had proven at Monaco, but the high speeds of Spa were an entirely different animal. He found it difficult to feel when the car was at its limit in the sweeping turns, which didn't inspire confidence. In the factory Lotus camp, Rindt did all of two laps in the 72 they'd reclaimed from Georgie, before switching to his Lotus 49C they'd brought as his spare car, citing the same issues with the newer chassis.

After practice, Miles begged the track officials to let him drive slowly around the circuit a few times in a road car, which they finally agreed to. He'd only managed to walk one lap on Friday morning as the track was so long, but three more times around helped him become more familiar with the details. When he returned to the paddock with the sun setting, he found Phil and Tina hard at work on the chassis.

"Mr Chapman came by with a few suggestions of things for us to try, so we're changing the geometry a bit," Phil explained. "He thinks it'll make the car feel more comfortable in the high-speed corners."

"I figured out a few things with the track too, so we'll be better tomorrow," Miles responded, feeling more confident. "Let me help you with the changes."

"Best thing you can do is get a good night's rest and be ready to go in the morning, mate," Phil insisted. "We'll take care of the car."

"He's right," Barney added. "Georgie is about to leave. Catch a ride with her. I'll stick around and help the lads out."

Miles reluctantly agreed, but felt guilty leaving the mechanics to what promised to be another late night for them.

The next morning was cool, but with clear skies and the forecast of a beautiful day. When Miles and Georgie arrived at the track, Martin van der Meer was already there, having driven from Holland early that morning.

"How do you like my chassis?" he asked Miles with a grin.

"It's better than me at the moment, sir, but I hope to improve on that today."

"I hear all the cars will qualify for this race with the McLaren team not here," he said.

"That's correct," Miles replied. "A tragedy what happened."

Martin shrugged his shoulders. "It is. But part of the game, right? You all know the risks."

Miles was slightly taken aback by the man's bluntness and seemingly casual attitude towards the drivers' lives, but he wasn't about to question the man who was providing the race car for him.

"Martin, so good to see you," Georgie said as she walked over. "You must have left very early to get here?"

Miles took the opportunity to slip away and chat with Phil about the chassis changes and their plan for that morning's session. Everything else was a distraction. He'd been as shocked as anyone on hearing the news about McLaren, but he had to put all thoughts and concerns about his safety aside. Anything less than one hundred percent focus while behind the wheel would render him more likely to become the next victim of a cruel sport. He knew 175 mph was over 250 feet per second. A lot could go dramatically wrong within a single second.

With the track being so long, one challenge about Spa was the number of laps the drivers could complete in each practice. Lap times were in the three-minute and thirty-second range, so with a couple of pit stops for adjustments, or a few moments to catch his breath and think about how to improve, Miles would only have a dozen laps to set a time.

When the track opened for the one-hour session, Miles followed the experienced Mexican driver, Pedro Rodríguez, out of the pit lane and tried his best to stay on the tail of the BRM. His first timed lap was 3:35.2. A solid time which placed him tenth fastest at that moment, but on the second lap, as he pushed harder to keep up with Rodríguez, who was steadily pulling away, Miles made a big mistake.

Eau Rouge consisted of very fast esses at the bottom of the downhill start/finish straight, which transitioned into a steep uphill in the middle of the series of turns. Renowned for being one of the most iconic and dangerous set of corners in Grand Prix racing, it was lined with unforgiving steel Armco guardrails, allowing no margin for error.

Miles had been lightly braking for the sweeping curves taken in third gear, but had noticed it appeared to be a spot where the BRM was pulling away from him. This time, he lifted off the throttle on the approach through the left curve but didn't touch the brake, going smoothly back to power before the compression, settling the car as he turned right. His apex speed was a lot more than he'd anticipated and as the car loaded the Firestones to their maximum and began sliding in a four-wheel drift, he knew he'd overdone it. He was running wide of the racing line, which would put him treacherously early into the final left-hand part of Eau Rouge.

Lifting off the throttle while the car was in the corner at its limit would pitch the weight transfer slightly forward, giving more grip to the fronts and taking away traction from the rears, causing the Lotus to violently oversteer. It would be a disaster. All he could do was wait, knowing he had to reduce speed in the split second between cornering to the right and transitioning back to the left. His timing would be the difference between a scary moment and the biggest crash of his young career.

Every nerve ending in Miles's body tingled and begged for

feedback through the steering wheel and the racing seat which cocooned his body. The subtle changes in effort through his hands connected him to the front tyres, telling him when they'd reached their maximum grip and if that had been exceeded. His body, strapped as one to the chassis, gave him the same feel from the rear tyres, and his neck muscles sensed the changes in g-loading in every direction. His brain, finely tuned to accept, process, and react to these inputs, fired out signals to his muscles at a remarkable pace.

At the exact moment Miles finished unwinding the steering wheel from the right-hander, the corner loads through the car reduced and he pounced on the moment to slowly lift off the accelerator. In that very same instance, he began turning left, or he'd never make the last part of the esses. As soon as the right-side tyres began building cornering load once more, he gently squeezed back on the throttle to prevent the Lotus snapping into an oversteer. With a touch of patience getting to the apex, he crested the hill in a four-wheel slide which took the car to the very edge of the road at the corner exit, where he stayed on the track by a fraction of an inch.

Up ahead, Rodríguez's BRM was pulling away in the distance as Miles had killed all his exit speed from Eau Rouge with his desperate, split second corrections, ruining his lap in terms of speed. But he'd survived, and avoided a crash in a Formula One car at Eau Rouge. Which would almost certainly be unsurvivable.

"What's the problem, mate?" Phil asked as Miles pulled into the pit lane after circulating slowly and recovering his wits. "Something break?" the mechanic asked, looking more than a bit concerned.

"I just needed a moment," Miles replied, still breathing heavily. "Sorry to worry you."

"Took so long to come around I thought you'd come a cropper, lad," Phil admitted.

"I almost did in Eau Rouge," Miles confessed.

"Bloody hell, mate. That ain't one to mess with."

"I'm alright now," Miles said, pushing the incident from his mind and focusing on the adjustments he needed to make for each corner. "I'll do a few on my own to get my confidence back."

"Alright, lad. Take your time," Phil said. "Is it better?"

Miles wasn't sure what he meant until he realised his mechanic was asking about the car set-up he and Tina had spent half the night changing.

"Yes," he replied, realising he might not have been able to save his mistake in Eau Rouge if the chassis hadn't given him more tactile feedback than it had the day before. "A good improvement, Phil. Thank you."

Phil shrugged his shoulders. "We just worked the spanners. It was Mr Chapman who told us what to do, but you're welcome."

After Phil and Tina gave the car a quick check over, Miles pulled away from the pits and rejoined the circuit. He spent the out-lap building up to speed and concentrating on being smooth and executing all the subtle line and technique adjustments he felt he needed. As he reached the start/finish line and the stopwatches started, Miles was determined to put a clean lap together, but he couldn't help holding his breath as he approached Eau Rouge.

This time, he eased off the throttle and gave the brake a light brush before hurtling through the compression and right-hand corner at the bottom of the hill. The Lotus 72 glided through the apex in a perfect slide, which placed him perfectly on line to stay flat out through the left and over the crest of the hill. With 100 more rpm than he'd exited on any prior lap, Miles grabbed fourth gear when the tachometer reached redline, and knew he was bettering his lap time all the way down the long straight as he hit fifth earlier than ever.

A quick glance in his mirrors before Les Combes showed a blue car several hundred yards behind. By the time he'd swept downhill through the countryside to the new chicane after Malmedy, the March of Jackie Stewart had halved the gap. Miles couldn't believe the Scotsman was catching him so fast. He was sure he was on a much better lap than he'd done before.

Through Stavelot, Stewart hadn't gained any more, but on the incredibly fast, winding run through La Carriere as the track made its way back towards the pits, Miles realised what was happening. Whether by clever planning or fortuitous circumstance, the canny Scot had positioned himself in the perfect position to benefit from an aerodynamic tow from Miles's Lotus. On each flat-out section where the cars reached their top speeds, Stewart was lining his March up directly behind where Miles's car was pushing the air aside as though he were punching a hole. With less wind resistance, the Scot was picking up more and more top speed the closer he got.

Miles knew about *drafting,* or *catching a tow,* as the method was called, but it had been a small factor in his racing to date. He drove alone around Hethel, and Monaco didn't have a long enough straight for it to make much difference. In saloon car racing, the effect was there with the boxy-shaped cars, but the top speeds weren't high enough for it to come into great effect. The reigning world champion was now giving him a crash course at 180 mph.

The two flew through Blanchimont nose to tail, and Stewart moved slightly right before braking for the hairpin at La Source, slipping past Miles on the inside. They finished the lap with only a few feet between them and Miles immediately recognised his next error. He was too close to take advantage of a tow behind Stewart. If he'd backed off around La Source and sacrificed the lap he'd been on, he could have started the new lap a perfect distance back to do exactly what the Scotsman had just done.

Instead, he tucked in behind, breathing off the throttle in the tow to stay behind Stewart and using the aerodynamic advantage to catch back up after a few corners where the March pulled away. Stewart pitted at the end of the lap, which Miles completed, having learnt a lot following the masterful veteran, as well as setting his best time of the session.

With the sun shining brightly all day, the afternoon practice was slower in the heat, as the track was slipperier and the engines made less power. Stewart was on pole position for the race with a sensational lap over two seconds faster than anybody else. It was the lap he'd drafted off Miles. Rindt was second in his Lotus 49 and Miles slotted in tenth, just behind the other first timer at Spa, Ronnie Peterson, and several positions ahead of the second factory Lotus of John Miles.

That evening, Miles was talking with Georgie about the day as the lads prepared the car for the race when Jackie Stewart and his wife Helen walked by.

"Are you the young lad driving the Lotus?" he asked, peering at Miles from under his tartan flat cap.

"Yes, sir. I'm Miles Preston."

"You're doing well for your first time here," he said in his broad Scottish accent.

"I learnt a lot from chasing you today," Miles replied. "That was an amazing lap you did."

Jackie moved closer and lowered his voice. "Do you mind if I tell you something?"

"Of course not, sir," Miles blabbered, completely starstruck. "I'd welcome any advice you could give me."

Stewart grinned. "No one else would've let me tow off them for a whole lap, laddie."

"I was happy to help, sir, and to be honest, I didn't realise that was what I was doing until halfway around the lap."

"You may be happy to help me, son," Jackie responded, "but I doubt Chapman will be as pleased with you. That tow was worth every bit of two seconds."

Miles's heart sank as it dawned on him that he was responsible for helping Ken Tyrrell's driver in a March chassis beat the factory Lotus to pole position. Jackie slapped him on the arm.

"I won't tell him if you don't, son," he chuckled and went to walk away, then paused. "One other thing, lad. At the end of that lap," he began, and smiled again.

"I should have backed off through the hairpin and towed off you," Miles said dejectedly.

Jackie winked. "Aye. I woulda let you have one for a wee bit."

18

BONAIRE

It was a little after ten by the time they arrived at the dive site, having stopped at a large hardware and building material store called Kooyman. The deck of the *Beste Leven* now looked more like it was part of a house renovation project than a dive expedition. A stack of assorted corrugated sheet metal lay next to a hefty mallet. Their plan was to bash the metal into the sand, but their hurriedly planned shoring scheme was purely experimental.

"I'm over the wreck, according to the GPS," De Konig said. "How do we find the buoy you set underwater?"

AJ picked up her fins and mask. "You're right over the site now?"

"Directly over it," De Konig confirmed.

"Okay, stay west of the wreck so you don't run me over," she replied. "Reg will tell you what to do from there."

Jumping off the side of the boat, she slipped her fins on in the water, then took the mask she'd looped around her wrist and slid it over her face. Dipping her masked face in the water revealed nothing but blue water turning to cobalt in the depths below. Figuring the line was being pulled by the light current and the gentle swells towards shore, AJ swam east towards the island.

They hadn't given much thought to the buoy on the ascent the previous day, and with the pull of the boat on the mooring line, the second line had disappeared from view by the time they'd reached the shallower decompression stops. Reg had been guessing how much line to pull in at the wreck, so she had no idea how deep the buoy had ended up. If he'd misjudged and the ball was below 60 feet, AJ might not even see it.

Farther from the wreck than she thought it would be, a pale white speck appeared in view, well below the surface. AJ swam until she was over the buoy, then waved to the two men on the pontoon, which idled towards her.

"How deep is it?" Reg yelled.

"Hard to tell," AJ shouted back, hoping it wasn't too far down.

She didn't consider herself a great freediver, and she was wearing shorter tech fins, not the extremely long style worn to descend on a single breath hold with minimal effort. Reg tossed her a line which he'd secured to a bow cleat while De Konig kept the boat idling in place ten yards from where AJ bobbed on the surface.

With the line in hand, AJ slowly filled and expelled air from her lungs, bringing as much fresh oxygen into her system as possible before holding her last inhalation and ducking under. Using her thighs to make long, sweeping strokes with her legs, she kicked down towards the buoy. The process would be easy if she'd donned a scuba tank, but she didn't need the extra dive on compressed air which would compromise her bottom time on the wreck. She was doing it the hard way, which wouldn't have been very hard at all if the buoy was the ideal depth of 15 to 20 feet down. Except it wasn't.

AJ's lungs burned, and she kept having to exhaust a little precious air through her nose into the mask to equalise the pressure as the frame squeezed against her face. Finally, at what she guessed was closer to 50 feet, she reached the buoy and threaded the line through the carabiner. Clutching the end of the rope, she kicked for the surface, which now looked impossibly far above her.

Halfway up, with her lungs screaming, despite the air

expanding as she ascended, AJ noticed a small green sea turtle on its way back down after taking a breath at the surface. The turtle moved with such ease and could stay down for hours at a time if it was resting. Unlike AJ, who felt like her lungs were completely out of usable air and she'd be desperate for a gulp at any moment. And then the line snapped to a stop in her hand, yanking it from her grip.

The rope had snagged in the carabiner, and the end she'd been holding now slowly floated back down as though it were running away from her. AJ's choice was either chase the end of the line or leave it, surface, and dive again. Annoyance and determination won out, and she kicked for the flailing rope, grabbing hold of the end after four fin strokes deeper. Turning, she wrapped the rope around her hand so she wouldn't lose it again, and as she passed her previous spot, the line tugged, but whatever had stopped it before gave way, and she continued towards the bright, inviting surface above.

Bursting into fresh air, she gasped and wheezed, sucking in all she could while treading water and trying not to swallow seawater.

"Took your sweet time down there," Reg shouted from the bow.

"Some... wanker... set it... too... deep," she spluttered between breaths.

Reg grinned. "Stop buggering about and give me the rope then."

AJ swam over and held the line up which Reg took from her. He quickly secured it to a second bow cleat.

"Shut the engines off," he told De Konig.

AJ swam around to the ladder on the starboard side and climbed aboard while the pontoon steadily drifted towards shore until the line came taut and the vessel pivoted around, leaving the bow facing the wreck.

"We have thirty minutes of bottom time planned again," Reg explained to de Konig as he stood at the bow about to splash in. "But we have some house-cleaning issues to take care of as well, so don't expect a lot of progress this morning. Hopefully, we'll put a bigger dent in the workload this afternoon."

"Leave the original mooring line down there," De Konig responded. "I'll buy TDS a new tank."

"That's not the way we work, sir," Reg countered. "We can't, in good conscience, leave rubbish on the bottom that we're responsible for."

De Konig looked like he wanted to further debate the point, but Reg took a giant stride into the ocean, letting him know their chat was over and the point was not negotiable. Floating next to AJ, who was already in the water ready to go, was an inflated lift bag. Reg pulled his deco tanks from the deck and clipped them to the D-rings on his Dive Rite harness, then nodded at AJ.

"Ready?"

"Waiting on your sorry arse," she grinned back.

"One-hundred-minute dive time," Reg shouted up to De Konig. "And make sure you scan all around the surface for marker buoys while we're down there. It'll be a sign something's not gone to plan. Most probably, one of us will be attached to the other end of it."

De Konig waved. "Got it. Be safe and bring me back footage, please."

Reg gave AJ the thumbs-down sign, and they both dropped below the softly rolling surface.

Releasing some of the air from the lift bag, their stash of sheet metal, held together with straps, descended with the two divers, guided by AJ who had one hand on the mooring line and the other holding the base of the lift bag. Once below the surface, the remaining air in the lift bag was compressed by the increasing water pressure, and the load gained more and more speed. The only way to slow the acceleration was to add gas to the lift bag, which used her precious breathing mix. Controlling her own descent by inflating gas into her wing, she used the regulator from her nitrox deco bottle to blow gas into the lift bag, pulling herself back to the line whenever she had a free hand. She was gambling on having a surplus of 50 percent nitrox from the 80 cubic foot tank they'd recover from the sea floor, otherwise she was cutting deeply into her reserve supply.

After three minutes, they were above the wreck and she released her grip on the payload, letting it drop on its own to the sand in front of the bow. Comfortable now leaving the line, they both kicked over the inverted barge and dropped to the sea floor next to where they'd been working the day before. AJ was immediately disappointed. The ever-changing and shifting sand had refilled much of the trough she and Laurens had made.

She signalled to Reg, tapping her chest and pointing east, indicating she'd begin retrieving the errant line and tank as they'd planned. He gave her an okay sign, then headed for the metal they'd dropped.

The grappling hook might have dropped to the sand off the stern, but the rope had fallen almost perfectly along the centre of the wreck, forming a distinct line across the brown coral growth on the hull. Ahead, the rope continued in the direction of the coastline, which fortunately meant shallower rather than deeper. Still, AJ rose to 190 feet to add conservancy to her bottom time and still be able to trace the rope. The farther she went, the more the line began to snake from side to side and about a hundred feet from the wreck, she spotted the tank amongst a pile of line. The negative weight of the full tank had acted like ballast, dropping almost straight down through yesterday's current.

She dropped to the sand and grabbed the tank by the neck below the first stage regulator, towing the line along as she finned back to the barge. She dropped the tank next to the pile of sheet metal, which Reg had already begun using. The lift bag lay deflated off to one side with the straps.

Reg's deco bottles also lay in the sand nearby, lined up dead centre with the bow ramp. AJ unclipped her own and left them close by. They'd be able to work far easier without the cumbersome tanks hanging from their bodies, and Reg had picked a perfect spot to retrieve them. Even if the whole area became silted out, they could find the spot by feel, just forward of the barge's bow ramp.

A hazy cloud drifted from the starboard side, telling her exactly where Reg was working. She finned that way, noting the gentle pace with which the silt was being dragged in an easterly direction, and reminding herself to keep an eye on that to gauge changes in the current. It had been mild on their descent, much like the previous morning.

Reg had made solid progress while AJ had been gone. He'd shoved metal as deep as he could into the sand around the area where they planned to access the cargo hold. As he removed the sand from the roughly six-foot by four-foot trough, he bashed the corrugated sheets deeper to stop more sand from sliding in underneath. It reminded AJ of some precarious mining endeavour, but it appeared to be working.

AJ checked her Perdix dive computer. They'd been down seventeen minutes of their planned thirty already. Reg gave her a few hand signals, indicating where he'd like her to help, and the two set about moving more sand and securing the small area at the side of the barge, which they hoped would gain them access. As AJ shovelled, scooped, and disappeared in a cloud of sediment, she felt a tinge of excitement about the project which she hadn't encountered thus far. Perhaps it was Laurens and his shitty demeanour, or simply the fact that they'd been hunting blind until this point, but she found herself eager to get under the gunwale of the barge. The idea of a fifty-something-year-old Formula One car lurking below was quite exhilarating.

When AJ's screen read twenty-five minutes, she nudged Reg. He checked his own computer and nodded, tapping his chest and indicating he would go to the stern and get the grapple hook. They left their spades in their newly shored trough, and went their separate ways. AJ moved to the bow, where she made sure the remaining sheets were tidied up, then re-clipped her deco tanks in place. The extra tank she'd recovered would be tricky to carry, as it was still secured to the line and didn't have any additional clips. Reg finned over the hull towards her with the hook in his hand attached to the other end of the line, which gave her an idea.

She checked her computer. Twenty-eight minutes. Reg arrived and pointed to the extra tank. AJ shook her head and signalled for Reg to go up the line with the hook. He frowned at her through his mask lens and she frowned back, pointing to the line then raising her hand in the water, telling him to go shallower. He shrugged his shoulders and did as ordered, so she quickly swam back to their work site. The haze hadn't cleared completely, but had certainly calmed enough that she could shoot a short video on her GoPro.

On a whim, she reached into the bottom of the trough and furrowed a hand under the gunwale like she'd done the day before. Sand fell over her fingers, spilling into the trough. She swept it aside and put her hand through one more time. She couldn't be certain, but it felt like less sand filtered past. Taking her dive torch from her leg pocket, she dropped it into the trough, then rotated herself upside down. The deco tanks dangled either side of her face and the gas gurgled to the highest point of her wing, making her feel like she was dangling from a balloon. She burped a little gas using the dump valve at the bottom of the wing, which was now the highest point. She dropped into the trough and let the top of her head rest in the sand.

Picking up the torch, she turned it on and shoved it under the gunwale. In the other hand, she turned on the GoPro, and poked it under the gunwale on its stubby handle until her hand was just inside. Moving both around as best she could, AJ hoped she was filming something underneath the barge. After about twenty seconds, the gentle current, combined with her precarious position, rotated her over and she began flipping to her back. Taking in a big lungful of gas raised her as she continued tipping over in slow motion, rising out of the trough so she didn't hit their new shoring.

It wasn't the most graceful exit, but she rolled herself over and once the gas settled in the wing and the deco tanks hung back in place, she finned towards Reg on the line, putting her torch and camera away as she went. Checking her Perdix, she noted she'd run over to thirty-one minutes, making her glad she'd sent Reg up, and that she'd spent her search for the extra tank at a shallower depth.

Reg must have figured out her plan to surface with the grapple then haul up the tank, as he didn't fuss anymore, but started his ascent as soon as she reached him. When they paused for their first decompression stop at 90 feet, Reg wrote something on his wrist slate, then swung out his arm so she could read it.

"You're a silly bugger."

AJ laughed into her reg, which wrinkled her cheeks and made her mask leak.

19

1970 – SPA, BELGIUM

For Georgie and the rest of the team members up and down the pit lane, Spa was a frustrating and nail-biting venue to watch the race. After the start, they waited nearly four minutes for the cars to appear at the exit of La Source, before flying past the pits and through Eau Rouge, then disappearing from view for another three and a half minutes. For twenty-eight laps. The announcers over the loudspeakers spoke in French, but with the heavy Belgian dialect and crackly broadcast quality, Georgie had a hard time following a lot of what they said despite speaking the language.

She'd seen Stewart make a poor start from pole, leaving Rindt then Amon at the front. Miles had been lost in a sea of race cars battling for the midfield spots when they'd crested the hill and vanished from sight. The fierce racing engines echoed in the distance around the mountains of the Ardenne, while the first mechanical casualty was Derek Bell, who broke a gear linkage on the warm-up lap and coasted down the hill to park his Brabham off the side of the track.

"I really think we have a chance of finishing in the points today," Georgie said, unable to bear the silence around her any longer. "Don't you think so?" she asked, looking at Barney.

"Absolutely," he dutifully replied. "If the car holds together, a top six is very doable."

Phil gave him the stink eye.

"Blimey, dad," Tina muttered.

"I didn't mean it like that, lads," he quickly apologised. "You know how hard this place is on engines and what have you."

"Miles and Peterson are the two who will likely get better and better as the race goes on," Martin said, diverting the conversation, much to Barney's obvious relief. "Being their first time here, they should improve their times more than the veterans."

"I dare say that's true," Georgie agreed, smiling at the Dutchman, who appeared completely relaxed.

The two of them had enjoyed a very pleasant dinner the night before in a quaint local restaurant before going their separate ways to their hotels. She found him almost impossible to read, which added a little to his mystique, but was also slightly frustrating. He'd spent the evening looking at her with his gorgeous eyes, which seemed to beg her to fall into his arms, but his words and actions never followed through. Georgie was in complete turmoil over whether she'd allow herself to become romantically involved with a business partner, but secretly she hoped the younger and very handsome man would put her in the awkward position of deciding.

The roar of the engines approaching La Source brought her mind back to the race, and she craned her neck to see the drivers fighting for rear grip as they accelerated out of the hairpin. Amon was leading and Stewart had recovered from his bad start to take second away from Rindt. Pedro Rodríguez had made good progress to complete the opening lap in fourth, from Jacky Ickx, Jack Brabham and Jean-Pierre Beltoise, who'd also made up a bunch of spots from row five. Behind them, a tight group of Stommelen, Courage, Peterson, and Miles wrestled over eighth through eleventh.

Georgie cheered for her royal blue car as it streaked by, tucked under the gearbox of Peterson's March, then watched in concern as

Miles backed off early for Eau Rouge, letting the other three pull away by five or six car lengths.

Cresting the hill out of Eau Rouge, Miles's heart thumped in his chest. The opening lap had felt far more hectic than the tight and twisting streets of Monaco. In practice, he'd been introduced to the true phenomenon of drafting, but that hadn't prepared him for the massive aerodynamic turmoil of a field of Formula One cars running together at top speed.

Having given himself a gap to Peterson on the approach to Eau Rouge, he now had the throttle pedal pinned to the stop as he grabbed top gear and chased the March down the straight towards Les Combes. While alone, the air being forced aside by his car caused the bodywork to rattle on its fastenings and vibrate. His head was shoved backwards as though a hand was pushing with all its might on the front of his helmet, straining his neck muscles. But in the tow, the wind and bodywork noise lessened so much it felt like he'd fallen into a void. The turbulent, disturbed air from the car in front buffeted his head around instead of forcing it rearwards. And the most amazing and terrifying effect was the engine rpm, magically increasing as the car kept going faster.

To Miles, as he closed on the back of Peterson's car, it felt like an otherworldly force was more in control of his Lotus than he was. The young Swede was also gaining on the two cars in front and pulled to the right just as Miles did the same thing. Miles quickly backed off the throttle, so he didn't hit Peterson in the gearbox, and held the pedal at three-quarters open while still being drawn along at full speed as the duo passed Stommelen and Courage. Somehow, they all managed to fall in line before Les Combes, and with a quick check in his mirrors, Miles realised the two cars they'd just overtaken were now setting themselves up to return the favour in the long sweeping run to Malmedy.

Hoping he'd timed his move correctly, Miles pulled out from

behind Peterson as he pushed the throttle to the stop. The slingshot effect brought him alongside the Swede with Stommelen and Courage following Miles rather than risking going three wide between the grass-covered embankments and steel guardrails.

Braking for Malmedy, Miles completed his pass on the March, while Peterson fended off Stommelen, who lost momentum off the turn, falling back into the clutches of Piers Courage. On the run out of Stavelot, Peterson drafted back by Miles and the two stayed nose to tail up La Carrière, gaining on Jack Brabham, who'd dropped back from the group ahead.

On lap three, Stewart had surrendered his brief lead back to Amon, followed by Rodríguez and Rindt, who'd stretched away from Ickx and Beltoise, while Brabham now had Ronnie Peterson and Miles for company. Stommelen had fallen back, giving Miles breathing room, and on the next lap the unfortunate Courage retired to the pits with an engine issue.

Brabham had lost ground in the opening laps but gathered himself together and now set a blistering pace ahead of Peterson, while Miles settled in behind the two, deciding not to slow them all down by fighting amongst one another. By lap six, Miles was becoming more comfortable in the tow and with the strange sensation of not having his right foot hard on the throttle stop for much of the straightaways. For the first time since before the start, Miles glanced down at his gauges.

The simple dashboard of the Lotus had three round analogue gauges containing nothing but the basic information the driver needed. In the centre, the largest gauge was the tachometer, rotated so the 9,800 rpm redline was in the 12 o'clock position, allowing him to see it at a glance through the 12-inch-diameter steering wheel. On the left, a smaller split gauge read water temperature in the top half and oil temperature in the lower. On the right, another split gauge displayed oil pressure on top and battery volts on the bottom. Speed could be calculated back in the pits from the rpm turned using the tyre circumference and gear ratio, but a gauge with the number would have been superfluous and possibly a distraction on track.

With the briefest of scans, Miles noted the temperatures of the DFV engine both looked a touch high, but fine considering he was running in the draft with less air going through the radiators and oil cooler. The battery volts were good, but the oil pressure was on the low side of the normal operating range. Usually, the pressure ran closer to 60 psi at higher rpm and only dipped down to 40 psi, where it sat now, in the slower corners when the rpm dropped.

Quickly returning his attention to the two cars ahead and the Belgian countryside flying past him at 175 mph, Miles made a mental note to check again at La Source hairpin. That was until Jack Brabham, who had led the trio to the gearbox of Beltoise, shot to the inside of the Frenchman, with Peterson attempting to follow suit. Two wide at the exit, they drag-raced downhill past the start/finish line with Miles trying to decide whether to join the fray or hold back.

Playing the same trick as earlier, he decided to lift early for Eau Rouge, where Peterson nosed ahead of Beltoise. The two had compromised their entry into the fast esses, and with perfect timing, Miles drafted by Beltoise's Matra on the following straight. Ahead, he could see Brabham was closing in on the battle between Ickx, Rindt, and Stewart, whose engine was suffering from an intermittent misfire at high rpm. The long straights of Spa were brutal on race engines.

Proving the point, on the next lap with the seven cars running third through ninth chasing each other in a tight line through the back section of the circuit, Rindt's DFV began running rough. He dropped back a few spots in the train and just as Miles was about to move around the Austrian, his motor failed in a plume of grey smoke and oil, with drops of the hot liquid splattering over Miles's goggles and balaclava. It felt like his face had been set on fire and he furiously wiped at the goggle lenses with the back of his gloved hand, only succeeding in smearing more than clearing them.

Miles had no choice but to ease off the throttle, knowing the cars ahead would be braking for Stavelot at any moment while he flew blindly along, seeing little more than a blurry world rushing by. Managing to wipe a section of one goggle lens clean, he hit the brakes just in time to stop himself careening into the now too familiar gearbox of Peterson. He lost a little ground through the turn but at the exit managed to clean enough of the oil away to see properly and refocused on catching the group ahead.

By La Source, Miles was still five car lengths behind, but knew he'd pull back to them in the draft if he executed Eau Rouge well. Sweeping around the hairpin apex, he remembered to steal a look at the oil pressure gauge. As he powered off the corner, squeezing into the throttle as the rear tyres fought for traction, his mind tried to process what he'd seen. The oil pressure, which soon recovered as the rpm quickly rose, had been almost zero in the middle of the slow corner.

As he raced down the hill past the start/finish line where Tina hung his pit board over the wall, enthusiastically giving him a thumbs-up, Miles had a big decision to make. He was running in eighth place in his second Grand Prix with a strong chance of moving into the top six to score points and prize money for the team. The engine appeared to be running flawlessly. *So, was the oil pressure gauge going faulty?*

If it was, and he pitted the car, throwing away the potential of a great finish, he'd never forgive himself. But if he ignored the gauge and blew up Lady Ashford's engine she'd just purchased six weeks ago, it could cause extensive damage to the DFV, or even destroy it completely. The team was running on a minimal budget compared to the factory-assisted and well-funded privateer outfits. Losing the engine could end their season.

Hanging back once more through Eau Rouge, Miles double-checked the temperatures again. Both water and oil were 20 degrees higher than they had been in practice. He pulled to the right, giving up the tow and putting the Lotus in clean air, which smacked him in the helmet and rattled the bodywork. Returning to the racing line through Les Combes, he once again pulled out of the draft on the next flat-out section, watching the cars ahead steadily pull away. The water temperature was coming down with more air through the radiators, but the oil temperature was staying where it was.

Miles checked his mirrors. He was still well clear of Stommelen, who was caught up in a battle with Pescarolo in a Matra. At the chicane beyond Malmedy, Miles used third instead of second gear, so the rpm dropped lower than normal. He lost more ground to the cars ahead, but carefully watched the oil pressure. It didn't drop quite as low as it had in the hairpin, but still fluctuated below the safe operating level.

To Stavelot, he stayed in clean air, and after the right-hand turn he was so far back from Peterson that he was no longer getting much of a draft. Yet the oil temperature stayed higher than normal. He heard his father's voice echoing in his head.

"It's physics, lad. If the gauges tell you something's wrong, then something's wrong."

Mr Chapman had drilled into Miles to check his gauges at least twice a lap around Hethel, and immediately slow or stop if they were not reading the perfect levels.

"Better to stop and check things over than keep going and destroy an engine," he recalled the boss telling him.

Backing off the throttle, Miles pulled offline, and with a sickening feeling in his stomach, he cruised back to the pit lane, watching the other cars fly by. Shutting off the engine, he coasted down the hill to where the team anxiously waited.

"What's wrong?!" Phil yelled over the roar of engines on the track as he leaned into the cockpit.

"I'm losing oil pressure!" Miles told him.

"Lost, or losing?" Phil quizzed him.

"It drops really low in the slow corners and only gets up to around 40 psi at full speed," Miles explained.

"Start it up," Phil instructed.

Miles flicked the ignition switch back on and pressed the starter button. The hot engine spun over a few times before catching and firing up. It only took a few seconds of watching the oil pressure gauge for Phil to reach in and turn the ignition back off.

"Bugger," he swore, and undid Miles's belts. "Jump out, mate."

As Miles reluctantly climbed from the cockpit, Georgie and Barney rushed over, with Martin following.

"What happened?" she asked.

"I'm really sorry," Miles began, but Phil cut him off.

"The driver saved your engine, ma'am," he shouted from the rear of the car. "Catch tank back here is full of oil and he noticed the pressure was beginning to run low. Few more laps and we'd have stuck a rod out the side."

"How do you know that for sure?" Martin asked. "Maybe it could have made the rest of the race. Was it running rough or losing power?" he directed at Miles.

"No sir, but the oil temperature was high, and the pressure was almost zero in the hairpin. I didn't want to ruin the engine."

"What a shame," Georgie enthused. "You were doing so awfully well, too."

"Can the engine be fixed before Zandvoort?" Martin asked.

"That's only two weeks from now, and we were scheduled for a rebuild after the Dutch Grand Prix," Barney said. "But I'll call them first thing tomorrow and see."

"Does that mean we have a chassis to use for the next race?" Georgie asked, and Miles noticed she was giving Martin a sultry smile.

The man went to respond, then stopped himself and thought for a moment. "If you get the engine fixed, you can use my chassis again for Zandvoort. Then we'll see from there."

20

BONAIRE

AJ and Reg looked over De Konig's shoulder as he put the memory card in his laptop and hit play on the video. Although AJ knew the odds of her capturing anything meaningful were beyond slim, she couldn't help but feel excited. On the screen, the imagery flitted between complete darkness and heavy particulate illuminated by her torch as the beam swung across the camera's field of vision.

"Bollocks," she muttered, disappointed but not surprised.

"Oh well," Reg said, patting her on the shoulder. "It's not like you stood on your head and performed circus tricks at 210 feet to film this David Attenborough documentary-quality footage."

She shoved him with her elbow and the big fellow chuckled like a truck rumbling by.

"Two hundred and twelve, actually," she replied. "I was in the trough and my computer recorded an extra two feet."

"We need to consider that in the plan from here out," Reg said in a more serious tone. "We'll probably see 213 or 214 if we manage to get underneath the gunwale."

"At least you've proved one thing," De Konig pointed out.

"It's not hard packed with sand under the barge," Reg said, finishing the point.

The video played on, but the images were either too dark or filled with illuminated scatter to reveal anything more.

"Could you cut your way in?" De Konig asked. "With a gas torch or something similar?"

"It's an option," Reg replied, scratching at his thickly salt-and-pepper-bearded chin. "There are gas and electric torch options, but they're bloody expensive. I used a few different versions back in my salvage days. They were effective but cumbersome, although I'm sure they've come a long way since then."

"Not easy to get that sort of gear down to 210 feet," AJ added, watching the video for a second time. "Hey! Rewind it a bit."

The other two had become engaged in their conversation, but De Konig quickly paused the video, then rewound it ten seconds and hit play. All three stared at the screen, which began with the familiar scatter resembling a snowstorm at night.

"There!" AJ blurted as something else was visible through the particulate for a fleeting moment. "What was that?"

De Konig rewound and played the clip again. The camera appeared to swing farther to stern than it had before, and the torch beam pointed up at an angle.

"That's the deck of the barge," Reg said. "Play it again."

They all studied the video where, for a brief second, the picture became clear enough to make out the texture of a metal surface.

"What do you think that gap is inside?" AJ asked as De Konig played the footage over one more time.

"Really hard to say," Reg responded. "There's nothing else in the shot to determine scale."

"At least we know there's space from the sand to the decking," De Konig offered optimistically. "If you can open up the access more under the side of the barge, you should be able to get a better shot."

"Don't suppose you have any idea where on the barge this car was situated?" Reg asked. "I assume they lashed it down in some manner."

"No idea on either, I'm afraid," De Konig replied. "But I think it's safe to assume the car was tied by some method for the crossing."

"Unless the barge inverted just before hitting the seabed, there's little chance the contents would have landed underneath it unless they were strapped to the deck," AJ commented.

"True," Reg agreed, moving to the bow where he'd fixed the grapple hook line to a cleat. "Here, Coco the Clown, you can haul this bloody tank up, seeing as you left it lying around down there."

He left the line tied and began hauling the rope up. AJ hip checked him out of the way and took over, trying not to show how much effort it was taking.

"Step aside, old man," she quipped, wishing she'd waited longer and let the big man do more of the work.

Although their plan was to spend four hours topside before diving again, allowing their bodies to process more of the gases they'd absorbed, the idea of unmooring from the submerged buoy was too much hassle. Instead, AJ and Reg spent time sketching the barge as best as they could recall. Rewatching the first video they'd shot helped, and using photographs and schematics they found online, they estimated what hadn't been clear on the footage.

Laurens called De Konig and reported that he was done with the chamber and feeling much better, which was a relief, especially to AJ. The guy had been a jerk and had failed to follow any of the appropriate protocols when things went wrong, but she still felt a little guilty for not watching him more closely.

Shortly after AJ and Reg finished preparing their gear with the fresh tanks for the second dive, Reg's mobile rang. He answered the call and listened for a minute, occasionally grunting a "Really?" or "You don't say". Eventually, he moved on to asking about cutting equipment available on the island, and AJ figured he was talking to Bryan. Reg ended the call by telling him they'd see him first thing in the morning, confirming AJ's guess.

De Konig was lying down on one of the benches, resting his back, which had been giving him a hard time, but the pontoon boat wasn't that big, so he could still hear any conversations above a whisper. She was itching to ask Reg about the first part of the call.

"Alright. Time to get back in," Reg said, nodding towards the water, and AJ knew she'd have to wait to get any answers.

De Konig sat up on the bench and Reg looked over at him.

"Once we go under, John, start the engines and idle forward, keeping the tension off the line. Give us three to four minutes, then you can drift back and the line should grab. Shut the motors down and we'll see you in a hundred minutes. If on the odd chance the line doesn't grab, it means we didn't get the job done and have left for the bottom. Make sure you pull the mooring line up to the boat or it'll tangle in your props. Look for an orange surface marker buoy after an hour or so. It'll mean we're on our decompression stop at the submerged buoy. After that, we may drift, as we won't have a line to hang on, so follow us."

De Konig nodded, although AJ wasn't convinced the old man was following along completely, despite being given these instructions for the third time. They weren't a million miles from shore and the current had been running that way, so she decided it wouldn't be the end of the world if De Konig didn't keep up with them. Besides, they had a plan to quickly add 30 feet of line to the rope from the wreck, and if they did that successfully, all would be well. She was eager to get back to the wreck and see if they could make it under the gunwale.

The rope shuffle went smoothly and Reg also reaffixed the spare 80-cubic-foot tank of nitrox at the spot where the buoy had been. AJ noted it was at 53 feet, which made her proud of her freedive that morning. For someone who didn't dive without a tank very often, that wasn't a bad depth to reach, especially with several tasks to be performed. The rest of their descent went fine, but they arrived at the wreck with almost five minutes of their bottom time already ticked away. That was okay. This was dive four over two days to more than 200 feet. Adding more conservancy to their profile wasn't a bad thing.

The corrugated sheet metal had successfully held the sand back, so they ditched their deco tanks and collected a couple more sheets to continue digging. Every task was becoming more difficult now their trench was deeper. Shovelling sand underwater is nothing like moving it on land. The grains simply float away and fill the surrounding water with scatter, much of it eventually settling back down where you'd just removed it from. Treasure hunters and salvagers often used vacuum systems to remove large quantities of sand and to bring up small artefacts which mixed in, to be sorted topside with strainers. Best they had was a bucket they'd brought down this time. AJ found if she loosened up the packed sand then scooped it with the bucket and kept it moving by handing it up to Reg outside the trough, they could remove most of what they'd dug up.

It was slow going, and their thirty minutes seemed to fly by, but with four minutes of bottom time remaining, they stopped work and let the haze settle. Much of the sand removal was now from under the barge, and although there wasn't enough room to crawl under the gunwale yet, AJ could easily reach her hands inside to film. Holding both the torch and the camera as high as possible towards the decking and away from the seabed, she lay on her side and filmed blindly again. By moving them both around, she hoped to capture a clearer shot than last time, and kept the camera rolling until Reg reached down and tapped her shoulder.

Without wasting any time, they made sure their equipment and remaining sheet metal were secure, clipped on their deco tanks, and headed for the line. On each dive, the smaller snappers, grunts, and goatfish had kept them company while they'd worked, but otherwise, once clear of the wreck, the waters had been generally sparse. This time, as they ascended alongside the mooring line, five African pompanos cruised by, their blunt nosed, silvery disc-like profiles distinctive, glimmering in the deep blue water.

Following AJ's computer's deco plan as she'd been a few feet deeper for most of the thirty minutes, they made brief stops in 10-foot intervals beginning at 100 feet, and at 70 feet they switched from the trimix back gas to the 50 percent nitrox deco bottle. Once they'd adjusted their computers to the new gas, Reg began writing on his wrist slate. When he was done, he held it out for AJ to see.

"Bryan checked on DK. Renting boat. Not live here."

AJ reread the words a few times. Reg had run out of room on his slate, so she figured he'd finished in clipped English. They'd both assumed De Konig lived on the island, but apparently not. They moved on to 60 feet, where they'd spend three minutes.

AJ flipped her own slate over to the second leaf and began writing, showing it to Reg when she was done.

"How did he know about it?"

Reg wiped his slate clean with the back of his hand, wrote a new message, and showed it to AJ.

"Maybe he knew the guy."

AJ quickly scribbled a reply.

"Said he didn't."

Reg moved more slowly, cleaning his slate and thinking before he wrote his reply.

"People lie."

21

1970 – ZANDVOORT, HOLLAND

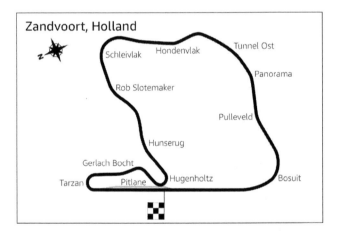

Georgie spotted Barney coming through the front door and waved. She'd felt a little embarrassed sitting alone at a table for six in the busy waterfront restaurant in the seaside town of Zandvoort, wondering why everyone was late.

"I'm so sorry," Barney began, out of breath. "With all the mayhem, I completely forgot about the dinner."

"Have a seat," she replied. "I'll get you a drink and you can tell me what's going on."

Georgie raised a hand to summon a waiter.

"I can't stay, I'm afraid," Barney continued, leaning on the back of a chair instead of sitting. "We only received the engine a few hours ago. It'll be a late one for the lads. I drove here to tell you, and to pick up some grub for them."

"Oh my gosh," Georgie responded.

She'd arrived earlier in the day, checked into the hotel, then looked around the little town before coming to the restaurant where, before leaving England, she'd booked a table for a team dinner. She knew Cosworth had been overwhelmed after Spa, but last she'd heard, their engine was supposed to arrive in Holland to meet the team transporter on Wednesday. It was now Thursday evening.

"Order the chaps whatever you think they'd like," she said, finally getting the waiter's attention. "I'm sure they can wrap it up and let you take it away."

"There's a little place down the road which looks a bit more like a fish and chip shop, ma'am," Barney replied awkwardly. "That'll be easier for them to eat while they're working."

"What about Miles?"

"He's at the track too, ma'am. He sends his apologies, but he wants to help the lads."

"How may I assist you?" the waiter asked in perfect English.

"Oh," Georgie stuttered. "It appears we won't need a table for six, after all. I'm sorry about that. It'll just be two of us."

"Very well, madam," the waiter replied. "I'll check with the maître d' and be right back."

"Martin hasn't arrived?" Barney asked.

"I'm sure he'll be here shortly," Georgie replied, although she wasn't sure he would at all, and felt rather deflated.

She was certainly sympathetic to the long hours the mechanics and Barney often endured both at the workshop and the track, but the life of a Grand Prix team owner wasn't turning out to be as glamorous as she'd hoped. Barney left and as the waiter reseated her, she spotted a pair of drivers across the restaurant, enjoying a decent meal before the weekend began, and wondered if they even knew who she was. Probably not.

Jochen Rindt and Piers Courage appeared relaxed, and the Lotus driver, who Georgie had only seen as being solemn and focused at the racetrack, was actually smiling with his close friend. Courage laughed and his head turned her way. He nodded, and she smiled in return, slightly embarrassed to be caught staring at the two. Maybe the English driver was being polite, thinking she was a female admirer, or maybe they did know who she was. Another quick glance, and Georgie was sure they were now discussing her, Rindt nodding to his friend as his eyes flicked her way. Perhaps they recognised her as a team owner after all. The idea made her blush a little with a warm feeling inside, running off her moment of self-pity.

Reseated at a smaller table, Georgie decided to wait another fifteen minutes and then order food if she was still alone. Martin van der Meer continued to be an enigma. He'd called her once since the race in Belgium. They'd had a brief conversation, and he'd suggested the restaurant when she'd mentioned the idea of a team dinner before the race weekend. Apart from that, he'd wanted to know if the engine would be ready and once she'd confirmed it would, he'd hurriedly made an excuse to get off the phone. She'd tried the number in Holland he'd given her a few times since, but it rang with no answer.

After giving it twenty minutes, and another glass of wine, Georgie was about to order her meal when she finally saw Martin walk in. Wearing jeans, a collared shirt with a few buttons undone, and a pale blue blazer, he cut a dashing figure, and she noticed several heads turn his way as he walked towards her.

"My apologies for being late, Georgie," he said, taking his seat. "I ran into more traffic than I expected."

"I'm afraid the team couldn't make it," she explained. "The engine arrived late and they're still at the track working."

"Then I have the pleasure of your company all to my myself," he replied with a devious smile, and all at once she didn't feel alone anymore.

Martin quickly chose the fish special and Georgie, having pondered the menu and specials board at length while she was waiting for someone to eat with, changed her mind and ordered the same. He asked for a Martini while Georgie stuck with her wine, as she'd bought a bottle for the table and was already halfway through it.

Conversation came easily, and Martin had an amiable way of making Georgie feel like the two of them were the only people in the room. He focused on her as though she were the most interesting person he'd ever met and she found herself spilling her secrets of why she'd never remarried and how her family's old school English heritage was still flourishing in a modern world. In return, he revealed glimpses into his upbringing as an orphan of the war. His Jewish parents had been herded to a concentration camp from which they never returned, like so many others, and he'd been raised by a family friend under false papers.

He revealed few details, but Georgie was reticent to pry into what she assumed to be painful memories. His money came from buying, selling, and trading goods throughout Europe. He had no office, warehouse, or employees. He facilitated supplies to meet demands, wherever he found a need, taking a percentage for his services.

After a splendid meal, they left the restaurant and walked along the main street towards his hotel, where he said there were usually taxis waiting. Georgie felt young again. While she was ageing well and most believed her to be ten years younger than she was, it had been a while since a youthful spring had returned to her step. She didn't want the evening to end, and when they reached his hotel, they passed by the waiting taxis, and her wonderful evening continued in Martin van der Meer's room.

The three practice sessions were dominated by the impressive speed of Jochen Rindt in the Lotus 72, which he was finally happy with. John Miles also set a solid time in the second factory car, good enough for eighth on the grid, one place ahead of Miles. The McLaren team had regrouped with American Dan Gurney taking over Bruce's car, and with their additional entries, twenty-four cars attempted to qualify for twenty spots, per the latest rules.

Sunday began with overcast skies and threatening rain, but began clearing before the earlier than usual start, moved forward to avoid conflicting with the World Cup football final that afternoon. Having never driven a single-seater car in the wet, Miles was glad the precipitation held off. He was nervous enough, starting from the fourth row alongside Piers Courage with the main championship contenders just a few places ahead of him.

The start of the race was a mess. The official with the flag appeared to become confused after all the cars were set in position on the grid, and held them there with the drivers poised just below the biting point of their clutches. Some crept forward and had to dip the clutch again and brake before the man finally waved the flag and the field took off towards Tarzan, the slightly banked 180-degree first corner. Ickx beat Rindt away, with Stewart falling in behind Jackie Oliver, but Chris Amon had fallen foul of the start line delay and fried his clutch, ending his day before turn one.

Miles made a respectable launch, tucking in behind Piers Courage with the pair getting ahead of a slow-starting Clay Regazzoni who was making his Formula One debut in the Ferrari. It didn't take long for Rindt to command the lead, and Stewart passed Oliver for third, but was unable to gain on Ickx although the three cars at the front pulled away from the rest of the field. Rodríguez and a hard-charging Regazzoni ran fourth and fifth with a gap back to John Miles, who held a pack of snarling competitors behind him.

On lap fifteen, Courage finally found a way past the Lotus with a good tow down the front straight and a daring late-braking move into Tarzan. Miles opportunistically snuck by at the same time when John Miles went wide trying to defend his position. From then on, Piers Courage was driving like a man possessed, sliding his De Tomaso to the very edge of the road through every turn in his pursuit of the cars ahead. Miles hung gamely on, using the tow on the long straight to make up any ground lost around the rest of the lap.

The 2.6-mile Zandvoort circuit had three slower corners at the beginning of the lap, then nothing but fast, sweeping corners as the track wound its way around the undulating sandy hills of the Dutch coast. Only a few Armco barriers lined the track, which was mostly contained within natural earthen embankments. The ocean breeze sporadically brushed a dusting of sand across the road, making the turns unpredictable on every lap.

The pace was furious, and Miles was glad he'd been training hard between races to improve his strength and stamina. Several times he found his Lotus unexpectedly losing grip mid corner with the front tyres understeering through a sprinkling of sand, before suddenly grabbing the track and rotating the car into an oversteer. His quick reactions with the wheel saved him each time, but after twenty laps of the scheduled eighty, he wasn't sure he could beat the odds over the full distance.

Two laps later, at the incredibly fast right-hand kink called Tunnel Oost, Courage's De Tomaso twitched while at full cornering load as he apexed the corner. Only three car lengths behind, with his eyes focused through the car ahead towards the track beyond, Miles sensed Piers getting out of shape and lightly breathed back on the throttle. The Lotus was already in a four-wheel drift at the maximum slip angle of the tyres when it too lost grip and snapped into a lurid slide. Miles fought the wheel, knowing he couldn't lift all the way off the throttle without losing complete control. Ahead, the De Tomaso disappeared from his field of vision, shooting off the outside of the track as Miles drifted to the very edge of the tarmac, barely keeping his tyres on the road.

Still holding his breath, he glanced in his mirror to see the car he'd been closely following only a split second earlier, tumbling along the embankment. Miles tore his eyes away from the crash as he rapidly approached Panorama, another fast right-hander. He stole a quick look in the mirror as he dabbed the brakes before turning in and saw a bright yellow and orange fireball consuming the outside of the racetrack.

Finishing the lap in stunned shock, Miles found himself unsure of what he was supposed to do. As he passed the pit lane, he saw his pit board hung over the wall as usual, and no one flagging the cars to a stop. The competitors ahead hadn't slowed as he wasn't catching them, and in the mirrors he could make out the Matra of Beltoise, who had passed John Miles's Lotus. White flags, indicating a slow-moving vehicle on track, waved through turns four, five, and six, and Miles slowed before passing an ambulance, lumbering around the circuit.

Marshals waved yellow flags, and Miles slowed again as he approached Tunnel Oost. Thick black smoke billowed into the sky and as he made the turn and the wreckage came into view, he couldn't believe the raging inferno covering a large section of the embankment. A pair of corner workers battled the grass fire with water while the remains of the De Tomaso blazed unattended.

Miles had a sickening lump in his throat as he accelerated away and continued at speed. Once more past start/finish and no track officials tried to stop the cars. The race went on. For another fifty-six laps. As had been common practice in Formula One and other European racing, local yellow flags slowed the drivers past the incident site, but the event continued. The show must go on.

It was lonely and gut wrenching for Miles, as he presumed it had to be for the other competitors. He knew the crash was unsurvivable. Piers Courage was dead, trapped in the burning wreckage which the marshals were completely incapable of extinguishing. When the chequered flag fell, the fire had finally run out of fuel to burn, and all that remained was an unrecognisable pile of smouldering metal.

Miles rolled to a stop in the pit lane and the team gathered around the Lotus. Martin was the first to speak.

"Impressive run, mate. You're fifth."

Miles had no emotions left to be pleased with such a great result for the fledgling team, or angry at Martin for sounding so cheerful. He climbed from the car and Phil patted him on the back, but didn't say a word. Miles took off his helmet and balaclava, wiping his grimy face with a towel that Tina handed him. Rubber, oil, and soot from the fire had dirtied his balaclava and filtered through to his skin over the course of the race.

"He's gone," Georgie stammered, holding Miles's arms in her hands.

Her eyes were red and tears ran down her cheeks.

"I know," he whispered, and Georgie pulled her young driver into an embrace.

Miles allowed his own arms to wrap around her ladyship and felt her sobbing into his shoulder.

"I can't do this anymore," she said, her words barely audible. "I couldn't live with myself if something happened to you."

Miles wanted to tell her he was fine, and it wouldn't happen to him. But he couldn't. *What if he'd been ahead of Courage at Tunnel Oost, and hit the sandy patch first?* He felt like the soldier who'd kept on running as his mate alongside was struck down with bullets. Miles had no idea whether it was fate, destiny, or just dumb luck, but he'd survived the day, yet he felt no relief. Only guilt. He looked down the pit lane to where the winner of the race, Piers's best friend Jochen Rindt, sat on the rear tyre of his Lotus with his head in his hands, and Miles wondered whether the enormous risks of Grand Prix racing were really worth it.

22

BONAIRE

By the time AJ and Reg had finished their decompression stops and dropped their gear on the boat, it was nearly 6:00pm and the sun was low in the sky across the water. De Konig was full of questions, but Reg fended him off.

"Let's get unhooked and start in before we lose the light. We can watch the video on the way back."

The older man nodded and moved to the helm, where he started the outboards. AJ grabbed her mask and fins, catching her breath after lugging the heavy kit out of the water.

"Get on with it, then," Reg urged, grinning at her with seawater dripping from his mop of hair and beard.

AJ grumbled to herself but slipped her fins on and jumped in, holding her mask in place so it didn't become dislodged as she hit the water. She took a few deep breaths while De Konig idled forward, relieving the strain from the line, then she ducked under. Freediving down to a little over 20 feet felt like a walk in the park compared to that morning, and she soon had the carabiner unclipped from the buoy on the extended line. As she turned to swim back up, movement from below caught her eye, and she

hung to the line while a pair of curious spinner dolphins effort-
lessly glided her way.

The two circled around her while she watched in amazement
and glee, almost forgetting she was down there on a single breath
hold. Long before the dolphins needed air, AJ kicked for the
surface, hanging on to the line to the *Beste Leven* so it didn't get
tangled, and the pair swam away. As she clambered up the ladder,
AJ was about to tell the two men about her encounter but decided
to keep it to herself. Sometimes, she found her encounters and
experiences underwater were better left to her own memory.
Describing them could never do justice to the moment.

Reg took over at the helm so De Konig could put the memory card
in his laptop and play the video. In the fading light of the day and
under the pontoon boat's canopy, they could all see the screen, which
initially showed little more than the first footage under the wreck.
Scatter and haze filled the view, lit occasionally by the torch beam as
AJ had moved both around. But after a few moments, the water
cleared when AJ had reached higher up, away from the sand, and the
inverted deck of the barge came into focus. And then something more.

What appeared to be an angular box or crate sat close to the
gunwale, resting in the sand where it had fallen. Metal bars and
some sort of twisted line stuck out of the surrounding sand.

"That could be the railing," Reg suggested. "The gunwales
would have crushed it when the barge hit the seabed."

The video played on and something else appeared, farther
away, and harder to make out through the particulate stirred up by
their digging.

"There!" De Konig jumped, frantically rewinding the footage
and playing it again.

At the spot he'd seen, he paused the player, then advanced it
frame by frame. The high-definition recording was still incredibly
grainy with the poor light conditions, and the auto-exposure kept
jumping around between the scatter lit in front of the lens and
whatever lay farther away. De Konig stopped on a frame where the

focus had found an object on top of the sand, maybe five feet away from the camera, beyond the box.

"Could that be a tyre sticking out of the sand?" AJ blurted, pointing at the screen.

"I think it is," De Konig murmured, leaning closer. "And there, to the right of it. See that?"

Everything under the barge appeared to be the same colour. Although no coral could grow where the light couldn't reach, a dull, brown, almost furry coating covered everything, including the sand. AJ stared more closely.

"It certainly has a flat, uniform surface," she said, imagining whatever it was without the brown muck.

"I reckon it's the underside of the car," Reg offered. "Remember, everything is upside down, and if the straps broke or rotted, the race car would have dropped into the sand."

"Exactly," De Konig enthused. "We've found it!"

The old man quickly reined in his joy and continued playing the video.

"There's a chance it might be in decent shape," AJ said, as they watched to the end without seeing a better view.

"So, where's this chassis plate you were talking about?" Reg asked. "I'm guessing they didn't stick 'em on the underpan."

De Konig shook his head as he closed his laptop. "Inside the cockpit on the aluminium monocoque chassis."

"That'll be the part that's buried in the sand, right?" AJ noted.

"Yup," Reg confirmed, and ran a hand through his hair. "This is the point at which you might consider stopping," he said, looking at the Dutchman. "One thing we can't do is pull that race car out in one piece from underneath the wreck. Best we could do is to cut bits off and bring them up. Getting to the chassis plate will be a project by itself. I'd seriously consider pausing here and investigating a bigger salvage project to move the barge off the race car. Might be able to cut it away, or lift the barge off with big float bags."

De Konig held up a hand. "We're not stopping, Reg."

"But Reg is right," AJ added. "There's a chance the race car could be raised almost intact. I know nothing much will be usable after the impact damage and corrosion, but it'll be more like reconstructing it from a skeleton instead of one tooth."

De Konig nodded. "I hear what you're saying, but with all things considered, I need to press on. I'll point out a few key parts for you to focus on initially. They'll be particular to that race car and will prove its identity. I need you to think about how to disassemble the car."

Reg grunted, and he and AJ shared a look. She was sure they felt the same way. It seemed like madness to chop apart the race car if there was a chance of bringing it up without further damage.

"I asked Bryan about cutting equipment that might be available here on the island," Reg replied. "He knows a guy at the commercial dock with an underwater rechargeable reciprocating saw. He thinks he'll rent it to us."

"Perfect," De Konig said. "See if we can use it tomorrow."

"Okay," Reg responded. "It won't be cheap. Those things are expensive."

"Get the saw," De Konig reiterated.

Reg nodded. "We can dive again tomorrow, but then we'll need a rest day, okay?"

De Konig frowned. "Why? We're so close. I need you to dive more, not less."

"Doesn't work that way with deep dives," AJ responded, unsure whether the man was simply caught up in the discovery, or didn't care at all about his divers' wellbeing. "You can't keep doing decompression dives day after day on these gases without giving your body a break."

"You're after more money, aren't you?" De Konig scoffed.

"Hey," Reg quickly rebutted. "That's not the way we operate, mate. It has nothing to do with money and everything to do with safety. You didn't listen to us before, and your bloke took a ride in the chamber. You hired us to do the diving because we know what we're doing. If you don't think we're doing a good job, hire someone else."

De Konig glared at Reg for a moment, but his expression quickly softened. "My apologies to you both. I'm just excited. Of course, you're right. Whatever you say goes when it comes to the diving. Please see if you can get the saw for tomorrow, and hopefully you can get inside the wreck."

"I'll talk to Bryan again this evening," Reg replied, and they all fell silent as the pontoon skimmed across the ocean towards the marina with the sun setting off the starboard side.

AJ wanted to protest more about cutting up the race car, but it was De Konig's wreck. He owned the salvage rights and stepping up the operation would very quickly turn the budget from thousands of dollars into hundreds of thousands. Maybe a vintage Formula One car wasn't worth as much as she'd thought, but she made a mental note to spend some time later on Google exploring the subject. Which reminded her. She hadn't contacted the lady they'd met at Breeze 'n Bites about the night dive.

Digging Jo's card out of her rucksack, AJ sat on the bench and called her. A shallow dive to 20 feet wouldn't hurt their off-gassing in any significant way, and the two of them could use a fun dive to relax. They'd hardly seen any of the island so far, and tensions were rising on the job despite the progress being made. As the phone rang, she wondered again if De Konig was being honest with them. About anything.

23

1970 – LONDON AND CLERMONT-FERRAND, FRANCE

Georgie stared out the window of her two-bedroom flat overlooking Hyde Park in Knightsbridge. The sun peeked through the clouds, suggesting a hint of the English summer ahead as July approached. The people milling about the park and on the street below wore light jumpers and blazers instead of heavy winter jackets or raincoats. A moment after she spotted Barney's blue Ford Zephyr parked down the street, a knock sounded from the front door.

"Hello," she greeted her team manager when she let him into the flat.

"Good morning," he said, then glanced at his watch. "Um, afternoon, actually."

"I made a few sandwiches," Georgie continued as they walked into the living room.

Barney appeared startled to see Martin already there and bumbled a greeting to the Dutchman.

"Here, we'll sit at the dining table," Georgie said, leading both men to the long, elegant table where sandwiches, a pot of tea, and a tray of biscuits awaited.

For five awkward minutes, she poured tea and handed out delicate sandwiches on fine china plates while they made small talk about anything that didn't have to do with race cars. Georgie had left Zandvoort in a hurry after telling Barney she was done with the team. Martin had called her the next day, saying he was in London, and they'd dined together, but she'd still refused to discuss the race. The following morning, she had called Barney and asked him to join her for lunch, where they now sat, and Georgie was dreading the conversation they were about to have.

She also sensed Barney had picked up on the fact that Martin had stayed the night, which made her feel even more uncomfortable. Why it bothered her, she wasn't sure, although she'd been emotionally drained since Sunday, so perhaps it was simply her general feeling of malaise.

"I know I owe you both a conversation about the team," she began. "And I'm sorry it's taken me a day to sort myself out, but I've been trying to get my thoughts in order."

Martin sat patiently waiting without showing any emotion, but Barney made his usual polite comments about it being alright.

"I know we were all shaken by the accident, but for me it drove home the reality of what could happen to our driver. Carlos's crash was horrifying, and it was awful seeing him lying in a hospital bed, but Piers's death was simply too terrible."

Georgie paused, unable to shake the image of the Englishman laughing with his friend that night at dinner before the Zandvoort weekend. His polite nod in her direction. She closed her eyes and tried to push her thoughts of the man's poor wife aside.

"The idea that Miles could come to a similar end in a car I entered is too much for me to contemplate."

The three sat in silence for a few moments before Martin spoke.

"I think it's important and commendable that you do recognise the risks inherent in the sport," he said, and Georgie waited for him to continue. But he didn't.

She hadn't expected any support for her decision from either of the men at the table, although she'd presumed each would have different reasons for wanting to continue.

"Do you have another team who'd want your chassis?" she asked Martin.

He shook his head. "I'd planned to continue for the season with you, so I haven't asked, and I'm not sure I'm interested in finding another team to work with."

Georgie felt confused and a little conflicted. "You're considering pulling out of Formula One, too?"

"I hadn't," Martin replied, his eyes locked on hers. "But I thought I'd found the perfect situation for me, so I'll need to consider what's next."

"It did seem like our little team was a force to be reckoned with," Barney added.

Georgie kept her eyes on Martin's. The man was so difficult to read on both a business and emotional level. She knew her physical attraction for him was growing into something more, but had been reminding herself that he showed few signs of feeling the same way. His apparent reluctance to move on to another relationship in Formula One suggested he'd become more invested in the team than she'd believed… or was it more than that?

"I'd like to see Miles in a position to continue showing everyone what he's capable of," Martin continued. "But I'm not really sure how to do that. Someone like Rob Walker would need running costs as well as a chassis to add an entry to his team. Plus an engine, of course. I'm not ready to fund a ride to that level."

"It would be a shame to see Miles's talent fall by the wayside," Barney said, and Georgie frowned at him.

"It would be a bloody shame to see the young lad burnt to a crisp in fiery crash," she snapped.

"Of course. I didn't mean to…" Barney began, then mumbled a little more before giving up on explaining himself.

"Statistically, the odds are pretty good for the rest of the year," Martin offered. "I know it's callous to speak of these things in such a manner, but history tells us we lose one driver a year in Grand Prix, and another Grand Prix driver a year while they're competing in other events or testing. We've met that number already. I'm hearing the German Grand Prix is being run at Hockenheim instead of the Nürburgring due to safety concerns, and the Grand Prix Drivers' Association is starting to have more and more impact on key issues. Motor racing is inherently dangerous, but I believe the sport will become safer and safer over time as more measures are implemented."

Georgie thought about his words and knew he was making valid points, but the gamble wasn't a matter of losing equipment, pride, or money. It was lives. She glanced at Barney, but his attention seemed to be on Martin, and he didn't look pleased. Perhaps because the Dutchman was more eloquently pleading the case to continue, or maybe he simply didn't like the man, Georgie couldn't tell.

"I'm sure you're right," she said, turning back to Martin. "And I may well wish to return to the sport when it becomes safer for the drivers, but I don't think I can stomach risking Miles's life until then. Not in a car I enter."

Silence fell between them once more and although she guessed Barney was dying to plead his case to keep the team alive, he remained quiet, and it was Martin who spoke first once again.

"As a team owner, you're in a position to affect change, Georgie. You could make a difference. As a spectator, your voice won't be heard."

"No one will listen to me," she responded. "I own one of the smallest teams in the paddock, who only showed up this year. Besides, I'm a woman, and this is most definitely a man's world, even if they do allow me into their party."

"I think your voice would carry more weight than you think," Martin continued. "With the new rules expanding entries, they're looking for teams who'll be at every race, which you have been this year. What they don't want is a reputation for losing entrants because the sport is too dangerous. I agree, alone you won't be heard, but as an owner in support of the drivers as they campaign for their lives, you can make a difference."

"The drivers will most certainly be vocal after the weekend,"

Barney chimed in. "It is sad, but it often takes a tragedy to spur people into change."

Georgie sighed and sat back in her chair. She'd already decided to pay Barney, Phil, and Tina until the end of the season, even though they'd have nothing to do beyond stripping down the car to give Martin back his chassis, then selling the DFV, transporter, and other equipment. She felt an obligation to do so. But now Martin had thrust a different burden upon her. Instead of risking Miles's life, perhaps her actions could save many young drivers from a fate such as befell Piers Courage. An avoidable death if the correct barriers had been in place.

"I don't know," Georgie said, honestly expressing her conflicted mind.

"May I make a suggestion?" Martin asked.

"Of course," Georgie replied.

"Clermont-Ferrand is less than two weeks away," Martin said. "Why don't we continue to the race as planned. During the weekend, you can chat with other team owners and get an idea of what they're thinking on the safety front. I'm sure Jackie Stewart would be happy to discuss the issues as well. He seems to be the most vocal member of the GPDA."

Usually bold and decisive, Georgie was still unsure, and felt paralysed to make a decision. She loved the idea of making a difference to the future of the sport, but at what cost? Odds be damned, there were eight more races left in the season, which were eight more opportunities for disaster.

"Fine," she finally relented, unconvinced, but glad to be free of the decision. "We'll go to France and see from there."

With her mind made up, Barney rose to leave, and Georgie walked him to the door.

"Are you sure about this?" he asked quietly.

"I thought you were all for carrying on?" she questioned in surprise.

Barney looked down and shuffled his feet uncomfortably. "Of course I'd like us to keep racing, because, well, that's what me and the lads do. We're racers. But I want to make sure it's the right decision for you, ma'am, not something he's pushing you into," Barney said, nodding in the direction of the dining room.

"You don't seem to like Martin very much," Georgie responded, more curious than annoyed.

Barney scratched his head and awkwardly tried to smile.

"What is it that's bothering you, Barney?" Georgie persisted.

Barney leaned closer and whispered, "We really don't know anything about the man, do we?"

"Colin Chapman brought him to us, so he must think he's alright," Georgie pointed out.

"Chapman is in the business of selling cars, ma'am. He thinks anyone's alright whose cheques clear."

"That's a bit harsh, Barney."

"Perhaps," he admitted, "but I'm just saying Martin is becoming more and more involved, and we really don't know much about him."

Georgie was about to suggest that Barney was stepping over the line, but she stopped herself. Maybe her team manager's suspicions were based, at least in part, on jealousy, but he wasn't wrong. She was now in some form of relationship with the man, beyond their business ties, and she still had no idea exactly where he lived or any personal details of substance.

"I can't say I'm completely convinced I'm making the right decision," she said. "But I've made it, and I don't feel like I've been coerced or tricked in any way. We're going to race in France."

"Fair enough, ma'am," Barney replied softly. "You know I just want what's best for you and your team."

"I do appreciate that Barney," she said, then she moved a little closer and lowered her voice further. "If you'd care to do a bit of discreet investigating, perhaps that would put your concerns to rest."

Barney looked surprised. "Leave it with me," he replied.

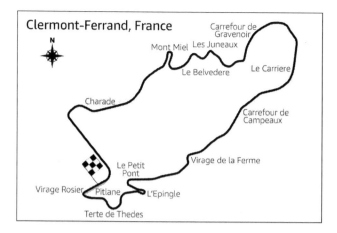

Wrapping around an extinct volcano in central France, Clermont-Ferrand was another circuit which utilised a mixture of public roads closed for the event and permanent sections of racetrack. Five miles of twisty corner complexes were strung together by faster curves, with only one straightaway that actually went straight between two corners. It was a complicated and difficult track to learn, putting the veterans at a distinct advantage throughout the practice sessions.

Despite arriving late after problems with their transporter and missing Friday's session, the Ferraris had great pace in both of Saturday's practices. Ickx set quickest time for pole in the afternoon session with a cooler front dropping temperatures and helping all the cars go faster. Beltoise took second in the Matra, then the two Marches of Amon and Stewart. Rindt, hampered by a rock in the face from another car dropping a wheel ahead of him, managed the sixth best time.

With his usual focus on preparation, Miles was fastest of the drivers who hadn't seen the track before, and he turned a few heads by qualifying two spots behind the factory Lotus in eighth. With both his own entries running the 72 chassis every weekend, Chapman was becoming slower to pass on the latest updates to Lady Ashford's team, yet Miles still outqualified the second works entry by a clear margin.

In the race, Rindt steadily worked his way to the front, helped by the engine expiring on Ickx's Ferrari while he was leading. Miles held his own off the start and battled with Denny Hulme and Henri Pescarolo throughout much of the thirty-eight-lap race until, with only five laps remaining, a puncture sent him to the pits. Phil and Tina changed the tyre as fast as they could, but the stop relegated him to tenth, one spot behind Jackie Stewart, who had suffered an ignition issue and pitted for repairs earlier in the race.

When their young driver climbed from the cockpit post race, the team's mood was one of stifled jubilation. Once again, Miles had proven the competitiveness of Georgie's little team, as well as his own ability, but they'd been denied points and extra prize money with a stroke of bad luck. As the race had worn on, Georgie had felt the old excitement and exhilaration of being involved in a Grand Prix. But once it was over, she sensed the pressure of expectancy from everyone. She'd told them one race and we'll see from there, and now that race was over and she faced a decision once more.

"Bloody shame about the finish," Barney said, standing next to her. "But nice to put in a solid showing and have a safe weekend."

Her team manager's lack of subtlety was slightly annoying, but she knew they were all worried about what was coming next. Over the weekend, she'd spoken with other team owners as planned, and they all shared her concerns with safety. Jackie Stewart had been most appreciative of her support of the drivers and urged her to continue voicing her opinions on their behalf.

"One swallow does not a summer make," she replied to Barney, still struggling with the idea of feeling responsible for a young driver's life.

Martin joined them and was about to add his thoughts when he paused, looking over Georgie's shoulder.

"Another strong weekend," Colin Chapman said, stopping next to them on his way to the podium. "It's only two weeks until the British Grand Prix, but we need to win on home soil, so call me mid-week. I'll do my best to get you as many updates as possible."

Without awaiting any response, the Lotus boss briskly strutted away, leaving Georgie saying thank you to his back.

"You realise what this means?" Barney said excitedly. "He thinks we might be able to win."

"Or at least fend off the Ferraris, Marches, and Matras so Rindt can keep on winning," Martin suggested.

They both turned to Georgie, who knew she was really on the spot now.

"Okay, okay. We'll keep going," she relented, despite her misgivings.

24

BONAIRE

"I hope we didn't keep you waiting," AJ said, placing her dive gear in the back of a four-door pickup truck.

"The timing should be good," Jo replied, and introduced AJ and Reg to her clients, Kristina and Kim.

Reg sat upfront, and AJ sat next to the American couple on the rear bench seat. Jo drove them north, heading through the township of Hato before the road jogged away from the coastline for a few miles. Another sharp turn took them back towards the water where the road narrowed considerably as it cut ninety degrees right when it met the ocean. Occasional small turn-outs were the only way two vehicles could pass each other, but the road appeared to be deserted.

They all chatted as the pickup bumped along the roughly paved road, and in the headlights, AJ noticed several of the yellow painted rocks which marked the shore diving sites all around the island. On their right, a bluff overshadowed the road, and at one point a rock outcrop actually hung over part of the single lane. After a few minutes, Jo pulled over opposite the third large yellow stone they came across, parking next to a small, abandoned concrete building.

On the drive, they'd discovered Kristina and Kim were both experienced recreational divers who'd travelled extensively to spend time underwater. Kristina was bubbly, fun and outgoing, while Kim had a similar tone to Eeyore, the donkey from Winnie the Pooh, but with a bone-dry sense of humour. They came to Bonaire most years around the same time and stayed in Den Laman condos next door to Sand Dollar, in the building where Breeze 'n Bites was located.

The group changed into their wetsuits, and with a competent group of divers, Jo kept her briefing simple.

"We'll walk down a flight of steps to the beach and watch the lower ones as they're pretty broken up," she began. "Then straight out into the water. We'll drop down once we're in ten feet or so and swim out to where you'll see a large patch of soft corals at about 20 feet. I'll flash my light a few times, which will be the signal for everyone to turn theirs off. Then give it a few minutes and the show will begin. I'm setting a lantern on the steps for a guide back in case we get separated. Sound good?"

Everyone gave her an okay, keen to get in the water, and the group waddled across the road with their tanks on their backs, strapped to their buoyancy control devices, or BCDs as they were usually called. AJ and Reg had grabbed their recreational rigs from the room, which were still Dive Rite backplate systems, but set up with single tank straps and smaller wings with the lower lift requirement. They picked their way carefully across the short, rocky beach, and waded in until the water came up to their waists, then lay on their backs and slipped their fins on.

The waning moon, only a few days after being full, lit the ocean's surface enough that they could make out each other on the surface, but once they descended, their five dive lights illuminated the sea floor all around them. As Jo had described, the sand gently sloped towards a garden of swaying soft coral and continuing deeper to the reef itself. The group gathered, and when Jo flashed her light three times, everyone turned off their torches.

For the first few moments, AJ was in complete darkness until her eyes slowly adjusted. The moonlight was just bright enough to provide a vague hint of an outline of the diver closest to her. She sensed their presence as much as visually located them. The only way to tell if she was drifting up or down in the water was by checking her dive computer, but the LED screen then glowed and ruined her night vision again.

After five minutes, AJ was beginning to think the whole thing was an elaborate hoax and she wished she'd looked it up on the internet after all. But Jo seemed really nice and unlikely to invite strangers she'd just met in a restaurant to venture out on a night dive where they'd see nothing at all. It was more likely, she decided, that these ostrocod creatures had stayed home for the evening.

As though a switch had been thrown, tiny specks of light began appearing all around her. Her first reaction was excitement that they hadn't missed the event after all. Her second thought was disappointment. The little beacons of light were nice, but nothing more than she often saw on night dives when select macro life forms illuminated themselves. AJ floated in the water and waved her hand back and forth, sparking more of the bioluminescent creatures.

And then something else appeared before her eyes. A spiral of light no more than a few inches long. They sprang up all around her, spinning like illuminated corkscrews. They reminded her of the icicle-style Christmas lights with their swirling effect. The scene was otherworldly. AJ suddenly felt like she was adrift in space, surrounded by a hundred Milky Ways. There was no way to tell up from down as the tiny creatures joined together in little chains to form their spirals and put on their best glow to attract their mates.

For ten minutes, the show continued before the lights slowly diminished and eventually disappeared altogether. The curtains of night-time closed once more, and the divers were left in pitch-black darkness. Jo flicked her light on and one by one, the others did the same. Their guide led them on a brief tour of the dive site, finding all sorts of critters who weren't usually seen during the day.

Lobsters and eels were roaming outside their hiding holes, and an octopus changed colours several times, trying to camouflage itself against the coral when it was caught in a beam.

AJ and Reg made sure to stay above the others at 20 feet so the dive didn't impact their bodies' processing of their deep dives that day, but still caught all the sights in their powerful torches. When the group finally surfaced close to shore, they all babbled at the same time, enthusing about the dive. Except Reg, as he wasn't the babbling type, but even he claimed it was one of the most unique dives he'd ever seen.

They made their way out of the water, collecting the lantern on the way, and climbed the steps back to the road. Reg was a gentleman and walked around the building while the women stripped out of their wetsuits and threw on dry clothes. They gave him a whistle when it was safe for him to return, having changed himself while away.

"Dinner plans?" AJ asked the group.

"There's a pizza place by Oil Slick Leap, if that sounds good to everyone," Jo suggested.

"I'm going to look like a pizza by the time I leave Bonaire," AJ joked, thinking of the flammkuchen she'd eaten two nights in a row.

"We can find somewhere else," Jo offered.

"I didn't say I didn't want to eat there," AJ quickly replied with a grin. "But you'll have to show me where the oil slick is."

Everyone else laughed, including Reg.

"It's the dive site at the corner before we turned along the waterfront," Kristina said. "You get in by jumping off the sea wall, hence the leap part."

"Bonaire rookie," AJ admitted.

"Which sites have you dived so far this trip?" Kim asked as they piled back into the pickup truck.

"Just one, actually," she replied. "Well, two now. Thanks to you."

"When did you arrive?" Kristina asked.

"Monday, and we've dived twice each day, but we're sort of working while we're here, so it's been one site."

"What kind of work?" Kim asked with interest. "It's great that you get to travel and dive for work."

"Yeah," AJ replied, smiling in return. "I'm afraid we're doing private exploration, salvage sort of stuff, and the guy hiring us is paranoid about the secrecy thing, so I'm not allowed to say."

"Wow," Kristina enthused. "Now I'm really fascinated. Maybe we can get you both drunk enough to spill the beans."

AJ laughed. "It's deep, tech stuff, so we'll be on a one drink limit tonight, but come to Grand Cayman sometime and you can buy us lots of drinks when we're home."

"Wait, wait, wait," Kim said, holding up both hands as Jo pulled into a restaurant with a small indoor kitchen and a patio for seating. "You two live in the Cayman Islands and are being paid to dive a super-secret whatever it is you're diving in Bonaire. That sound about right?"

Reg climbed out of the truck. "Hit the nail on the head, love. It's a sacrifice, but we do it for queen and country."

Kristina laughed, and Kim scoffed.

"Don't you have a king these days?"

"We do, but we're not quite ready to embrace that just yet," AJ replied as they walked to the counter and picked up menus.

Once they'd ordered, the group found a table and a waitress soon brought them their drinks. AJ had been chilled when she'd come out of the water but had warmed up already and they could feel the heat coming from the ovens in the kitchen. She slipped off her Mermaid Divers zippered hoodie and set it over the back of the chair.

"Ooh, I love your T-shirt," Jo said, reading the words aloud. "Peace, Love, Dive. That about sums it up, doesn't it?"

"I think so," AJ agreed with a grin, holding up her drink. "And cheers to Jo for taking us out for a dive we'll never forget."

"Cheers," they all agreed, clinking glasses.

The evening was just what the doctor ordered for AJ. A fun

dive, great food, and enjoyable company. Following the tensions of the past few days, the dolphins and the ostrocods had worked their underwater magic on her, and she felt tired but rejuvenated by the time she and Reg were back to the rented condo.

"Can't say I like the idea of cutting this car to bits," Reg said as they sprawled on the sofas, not quite ready for bed as it was still only 9:00pm.

"Me neither," AJ replied, pulling her back to the stress of the day. "But he's the boss on this one."

She picked up her tablet and open an internet browser, typing in 1970 Formula One car for sale.

"Didn't he say the barge sank in 1970?"

Reg nodded. "Yeah, but he didn't say what year the car was from, or what make it was."

"Right," AJ mumbled, looking through the search results. "Not too many Formula One cars for sale."

"Most teams don't sell them anymore," Reg replied. "I think they all hang on to them. Back in the day, Ferrari used to actually destroy the previous year's chassis so no one could ever get their hands on them."

"Bit extreme," AJ commented.

"Top secret stuff," Reg explained. "Especially back in the 60s and 70s when they were first understanding aerodynamics and putting wings on the cars."

"Hmm," AJ grunted. "Might explain why there aren't any 1970 Formula One cars for sale that I can find. Here's an interesting story though," she continued, reading the headline from the article. "The puzzling mystery surrounding the Ashford Motor Racing Team and the missing Lotus 72."

25

1970 – BRANDS HATCH, ENGLAND

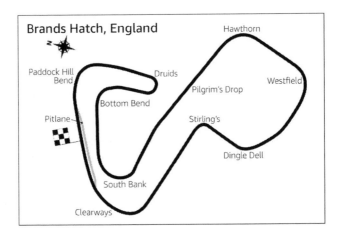

Miles had raced at Brands Hatch many times and even driven the full-length Grand Prix circuit once before. Finally, he felt like he was on a more even footing going into the weekend. He still walked several laps of the 2.6-mile permanent road course to refamiliarise himself and check if any details had been changed or updated.

While making notes, standing on the apex kerbing at Hawthorn's corner during his first lap of his walk, Miles was almost bowled over by a motor scooter zipping by. Jochen Rindt looked back with a wicked grin on his face as he zoomed off into the distance with his wife, Nina, hanging on as best she could. Miles had made it to the last corner, Clearways, a long sweeping downhill right-hand curve, when he heard the scooter approaching again. The Austrian, who was now the championship leader after his win in France, slowed this time and stopped next to Miles. He'd spoken to Rindt a few times before, once at Hethel and a couple of brief conversations earlier in the season, but Miles was surprised to see the man taking a moment to approach him.

"You have the suspension updates?" Rindt asked in accented English.

"We do, sir," Miles replied, although he had no way of knowing whether the parts and set-up they'd received from Mr Chapman were the very latest or not.

Rindt nodded. He was known as a man of few words who didn't waste time on small talk.

"You've raced here before?" he asked.

"Mainly on the club track, but once on the full course," Miles replied.

Rindt nodded again and Miles tried not to stare at Nina, who was stunningly pretty and paying attention to the conversation, although she didn't say a word.

"Good. I need you to qualify well," Rindt said flatly.

"I'll be doing my best, sir," Miles responded. "I'm sure John will be up there too," he added, referring to Rindt's Lotus teammate.

The Austrian looked thoughtful for a moment and appeared ready to say something more, but must have decided against it, as he surprised both Miles and Nina by accelerating away. Miles watched the man disappear around Clearways and enter the pit lane. He already felt a ton of pressure to perform well at his team's and his own home race, but now the championship leader expected him to have his back as well. A shiver ran through Miles's body despite the warm, early summer day.

The race weekend started on Thursday, with the race itself on Saturday, unlike most Grand Prix, which were held on Sundays. The only practice on Thursday was delayed by the pre-event technical inspections taking longer than anticipated with the larger entry. The organisers had announced that all entries would start the race, which drew extra teams and drivers.

Miles got up to speed quickly around the familiar circuit, and with overcast skies the lap times for everyone were fast. Jochen Rindt set the pace with a 1:24.8, lowering the track record, and eight-tenths quicker than his closest rival. Miles was ninth fastest with 1:26.7, putting him just ahead of John Miles in the second factory Lotus. Lady Ashford and the team were delighted, but Miles couldn't help being a little disappointed in front of his home crowd, and especially his family.

That evening, after the support series practices were done, he walked the track again, making more notes and thinking about ways to improve his line and technique at each turn. When he returned to the paddock, he also had a clearer idea of what the car needed to help him go faster at different corners, but those needs conflicted each other. Phil and Tina were almost finished with their evening checks and maintenance, so Miles sat on the front tyre and didn't say anything. He didn't want to make another late evening for the crew, especially when he wasn't sure of himself.

"What'd you figure out then?" Phil asked, looking up from where he was checking the rear brake lines and pad wear.

"I noticed a few spots where I'll try adjusting my line tomorrow," Miles replied.

Phil paused his work, wiping his brow with the back of his hand. "That's good. What else?"

"I need to get the car more settled for Paddock," Miles replied, thinking about the notes he'd made. "I think I can do that with a softer brake release before turn-in."

Phil looked up at him. "What can we change to help that?"

Paddock Hill Bend was one of the trickiest corners on any circuit. The front straight never actually went straight, but undulated and curved, rising over a crest before steeply plummeting into the very fast right-hand corner which dipped into the bottom of a valley at corner exit. The entry was completely blind and the race cars were far more interested in skating off into the railway sleepers which awaited a few yards beyond the grass lining the track than sticking to the road over the hill.

"I'm not sure we can make the car perfect for Paddock," Miles replied, thoughtfully.

"You're right about that," Phil said. "So let's make it the best it can be everywhere else and let you sort out Paddock as best you can."

His mechanic's words sparked a light bulb in Miles's head. "Of course, you're right," he said.

"It does happen occasionally," Phil replied with a grin.

"Rarely, but occasionally," Tina ribbed from under the left rear suspension.

"So, what does the car need to do better in the other corners?" Phil asked.

"I need the front to be more positive mid corner," Miles replied. "But I'm so worried it'll be too much over the crest into Paddock that I'll be backwards before the apex."

"So do your soft-release braking business and get the weight off the front tyres over the crest," Phil said, picking himself up and sitting on the rear tyre facing Miles. "Is the rear stable on entry elsewhere?"

The young driver gave himself a few moments to reply, running a lap in his mind. One of the challenges of the Brands Hatch circuit was the elevation changes. Winding around the hillsides of Kent, the road was never on even ground during the lap. Consequently, the corners were a wide mixture of on and off camber as well as uphill, downhill, and a mixture of the two, with Paddock Hill Bend being the most extreme.

A car gained grip through its tyres with vertical load pushing them into the ground, so when the driver braked, transferring the weight of the vehicle more onto the front tyres, it gained turning ability while losing grip in the rear tyres as the vertical load lessened. This, combined with the undulations and camber of the circuit, made maintaining balance and control of the car at the limit incredibly challenging. Along with finding the right adjustments to the set-up.

"I believe I can manage the entry oversteer, so let's focus on finding mid-corner front-end grip," Miles said, having made up his mind with the prompts from Phil. "We can't lower the front ride height as I'm already touching the ground in braking up the hill to Druids, and softer front springs will do the same unless we raise the car, so maybe we need to stiffen the rear springs."

Phil thought it over for a moment. "I'd like to try something else if you're open to the idea?"

"Of course," Miles replied without hesitation.

"I'd like to reduce the toe-out on the front," Phil said, and both Miles and Tina stared at him in silence.

Recently, the trend in front alignment had been for the wheels to be toed-out more to help the car turn into the corners.

"I think that's what Chapman is doing on the factory cars," Phil added.

"Won't that make it dart around on the straightaways?" Tina asked.

"What straights?" Phil countered.

Miles laughed. "That's true. I almost never have the wheel straight around here."

"We've been toeing out the front more and more to get the car to point into the corners," Phil explained. "But I think we might be sacrificing mid-corner grip. With toe-out, the inside front is turned more than the outside front, which is correct for the radius it's on relative to the outside tyre, but not the slip angle. When the car rolls on its suspension and loads the outside tyres, their optimum slip angle is higher, but the inside tyre's is less."

"I think I follow," Miles said. "You're saying it's about increasing grip of the inside tyre."

"Exactly," Phil replied. "With the wings we're running, there's more downforce on all four tyres than ever before. I think we can make the inside front tyre do more work for us."

Miles grinned. "I'm all for it. What do we need to do?"

"You need to go to bed," Phil said, standing up. "The lad and me'll get to work on realigning the front end."

"That'll take a while," Miles responded. "Let me stay and help."

"If it makes us go faster, it'll be worth it and then some," Phil said, giving Miles a wink. "Now bugger off and get some kip."

With a combination of improvements in his driving and the set-up changes Phil fine-tuned, Miles bettered his lap time in Friday's session to a 1:25.7, putting him sixth on the grid. By a mere tenth of a second, he'd beaten Ferrari's very rapid newcomer, Clay Regazzoni, who was back for another race, and two-tenths ahead of John Miles. Also behind him were Jackie Stewart and Mario Andretti, which gave Miles a serious case of nerves when he looked in his mirrors as he sat on the grid.

The sloping front stretch at Brands Hatch made the standing start incredibly difficult, as each driver had to keep the ball of their foot on the brake while simultaneously revving the engine with the side of their shoe on the throttle. If the car rolled forward of their grid spot line painted on the track, they'd be penalised. When the flag dropped, the field of drivers slipped their feet off the brakes and tried to judge the amount of throttle needed to launch the car without stalling or spinning the tyres too much.

Miles got away quite well, much to his relief, but a hard-charging Regazzoni kept the middle line into Paddock Hill Bend, pinning him to the inside, where he had to lift to make the corner. Slotting in behind the Ferrari, the cars ahead and behind fanned out across the track as they sped steeply uphill towards Druids Hairpin. By the apex of the tight, first gear corner, everyone had sorted themselves out and a single file train of screaming Formula One cars which dived down the hill and slid through the off-cambered corner aptly named Bottom Bend.

More relieved to have survived the first few corners than annoyed to have lost a spot, Miles chased Regazzoni through South Bank and over the hill to Pilgrims Drop, the fastest part of the circuit leading to the right-handed Hawthorn Bend. Jacky Ickx had grabbed the lead from the outside of row one and Miles could see Rindt was running third behind Jack Brabham, but they were both losing ground to the red Ferrari.

By the time the field reached Clearways, Regazzoni was all over the gearbox of Denny Hulme in the McLaren and Miles had pulled one second away from John Miles in his identical Lotus 72. Carefully timing his exit onto the curving front straight, Miles pulled closer to the Ferrari who'd mistimed his own attack on Hulme. But instead of drawing alongside Regazzoni, Miles watched the 12-cylinder Italian machine edge away from him with superior power over the Cosworth DFV.

Tucking into the draft, he chased the cars ahead, watching Regazzoni charge up to the back of Hulme underbraking for Paddock Hill Bend. Miles braked hard, downshifted to third, and began easing gently off the brake pedal as he crested the hill. Using the gap in the outside wall where the ambulance parked as his marker, he was completely off the brakes as he urged the steering wheel into the fast corner. The car went light over the crest, and by the time Miles could see the tarmac again, he was aimed perfectly through the apex with his right foot squeezing into the throttle.

The compression in the valley felt like the car weighed more than the transporter that brought it to the track, and the chassis scraped on the road with the forces exaggerated from a full fuel load. But his plan had worked. The Ferrari rode up the exit kerb as the Italian fought the wheel to stay on the road and Miles pulled to his right up the hill and was alongside the Ferrari before the braking zone. Both drivers waited to the last possible moment to brake as hard as they could, heel and toe downshifting through the gears to first.

Miles had the inside line, but it made for a very tight turn around the hairpin. Regazzoni had the ideal approach, but the Lotus blocked his turn. They surged into the corner side by side, but Regazzoni hung on his brakes a little too hard, too long, and locked his right front tyre, leaving a plume of tortured rubber smoke behind him. Miles slipped by into sixth place, now setting his sights on Denny Hulme.

By Clearways, he was within a car length of the Kiwi, and another good run through Paddock placed him ready to pounce with no pressure from a recovering Regazzoni two seconds behind. But Hulme was driving smoothly as he found his rhythm and without a mistake he'd be difficult to overtake around Brands Hatch, which offered few good passing spots. On the back side of the circuit, exiting Westfield, Miles was thinking ahead to the hairpin and calculating what he'd have to do to challenge Hulme.

Brushing the brakes for the right-hand Dingle Dell, he felt something strange in the front of the car. An odd vibration and the car veered slightly left, upsetting the balance at turn-in. He lost a car length to Hulme but knew he should brake early for Stirling's in case the issue happened again. It did. The Lotus leapt left as Miles braked firmly and the front of the chassis shook. Able to slow the car enough to make the turn, he released the brakes as soon as he could and slid through the corner, riding the kerb at the exit.

Regazzoni was alongside soon after they exited the turn, but Miles could do nothing about it. With his hand raised in the air, he stayed off the throttle and coasted down the hill, staying right and entering the pit lane. A mixture of anger, disappointment, and panic ran through his mind. *Could it have been debris on the brake disc which made them shake? Maybe if he'd stayed out, it would have been fine?* Miles touched the brakes again as he approached his team and the front of the car shook and the steering wheel tugged left in his hands.

"What's wrong?" Phil shouted, as Miles came to a stop.

"Something in the front brakes!" he explained, pointing. "The left front."

Miles left the engine running while Phil leapt to the front of the car and inspected the suspension. He grabbed the halfshaft which connected the wheel and hub assembly to the innovative inboard brakes, and Miles watched the shaft rattle in his hand. Miles switched off the engine and unbuckled his belts.

"What broke?" Martin asked, speaking loudly to be heard over the race cars flying by on track. "Can't you fix it?"

"Looks like the universal joint on the halfshaft, or the halfshaft itself," Phil explained as he and Tina began removing the body-work for a better look.

"What the hell is that?" Martin demanded. "Don't you inspect and check all these things?"

Phil glared at the chassis owner and continued working without replying.

"It's a new system Lotus designed this year," Miles began, steering Martin away from the car. "Moving the brakes to the chassis side reduces unsprung weight and helps cornering performance. But it means running a shaft from the upright to another hub which carries the brake disc. That's where the problem seems to be."

Miles slipped off his helmet and balaclava, joining Phil at the front of the car. Phil rattled the halfshaft, the inboard end moving inside the universal joint.

"I'm really sorry, mate," Phil said. "I pulled the rubber boots back and looked at the UJs last night. If there was a problem, I missed it."

"This isn't your fault, Phil," Miles quickly responded. "We'll show Mr Chapman the parts after the race and see what he says."

Barney crouched down beside them. "Another bloody good run, lads. We'll get 'em in Germany in two weeks."

"If we get to go," Phil countered, glancing up to the pit garage where Lady Ashford was in deep conversation with Martin. "What's with that bloke, anyway?"

"Good question," Barney replied, just loud enough for the crew to hear. "I've been checking into him, and you know what I discovered?"

"What?" Phil asked, as Tina and Miles leaned in closer.

"Absolutely bugger all," Barney replied. "Our import–export man, Martin van der Meer, doesn't seem to exist, despite the fact he's standing over there."

26

BONAIRE

When De Konig showed up at 7:00am, he brought with him two surprises. The first was Laurens. He appeared to be fine and just as unsociable as he'd been prior to spending two shifts in a recompression chamber. The other news was the back of the van was already full of tanks, so they were going straight to TDS. AJ doubted his doctor would approve of Laurens lugging dive tanks around, seeing as part of the rehabilitation for decompression sickness was rest and no strenuous activities, but she was glad it was done.

Bryan had come through once again and had a well-used underwater reciprocating saw sitting on the counter for them, along with several spare blades of different tooth counts. De Konig forked over a two thousand-dollar damage deposit and another five hundred for the daily rental. He paid both with cash. From what AJ knew of the specialised tool, he'd just slapped the cost of a new saw on the table, but she doubted he could buy one and get it here in a timely fashion. And time seemed to be a factor. Perhaps, due at least in part to the fact that she and Reg were scheduled to go home in four days.

Bryan efficiently topped off the tanks, blending the gases to hit the same mix they'd been using.

"How's my spare 80 doing?" he asked with a grin.

"Hanging at 60 feet, happy as you like," AJ replied, matching his smile.

As they made their way back to the boat and motored out to the site, De Konig explained where inside the cockpit they'd find the chassis plate, but went on to stress that the divers should focus on other components which could identify the chassis first.

"Do you know what a radius arm is?" he asked, as the pontoon boat motored south.

"No idea," AJ admitted.

"Part of the rear suspension, isn't it?" Reg replied, and AJ looked at him in surprise.

"Blimey, where did you learn that?"

"I had a mate who raced a Formula Ford back in Blighty. I helped him out a time or two," Reg explained.

"Good," De Konig continued. "This particular car only has one radius arm on each side, in the upper position."

"So what do these arms look like?" AJ asked.

"If Reg knows, perhaps it's better he's the one to get them for me," De Konig replied a little too dismissively for AJ's taste.

"See the size of him?" she countered. "Which of us do you think is more suited to crawling through small holes under upside-down barges?"

De Konig smiled. "I see your point. Radius arms are long steel tubes with rose joints at each end. They connect the upright to the chassis at the rear of the car, as Reg mentioned."

"Sounds like those parts will be buried in the sand with the car being upside down," AJ pointed out.

"Most likely," De Konig confirmed.

"And what's a rose joint?" AJ asked. "Apart from sounding like a flowery narcotic."

Reg laughed. "Americans call them rod ends. You've seen them on some boats. Threaded part sticking out of a ball joint with a hole to bolt it to something. They're used for attaching rods and tubes to things at odd angles. Usually things that need to move or be adjusted. They used to use them all over the suspension on race cars."

De Konig nodded as he slowed, watching the GPS. "Exactly. And they're the parts you'll saw through."

AJ grabbed her mask and slipped her fins on, preparing to free-dive to the buoy and tie them in. Reg stood next to her at the railing.

"Guess you need a lesson on using the saw, seeing as you volunteered yourself."

"I'm thinking I'll need an extra long hose as well," she replied.

Reg nodded. "I'll dig one out of the bag. I had Lamar at Dive Rite make me up a 12-foot Airflex hose for just such occasions."

"Perf…" she began, which morphed into a yelp as Reg nudged her off the boat.

Without the need for stops on the way down, AJ and Reg descended to the wreck in under three minutes. They dropped their deco tanks by the bow and moved directly to the work site where the sheet metal had held up. Even AJ's last-minute scraping under the gunwale hadn't refilled. But to access the underside of the barge, they still had a lot of sand to move for her to fit underneath.

She unbuckled her harness and lowered her rig to the sand just outside the trough then took her fins off. Taking the reg out of her mouth, she unwound the long hose Reg had set up for her then popped the reg back in and dropped into the trough. He waited at the end of the trough to take the bucket from her each time she scooped, and so began the same laborious process as before, at 210 feet below the surface.

The small fish soon showed up, but now confident they'd stay out of harm's way, AJ industriously dug, shovelled, and scooped. After fifteen minutes of run time, she had a doubled-over sheet shoved under the gunwale at the ramp end, cleared the sand back to the box they'd seen on the video, and awkwardly wedged another doubled-over sheet under at that end. She now had a 10-inch-high gap under the barge, which sloped upwards once inside until it met the level of the sand underneath. She ducked down and shone her torch inside, seeing little more than scatter and haze from her efforts.

If she was going inside on this dive, it was now or never. AJ reached down and took her GoPro from her leg pocket and placed it under the wreck by the box they'd seen in the video. Reg handed her the saw, and she shoved that next to the camera. Giving him a nod, she then squirmed under the gunwale, face down, almost knocking her mask strap off as she wriggled her head to the other side. The back of her wetsuit brushed against the rusty metal as she squeezed her breasts past the narrowest point and shimmied on her stomach up the slope. Now arched in a precarious position, her backside wedged against the gunwale and her cheek was flat against the sand in the pitch-black underside of the barge. AJ wondered what Lamar at Dive Rite would say if he could see her now with one of his high-tech regs shoved into the sea floor, and she made a mental note to thoroughly flush the XT topside.

Hoping she wasn't shredding her wetsuit, she wriggled again, digging her body a little deeper into the sand until her bum slipped through the constriction. Fighting back the urge to panic in the incredibly narrow space, she fumbled for the torch, banging her hand against the box, which felt like it had crumbled under her touch. AJ finally found the torch and turned on the light, but all it did was illuminate the hazy scatter she'd stirred up, making her feel even more claustrophobic. She quickly closed her eyes and took a few deep breaths.

Making her jump, she felt two taps on her foot. She knew it had to be Reg, but it still made her heart jump. Two taps was their code for okay. In this case, he was asking if she was. AJ didn't feel particularly okay, but she lifted her foot up and down twice so he wouldn't scare the shit out of her again.

Sensing the particulate should lessen if she moved farther in, AJ shuffled to her right and pulled her legs in behind her. Looking back, she could now make out the glow of light from the entryway she'd made, which calmed her nerves. Shining the torch up revealed the deck of the barge and she realised there was room enough for her to sit up on her knees. The visibility was better away from the sand and her heart rate settled. Ahead of where she sat, the tyre they'd seen on the video protruded from the sand and to her right, just behind the box, which appeared to be a wooden crate, was the other front tyre. Between the two, the flat underside of the race car stretched away from her.

Unsure whether to clamber along the belly of the car, or stick to the sand off to the side, she reached forward and gently touched the underside. A darker brown layer of sediment wafted up from the surface, which felt squidgy to her touch. She pressed a little harder, and the material indented. That made her decision easy, as apparently whatever the front nose was made of had significantly deteriorated, so the sand it would be. Carefully edging around the tyre, she tried her best not to disturb more sediment as she wondered if De Konig was right to bring up pieces. Maybe the car had rusted and rotted away and was unsalvageable whole.

Almost to the centre of the car, AJ noticed more parts stuck out either side, and behind those she spotted the rear tyres. She also realised she'd forgotten to bring the saw along. Now she had to reach across the belly of the car, trying not to touch the brown, fuzzy covering of sediment and algae. With one finger resting on the middle of the underside of the car, she risked applying a little weight as she stretched for the tool. Getting her hand wrapped around the body of the saw, she pulled herself back, and noticed the part of the car she'd pushed against with her finger was firm. So maybe it hadn't all decayed.

AJ jumped again as two knocks echoed through the confined space of the inverted barge. Reg was checking on her again by tapping on the wreck. She reached up and knocked twice on the deck above her, cussing him under her breath. She checked her

Perdix. Twenty-two minutes of run time. That didn't leave much to get out, don her gear, pick up the deco tanks, and leave the depths. Latest leave time of twenty-six minutes, she told herself, knowing that would still be cutting it close.

Shuffling forward again, she skirted the parts sticking out from the main chassis, which resembled scoops of some description. Taking one more knee-shuffle forward to bring her alongside the area in front of the rear tyre, her regulator suddenly jerked out of her mouth. She'd run out of hose. There was an arm-sweeping protocol for recovering a regulator attached to a tank on your back, but that didn't work when the tanks were outside the wreck. Rather than fling her arms around, AJ turned the torch on the sand around her, but the area was billowing in brown muck and sediment. Reaching towards where she knew the race car to be, figuring the hose must have made all the mess, she carefully felt around, urging herself to stay calm.

Typical of how things go wrong. She'd just exhaled when her air supply had been yanked away, and now her lungs burned, begging for fresh oxygen. Her throat convulsed, and she closed her eyes again, willing her brain to realise it still had enough gas in her lungs to survive for a while longer. Her hand finally stumbled over the hose and AJ ran her fingers along it until she grasped the reg, which she quickly stuffed in her mouth and purged.

After a few gulps, she settled herself down, and figured there was no option now but to turn around. With a gentle pull on the hose to verify it was indeed out of length, she found it reached another foot or so. Reg must have moved her rig into the trough to give her more hose.

Turning back to the rear suspension, AJ shoved her hand into the sand and instantly found the tube De Konig had talked about. The rear of the race car was held out of the sand a lot more than the front, due to the car's wedge-shaped profile, and the radius arm was only a few inches below the surface. In fact, she noticed it was out of the sand where it met the upright which held the wheel on. AJ grabbed the saw and leaned forward, dropping the blade onto the closest part to the upright, hoping underneath the muck and corrosion lay a rose joint. The regulator tugged at the edge of her mouth, letting her know she was at the end of her tether, but didn't dislodge, so she gripped it tightly between her teeth.

Pulling the trigger on the saw, all hell broke loose. Sediment and small shards flew, and despite the hefty watertight body encasing the motor, the noise of the electric saw echoed all around her. She let go of the trigger. To put any weight on the cut, she needed to be closer so she could use two hands. She gently placed the torch down in the sand facing the radius arm, then after taking a long pull of gas from the reg, she removed it from her mouth and set it down next to her. With both hands available, she pulled the trigger and leaned over the cut as best she could.

The saw was powerful and kicked and bucked, making a horrible noise as it ripped corroded metal and flung sediment all over the place. But in short order, AJ fell forward when the saw cut through the thread of the rose joint. Picking up her regulator, she breathed again while shuffling backwards alongside the air scoop and fumbling in the sand for where the other end of the arm met the chassis. With no point worrying about the visibility in the already silted-out haze, she swept the sand aside, and dropped the blade onto what she hoped was the second rose joint. Ready for the power this time, she leaned over the blade and pulled the trigger. Cutting at an awkward angle with the blade punching into the sand below took longer, but the saw kicked and she felt it hang up for a second before ripping through the last part of the metal.

The underside of the barge was now a complete mess. Her torch was useless, illuminating nothing more than thick scatter right in front of her face. Her exit was a faint glow which she quickly headed for, flinging the saw, radius arm, and torch ahead. She bumped into the protruding front tyre, then shimmied around it and banged the saw with her knee. Picking it up, she tossed it through the gap where she could now just make out something, or more likely someone, moving. She hoped it was Reg getting her gear out of the way.

Checking her dive computer at this point was superfluous as her plan was to exit and ascend as quickly as possible, regardless of the information on the screen of the Perdix. Either from her wriggling under the gunwale earlier or Reg doing more scraping while she was inside, the gap was now large enough that she slipped through, carefully pulling the long hose with her so it didn't snag on anything under the wreck.

Reg held her harness with the tanks resting on the shoring, so by standing up in the trough, she was able to quickly don her rig and cinch the waistband. She took her fins that he'd set just outside the trough for her and slipped them on her feet, then popped a little gas in her wing to lift her out of the hole, grabbing the saw and radius arm as she rose. She was out of hands for her torch, so she left it in the trough, glad she'd turned it off.

Finning towards the bow, she found Reg pushing off the sand with all four deco bottles. He'd clipped his own in place, then carried her two, one under each arm. From his haste, she gathered their bottom time had exceeded the plan, or he'd never risk dropping a deco tank. The hit going back down to retrieve it would be worse than the thirty seconds for her to gather them in the first place. But when they reached the line and began ascending alongside each other, she noticed he had her tanks clipped by one of their bands to his.

AJ finally peeked at her computer. They were scheduled to be at their first brief decompression stop at 100 feet at 34 minutes of run time. Her computer showed 35 minutes and change, and they were just passing through 150 feet. Looking at the time to surface and adding it to the run time told her the few minutes extra at the bottom had added nine minutes to their decompression obligation.

It was little more than a pause for 20 seconds at 100, but when they reached 90 feet, Reg carefully handed AJ her deco tanks one by one, which she clipped in place while he strapped the saw to his harness and held the radius arm. Reg ran a hand down the one-inch-diameter tube, sending over fifty years of muck, grime, and algae into the water column. It smeared as much as cleaned, but he continued carefully wiping the surface and soon AJ could see the metal below was dull, pitted and more rusty in some spots than others.

Reg handed her back the arm, as they moved up to 80 feet. When they levelled off, he flipped over his wrist slate, twisting his arm so she could read it. He'd left his note on there from the previous morning.

"You're a silly bugger."

This time, AJ didn't laugh. He was right. She'd just violated a list of key safety protocols of technical diving, and for what? A metal rod which looked like nothing more than an old rusty piece of scrap. Their eyes met, and she saw the concern. She'd put Reg at risk too, as he never would have left her down there on her own. She took hold of his arm and with the slate pencil wrote underneath his words.

"Yes. Sorry."

He nodded, then they opened the valves on their nitrox deco tanks in preparation for their next stop at 70 feet.

27

1970 – HOCKENHEIMRING, GERMANY

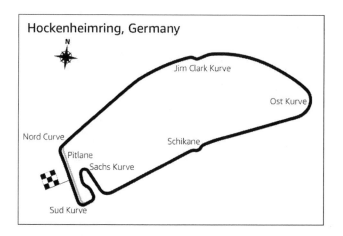

Georgie watched Miles get smaller in the distance down the pit lane at Hockenheimring as the final practice began. It was the first time the German Grand Prix had been held at the circuit after the daunting 14-mile Nürburgring track refused to make the safety upgrades the drivers asked for. Not that Hockenheimring was considered exceptionally safe, but after the legendary Jim Clark's death in 1968, they'd added two chicanes to slow the cars through the long forest section and installed more Armco barriers.

For Georgie, the lead-up to the event and the weekend so far had been a mixed bag of emotions. Martin van der Meer had disappeared. She was a big girl and could handle the personal slight, at least on the exterior as far as anyone could see, but the professional stress on her race team was more annoying. He had left Brands Hatch saying they'd speak in the week and they'd agreed to prepare the car for the German Grand Prix but finalise plans when they spoke. He hadn't answered the only number she had for him and was yet to appear at the track.

On the other hand, Miles had learnt the track remarkably quickly and had shown good pace in the previous practice sessions, leaving Georgie hopeful of another top ten start for Sunday's race.

Miles felt comfortable with the car. Mr Chapman had shared set-up information with them before the weekend and Phil had done a good job tweaking the chassis in the practice sessions. But the track was really fast, and even with the added chicanes, horsepower and drafting were worth a lot of lap time. The Ferrari and BRM 12-cylinder engines had the DFVs beaten for power, but the track offered four long, wide-open throttle stretches where carefully planned or fortunate slipstreams could more than make up for the horsepower deficit. The Lotus camp had discussed helping each other for better laps, but the three factory cars had left the pit lane scattered amongst the rest of the field and Miles couldn't see any of them.

Chapman had brought two Lotus 72s to the race for Rindt and John Miles, plus a heavily upgraded 49C for Brazilian newcomer Emerson Fittipaldi. Miles was confident that Lady Ashford was pleased with his performance to date, but racing was a fickle business, so another young driver in the Lotus stable meant more pressure on the Englishman to perform. If he stood a chance of qualifying well, he needed to find a dance partner for the drafting games.

The drivers were already behaving erratically on the out lap, positioning themselves in the ideal gap behind a competitor, only for the other car to slow down and play the same lark with somebody else. Miles passed several of them in the hopes of coming across another Lotus driver, but instead ended up chasing a pair of McLarens. After five laps of them falling all over each other and holding themselves up more than going faster, Miles pitted.

"I think the car is fine, Phil, but I can't get a decent lap together. Are any of the factory Lotuses in the pits now? Maybe I can follow one out and trade tows."

Phil stood and surveyed the pit lane while cars whistled by on the start/finish straight.

"Only John Miles, but you need someone faster than that to chase," Phil said, leaning back down and yelling over the raucous engines. "But Rindt just went by, so we'll wait a minute and a half, then send you out in front of him, okay? You'll have to watch your mirrors. Maybe if you give him a good tow, he'll return the favour."

Miles nodded and slipped his goggles back in place while Phil kept an eye on his stopwatch. In the cockpit, Miles felt cocooned in his own world. His helmet muffled sounds from the outside world, and distractions only came his way if he allowed them. All the team understood. He wasn't being rude if he didn't look their way or react to what they were doing, like Tina checking the tyre pressures and inspecting the front suspension. In Miles's mind, he was visualising the circuit, taking a corner he knew he could improve upon, feeling his feet on the pedals although he wasn't touching them at that moment. Drivers found lap time by gaining familiarity with the track while making more laps, but when that levelled off, stopping and thinking about it was often the only way to improve.

Phil's swirling hand brought him out of his trance, and Miles fired up the V8 engine, feeling the whole car vibrate underneath him. His mechanic waved him on, and Miles dropped the Hewland gearbox in first and pulled away from the pit stall, checking his mirror for other cars. At the pit lane exit, all the way around turn one, he accelerated, shifting gears at the redline on the rev counter and watching his mirrors for the red and gold Lotus of Rindt. He braked very early for the new Clark chicane, named after the man who'd lost his life at that spot two years ago, and the next car was still a speck in Miles's mirrors but gaining fast. After cruising slowly through the corners, Miles looked again as he pushed the throttle down at the exit. Rindt was now only 100 yards back and pushing hard.

From the chicane, the circuit gently curved right, taking the Grand Prix cars thundering through the forest down a river of tarmac lined by a grass border and steel barriers. Miles had his foot to the floor in fifth gear, hugging the inside of the track, taking the shortest route possible with Rindt gaining on him as he began picking up a slipstream. Easing to the left side of the track, Miles braked hard for Ost, the complex of esses at the far end of the circuit. Focusing ahead, he clipped his apex points perfectly through each of the three curves, compromising the middle part to set up a better exit onto the next straightaway. The Lotus fought for traction as Miles squeezed the throttle while he gently unwound the steering wheel until the left-side tyres rode the exit kerb. Glancing in the mirror, he couldn't be sure, but he thought he'd actually pulled a car length or so on Rindt through Ost.

The two Lotuses screamed along the back straight, watching their rev counters steadily climb as the cars reached their top speed. Miles checked his mirror several times and knew the championship leader was now getting a good draft and gaining quickly. They reached the second of the new chicanes, and again Miles stayed disciplined, braking at the mark he'd established, refusing to over-drive the entry under pressure. He cleanly blipped the throttle as he downshifted to fourth, third, and then again into second gear, before softly easing off the brake pedal as he pointed the front tyres at the apex of the left-hand jog. Whipping the wheel back to the right, he clipped the lower part of the sloped apex kerb. Once he felt the rear suspension compress on the other side, Miles began feeding in the power as he slid the Lotus through the last left jog and onto the final long straight before the stadium section.

Rindt had remained about ten car lengths behind, but as the two cars accelerated once more and Miles shifted the Ashford Motor Racing Team 72 into top gear, the number 2 of Rindt began closing once more. One hundred yards before the braking zone, Miles eased right, leaving just over a car's width on the left side of the track. Rindt followed in his wake, gaining now at an alarming rate as the race cars topped 180 mph between the steel barriers and trees. Just before the braking mark, Rindt pulled to the left, using the ideal approach line Miles had left him.

Miles didn't challenge the man into the right-hand turn, but gave him room and exited three car lengths behind. Hockemheimring's stadium section was a unique and marvellous design, with tall grandstands wrapping around a pair of 180-degree corners, giving the spectators an amazing view of the drivers battling in the last few turns before the start/finish straight. Miles chased the Austrian in awe of his ability to hustle his car at the absolute limit. Their styles were different, Miles favouring smooth hands and pedal transitions, whereas Rindt used a more aggressive technique, wringing more than coaxing every last ounce of performance from the Lotus.

Across the line, Miles had carefully dropped back a hundred yards, hoping the lead Lotus driver would grant him the same favour in return. Ahead, Rindt flew through the third gear turn one, accelerating back into fourth then fifth gear down the longest of the four straights. The one Miles hadn't helped him along. With his heart racing almost as fast as the two Lotuses were travelling, Miles realised if he'd gapped himself correctly, he'd be the beneficiary of a tow on all four straights compared to the three he'd assisted Rindt along.

But by the time they reached Ost, he realised he'd done a far better job in front than behind. Rindt moved to the right, leaving Miles room to pass on the left underbraking as he'd already caught the Austrian. Miles ran as hard as he could until the line, watching Rindt pull into the pit lane in his mirrors, and crossed under the chequered flag for the session. Once Miles had made it back around to the pits himself, he was greeted by his enthusiastic team, excited by the news he'd qualified eighth.

"Where did Jochen qualify?" Miles asked, climbing from the Lotus.

"You got him second, mate. Only two-tenths behind Ickx in the Ferrari," Phil told him.

Miles hung his head. "We could have been right there with him," he said despondently. "I screwed up again."

"We're top ten, Miles," Georgie said cheerfully. "I couldn't be happier."

Miles lifted his head. "Thank you, ma'am. But you deserve better. Rindt returned the favour, but I didn't gap him enough starting the lap."

"Solid job," they heard Colin Chapman say, and turned to see him walking by with his driver.

Rindt paused and stepped over to the Ashford car.

"Thank you," he said dryly and was about to turn away, but stopped. "I would have given you a third straightaway," he added.

"I appreciate it, sir," Miles replied. "I timed it wrong."

"You'll learn," Rindt replied with a slight grin, and rejoined Chapman.

Phil slapped Miles on the arm. "Bloody hell, lad. You know you're doing alright when this year's world champion stops to thank you."

"He's not champion yet," Barney corrected. "We've still got six races to run, including this one."

Phil smiled at the team manager. "Put a tenner on it, then. I'll take Rindt for the title."

"I didn't say he won't win it, Phil. I said he hasn't won it yet. Think I'll hang on to my tenner, thank you very much."

"I'm telling you, there's nothing that'll stop that bloke this year," Phil added as they watched the two men from Lotus walk down the pit lane, deep in conversation.

Georgie slept poorly on Saturday night, but her own excitement was to blame more than anything else. Her little team was mixing it up with the big names in Grand Prix racing, and she lay awake plotting and planning how she might be able to leverage her family's contacts for sponsorship. By the time she sat down to breakfast with Barney, he struggled to keep up making notes, let alone eat his toast and jam, as his boss unveiled their new to-do list for them both.

The entire facility was a-buzz when they arrived, a massive crowd making their way to the grandstands and emerging from the various campgrounds sprinkled around the countryside. The atmosphere was truly electric and Georgie had already forgotten about her lack of sleep, running on coffee and enthusiasm. Until Phil pulled her to one side.

"I'm worried about the engine, ma'am," he said in a hushed tone. "One of the plugs didn't look right last night."

"Well, I'm sure you changed it," she responded.

"Of course, ma'am, but the spark plug isn't the issue. It's what made the plug look that way that's the worry."

"Which is?"

Phil shrugged his shoulders. "No way to tell, I'm afraid. Best case, it could be a bad spark plug, but worse case, it could be a valve or a piston ring on the way out."

"You know you're talking Chinese to me at the moment, Phil. Just tell me what I need to do."

Phil shook his head. "I pulled the valve cover and checked the gaps, ma'am, and did a leak down on the cylinder. It all seemed fine."

"Still talking Chinese," she replied. "What does this all mean?"

"It means we might have a problem, or it might be nothing and everything's fine," Phil said. "I wish I could tell you more, but these DFVs are more complicated than I'm used to dealing with, ma'am. We could withdraw and send it back to Cosworth. They'll be able to tell, I suspect, when they strip it down. Or we race, and keep our fingers crossed."

"Isn't it due for a rebuild after this race?" Georgie asked, already sure she knew the answer.

She didn't understand the technical jargon, but she did keep a close eye on the schedule, especially when it affected the budget.

Phil nodded. "We have a basic rebuild slated for next week before Austria."

"That's a tight turnaround," she remarked.

"Bloody tight," Phil replied. "Pardon my French, ma'am."

"Then we have to race," Georgie said emphatically. "We can't pack up and go home based on something that only might happen. Lord knows, there's a million things that might happen today, Phil. We *might* win the Grand Prix. But don't say a word to Miles. We don't want him worrying about it for no reason."

Phil smiled. "That's one of the reasons I really like working for you, ma'am. You're not here just to pose about the paddock and make up the numbers."

"Thank you," Georgie muttered to herself, as Phil sped off to finish getting the car ready. "I think."

Miles was more nervous before the start than he had been at Monaco, or any other Grand Prix so far. He didn't know why, but something felt special about the day. The car was fast, and with the drafting, passing would be furious and often, so if he drove a smart race and timed things better than he had in qualifying, he could net a good result. He'd also managed to refrain from blushing when Lady Ashford gave him her good luck kiss.

The officials arranged the grid in a two-by-two format, as the front straight wasn't particularly wide, so Miles started from the outside of row four. From the drop of the flag, he began moving forward, surging around the outside of Jackie Stewart in turn one. On the long run to the Clark chicane, the cars ran in a snaking line until halfway down the straight when everyone picked up a tow from the car in front and the drivers began pulling out and jostling for positions.

Miles slipped by Henri Pescarolo's Matra into the chicane and at the exit gained on Amon and Siffert, who battled side by side. By the time those two sorted out their tussle, Miles was alongside Amon, with Stewart now drafting behind Miles, hoping to pass the pair. Amon lunged back ahead in the breaking for Ost, but he missed the first apex in his haste, leaving room for Miles to nip ahead in the last open and fast part of the esses. With Siffert now four car lengths ahead, Miles had a great draft on the run to the second chicane, but Amon and Stewart were tucked in, building a run behind him.

Miles grabbed fifth gear and immediately knew he had a problem. The engine made an odd sound and stuttered. He quickly steered left, moving away from the ideal line for the entry into the chicane, but the two cars behind must have thought he was trying to shake the draft and moved with him. He stuck his hand in the air to warn them and watched in his mirrors as, thankfully, Amon and Stewart pulled right. Miles immediately lifted off the throttle and watched a plume of oil smoke trail behind his Lotus.

Staying clear of everyone, he let the field go by before coasting down the final straight, staying away from the racing line in case he was dropping oil, and pulled the Lotus off on the right before the stadium section. Dejected, and worried he'd over-revved the engine and caused the failure, Miles climbed from the car and helped the marshals wheel it behind the barrier.

Walking back, he signed autographs for anyone who asked, and watched Rindt and Ickx battle away for the top spot. He looked up in awe at the grandstands packed with people, and was soon surrounded by race fans as he tried to keep moving to the paddock area. The race was fifteen laps in by the time he made it to the back of the pit lane, where the security guards stopped the fans from following any farther.

Miles jogged across the paddock, weaving between transporters, road cars, and service vehicles until he reached the Ashford lorry. Parked by the transporter was a black Mercedes he didn't recognise, and standing behind the pit garages was Lady Ashford, talking with a man in a suit. Glancing into the windows of the Mercedes as he walked by, Miles noticed a uniformed policeman in the driver's seat.

"Engine?" Phil asked, looking like he was ready to tear his hair out.

"I'm afraid so," Miles replied. "I'm so sorry, Phil, but I don't know when I might have over-revved it. The opening lap was pretty frantic, but usually you know when you've run it too hard."

Phil rested a hand on the young man's shoulder. "I doubt you did anything wrong, mate. There were signs of trouble with that motor last night, but her ladyship wanted to race. I'm sorry I couldn't do anything to fix it."

Miles thought he should feel relieved, but somehow didn't. He knew what this would mean for the little team. The Austrian Grand Prix was only two weeks away, and with Cosworth's struggles to keep up lately with major rebuilds and parts, they wouldn't make the next race. There was also the added expense to be considered. Lady Ashford was trying to keep their financial woes hidden from Miles, but he knew things were tight.

"What's all this about?" Miles asked, looking at the man who appeared to be grilling Lady Ashford with questions.

"German bloody police showed up just after the start," Phil explained. "Something about an Interpol alert, but I haven't heard a reason why. It seems they're looking for our elusive chassis owner, Mr Martin van der Meer."

28

BONAIRE

De Konig held the radius arm in his hand as though it were the Holy Grail.

"This is fantastic," he enthused, and even Laurens almost smiled. "It's in better condition than I'd hoped."

"Pretty sure someone had smothered it in a grease or thick oil," Reg offered. "I wiped a lot of slime off as we came up."

"It was..." De Konig began before stopping himself and nodding his agreement instead.

"How can you identify the car from that?" AJ asked. "Doesn't seem to be very distinct at all."

"Oh, but it is," the older man replied, wrapping the radius arm in a towel. "Length, diameter, and other distinguishing details."

"And that will tell you it's from a Lotus 72, or maybe even the Ashford Lotus 72?" AJ ventured, throwing a dart based on the article she'd read online.

De Konig whipped around and stared at her. "What?"

AJ shrugged her shoulders as she peeled out of her wetsuit. "The missing Lotus Formula One car, right? I read an article about it."

"Have you said this to anyone else?" De Konig asked pointedly.

"Of course not. We understand confidentiality, sir. Hopefully it was one reason you hired the two of us."

The older man nodded and shared a quick glance with Laurens, who took the rod wrapped in the towel and placed it next to him on the bench.

"Can you get the second radius arm on the next dive?" De Konig asked.

"Possibly," AJ replied. "It'll be more awkward to get to, and visibility is a big problem under there."

"We pushed our luck on this last one," Reg added. "We're already doing things most divers would have the good sense not to attempt. I think it's safer to say we'll locate it and prepare to remove it on the following dive."

AJ appreciated her friend's use of 'we' when they both knew it was her actions which stretched their bottom time and ate into their safety margin. Those protocols were there for just such reasons, but leaning on them too often turned them from being safety margins to extended dives without the appropriate margins in place. A good way to die underwater.

"And you'd like to take tomorrow off, correct?" De Konig responded.

"It's not a case of *like to*, John," Reg replied. "It's standard practice with deep, technical dives. You can't keep going down a couple of hundred feet every day without giving your body a break."

De Konig nodded again. "I understand. As you can imagine, this is incredibly exciting for me, so I'm eager, that's all."

"We get that, sir," AJ said. "And we'll try to bring up the second one this afternoon. We promise we'll do our best within the bounds of safety."

"That would also allow us to focus on the chassis plate on Saturday," Reg pointed out. "'Cos that'll be even harder to get to."

"Of course," De Konig replied. "That all makes sense. We'll head in for the surface interval and lunch, if you don't mind. I'd like to get this radius arm into a solution to preserve it as best we can."

"Okay," AJ replied, picking up her mask and fins. "I'll unhook us."

She was just beginning to dry in the warm air, but lunch ashore sounded better than the pre-packaged sandwiches the Dutchman had brought along as the provided meal. And sitting on the *Beste Leven* for four hours. De Konig started the outboards, and once he'd idled forward to relieve the tension on the line, AJ dived in.

———

"He just about jumped out of his skin when I mentioned a Lotus 72," AJ said once Reg had driven them away from the marina in the van.

De Konig had suggested they refill the tanks used that morning, which didn't seem like a great idea to AJ and Reg as they'd still have to go back to fill the afternoon's, plus they had a rest day on which to do it, but they were happy to get away for a few hours. The Dutchman had another vehicle at the marina to use for him and Laurens, so it also meant they could stop at their own choice for lunch.

"He's got his knickers in a twist about keeping all this secret," Reg replied. "Which is understandable, I suppose."

"Did you notice he was all about the chassis plate at first?" AJ added. "But now all he seems to care about is cutting pieces off."

Reg drove through the roundabout where they'd seen the goats the other day. "His circus, and we're his monkeys at the moment."

AJ stayed quiet while they continued past Sand Dollar towards the resort and TDS. As Reg slowed the van and turned into the driveway, she spoke up again.

"I was thinking," she began.

"Bloody miracle," Reg teased.

"I'll give you that one based on my performance this morning," she acknowledged. "Which is what I was thinking about. Our biggest problem, as we know from our contingency gas plans, is with 100 percent oxygen as our second deco gas. If we'd been much longer on the bottom, we'd have overstepped our oxygen intake and risked toxicity. Maybe we should get a couple of 80s filled with 80 percent O_2, even if we hang them at 30 feet."

Reg parked the van and sat still for a few moments. "Yeah, I agree. I was thinking about it too. I think the risk of being blown off the site is really low, so I think it's safe to hang them on the line."

"Might sink that buoy with three full tanks on the rope," AJ said with a laugh. "Especially if we get a bit of current and have to hold on ourselves."

"That buoy took some pulling to get it under the other day," Reg retorted. "Underwater, those three tanks are about the equivalent of six or eight pounds of weight. I think the buoy will be fine, but we'll check it when we attach them. Clip a lift bag on if needed. That'll keep that line tight."

They grabbed their deco tanks and walked into the shop, where Bryan was surprised to see them.

"Done for the day already?" he asked.

"Halfway," AJ replied. "And we wanted to grab a pair of 80s with 80 percent O_2 if you wouldn't mind? Figured we'd top these off while we were here."

"No problem," Bryan replied, and Reg gave AJ a wink.

She'd figured it was easier to use the deco tanks as an excuse than try to explain why they were making extra trips. Bryan took two of the tanks to the fill room while AJ and Reg returned to the van with a cart and collected the doubles. The entire process took about forty minutes to complete, including checking the fill percentages and labelling each tank. Bryan and AJ chatted about diving in the Florida caves while Reg listened in, but he made sure to ask the local for a lunch recommendation.

Back in the van, Reg followed Bryan's directions, and as he'd explained, they turned down a narrow lane next to a marine supply shop that felt like they were in the right place to make a delivery instead of eat lunch. The lane jogged right behind the building and revealed a small thatched kitchen on the left with a seating area and a car park before them.

A friendly Hispanic woman greeted them at the counter of Yhanni's Arepas and handed them menus. Bryan had recommended they try the arepas, which are Venezuelan corn griddle cakes, split like a pocket, and filled with various meats, beans, and vegetables. AJ had been looking around for one of the local 'snacks' as the food huts were called, but the Bonairians were keen on their meats, so they didn't have much choice for a pescatarian. She was excited to choose her fillings for the arepas.

They sat down to wait for the food with a bottle of water each, and AJ spotted a bird with a bright orange body and black wings and head fly to a nearby branch.

"I saw one of them the other day," she blurted. "They're so pretty."

"That's a troupial," a pretty woman at the next table said. "They're from Venezuela."

"Do they fly all the way here for the arepas?" AJ asked with a big smile.

The woman and her husband both laughed. "Some of the flamingos fly back and forth, but I don't think the troupials do."

"Wait, the flamingos, which we haven't seen yet, by the way," AJ exclaimed, "fly to South America and back?"

"Well, it's only about 55 miles," the lady explained. "There used to be a legend about them flying daily to overnight in Venezuela and then return in the morning, but that's been debunked. Still, some do make the commute quite often."

"Wow," AJ responded, extending her hand. "That's a lot of flapping. You don't think of flamingos as being keen on flying. They seem more of the stand in the water and eat shrimp types."

The couple laughed again.

"I'm AJ and this is Reg. We're here for a week doing a bit of work."

"You're not with customs are you by any chance?" Reg asked, offering his hand between the tables. "This one keeps getting us in a bit of bother about the work thing."

"I'm Tricia and this is my husband, Alan, and we hold no official capacity, I promise."

"Here from England?" Alan asked and AJ noted his distinctly Scottish accent.

"Originally," AJ replied. "But we live in Grand Cayman."

"Divers, I assume?" Tricia asked.

"Bit of a giveaway when we live in the Cayman Islands and travel to Bonaire, huh?" AJ joked.

"Two of the best spots in the Caribbean," Tricia agreed.

"And you?" AJ asked. "How long have you lived here?"

"About six years or so," Tricia replied. "Fell in love with the island on a trip here. We're both divers too."

"And what do you do?" AJ asked.

"I'm a writer," Tricia replied, "and Alan helps run the business."

"Blimey," AJ enthused. "You write books?"

"I do."

"What kind?" AJ asked.

"Fiction," Tricia shared. "Fun, fantasy, paranormal, touch of romance type stuff."

Everyone's food arrived at the same time, and Tricia invited AJ and Reg to join them at their table, so they moved over. The arepas were so hot no one could take a bite for a minute, so their conversation continued.

"Okay, so sorry to pepper you with questions, but I've been wondering about a few things," AJ said. "What are the lovely little yellow and black birds about the size of a finch?"

Tricia smiled. "The locals call them chibi chibis, but you're right, in English they're a saffron finch. Have you seen one of the local parrots flying around? They're called loras."

AJ leaned over and smacked Reg on the arm. "Told you I saw a bloody parrot outside the flat."

"We're on a tropical island and you were jumping up and down because you saw a parrot," Reg said, shaking his head.

"Well, she's sort of right to get excited," Alan responded. "The lora is endangered, so you don't see that many of them. It's a yellow-shouldered Amazon parrot, if we're using its official name."

"I like lora better," AJ replied, blowing on her arepas as her tummy grumbled in anticipation.

"Were you two diving this morning?" Alan asked.

Reg nodded as AJ risked her first bite. "Yeah. We're going pretty deep, so a long surface interval before the second dive this afternoon."

"You're not the tech guys diving off Lighthouse Point, are you?" Alan asked, and Reg and AJ looked at each other, her with a steaming hot mouthful of arepas she was trying to manage.

"Word travels fast," Reg commented.

"Small island," Alan replied with a grin.

Reg laughed. "Yeah. It would be the same back home," he said, then nodded. "That's us."

"How's your buddy?" Tricia asked. "Took a ride in the chamber, didn't he?"

AJ finally swallowed the bite she'd been working on and loved the flavour despite burning her mouth. "He's just as miserable as he was before he got bent."

"He's not really our buddy," Reg explained.

"You said you were working, right?" Alan queried. "What are you working on out there?"

AJ winced, feeling really awful they couldn't answer the question. The couple seemed really nice and had answered all her queries.

"Unfortunately, it's a confidential project, so we can't say anything about it," Reg said, saving AJ from having to.

Alan nodded and smiled. "Well, stay safe, and I hope whatever it is goes well for you."

AJ smiled at Tricia. "Maybe I'll call you when this is all over and give you a cool story for your next book."

"Will there be fae, magic, mermaids, or Scottish castles involved?" Tricia grinned in return.

"My dive op is called Mermaid Divers, but hopefully we don't come across any of the other stuff unless we get really narced!"

Tricia and Alan laughed.

"This one is pretty reliable at doing something daft," Reg added, nodding at AJ. "If you can use a silly bugger in a story..."

Tricia smiled again. "There's always room for a silly bugger in every story."

29

1970 – MONZA, ITALY

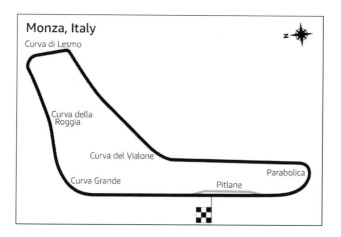

Missing the Austrian Grand Prix was devastating for everyone on the team, so it was with a sense of pride that Georgie was back in the paddock in Monza, Italy. The factory Lotus cars of Rindt and John Miles had both failed to finish in Austria. Rindt started from pole at his home Grand Prix, but was soon overrun by the 12-cylinder Ferraris before his Cosworth DFV expired. John Miles suffered a front halfshaft failure similar to the one the Ashford car had experienced at Brands Hatch, which indicated the upgrades Chapman had introduced were not sufficient.

A long Friday practice in the afternoon at Monza proved the Ferrari were again dominant around the incredibly fast circuit where power was a premium. Chapman began stripping the wings off Rindt's Lotus in an effort to reduce drag, and soon many of the competitors followed suit. Stewart in Tyrrell's DFV-powered March chassis was the most successful and proved to be the only non-12-cylinder-engined car to crack the 1:25.0 mark.

Saturday's session was also held late afternoon, but the day proved to be significantly hotter, making the track slower. Most teams experimented with different aerodynamic configurations, waiting for the cool of early evening to make a serious run at improving their lap times to set the grid. Georgie's team had trimmed their wings out as much as possible but not taken the step of removing them entirely yet, and an hour into Saturday's practice, they huddled to discuss the challenge.

"Rindt's running without any wings at all and he can't crack the top ten," Phil pointed out. "He's losing too much time in the fast corners to make up the gains on the straights."

"And every corner here is a fast corner," Barney added. "But maybe it's worth a run just to see? Stewart seems to be going faster."

Georgie looked at her young driver. "Miles. You're the one who has to drive it. What do you think?"

One of the most impressive things Georgie noticed about her driver, despite his youthfulness, was his patience. Both in responding, and working through issues, he took his time, and didn't panic or get upset.

"I think we have to accept that we don't have the pace to run with the Ferraris this weekend," Miles replied, after thinking for a few moments. "No one does. So the task is optimising the package we have in order to get the best result we can."

"I think that sounds logical," Georgie responded. "So does that mean we run with or without the bloody wings? Please excuse my French."

The crew laughed.

"I think we need to try running without them, so we have that data point," Miles said. "But we can't just pull the wings off and expect to see a fair comparison right away. We'll need to optimise the set-up, which will mean lowering the ride height or softening the suspension for less downforce."

"Agreed," Phil quickly responded. "And we only have two hours of practice left."

"An hour and a half," Miles replied. "The last half an hour will be the only chance we have to set a decent time once the track cools. We need to have made our decision by then and set the car in the best trim so we can go for a time."

"Fair point," Phil conceded. "So let's get on with it."

"Good show, chaps," Georgie enthused. "I like your plan."

The mechanics rushed back to the car and Barney followed to see if he could help with the changes. Georgie smiled as she watched her little team burst into action. The final three races of the season were all in the Americas, starting with Canada and ending the season in Mexico, with Watkins Glen, New York in between. She'd already made headway on her sponsorship search for the 1971 season, and although the team would stay overseas in the two-week breaks between each race, she would fly home and play courier for any parts they needed while continuing her proposals.

The prospect of elevating the team for the following season excited her, and a sponsor would mean being able to purchase her own chassis again, and perhaps even take a spare. Two engines in rotation, so they'd never miss a race again. Perhaps one more team member, even if they were part time, to help drive the transporter. With Miles behind the wheel and the support the team had received from the Lotus factory, Georgie truly felt like anything was possible.

"Hi," came a voice from behind her which took her breath away.

She swung around to see Martin standing there. Looking handsome as ever, and smiling at her as though he'd just arrived at the track like any other day. Behind him, another man, younger and rougher looking, leaned against the garage wall.

"I was beginning to think..." she begun, but trailed off, unsure what to say to the man.

He stepped forward and kissed her on both cheeks. "It's great to see you. Apologies for my absence. Business has been crazy."

Georgie placed a hand on his chest, pushing firmly, causing him to take a step back.

"Business has been crazy? That's the best you can come up with?"

Martin lost his smile.

"I haven't heard a word from you in six weeks," Georgie continued, her voice low to avoid making a scene, but still angry. "You weren't able to find a telephone and five minutes to make a call to let me... us. To let *us* know what's going on?"

Martin held up a hand. "You're right. I apologise. It's a poor excuse, but believe me, I've needed to focus on business for a while."

"Does that business have anything to do with why a German police detective visited us at Hockenheim, asking all kinds of questions about you?"

"That's all a load of nonsense," Martin replied. "They have me confused with someone else." He moved a little closer once more. "We can discuss all of this over dinner tonight, but right now, I'd rather focus on the team. How are we looking?" he asked, looking at his watch.

Georgie sighed. Her ebullient mood had been dashed, but if she refocused on the session, perhaps she could still enjoy the afternoon.

"Who's your friend?" she asked, looking past Martin to the man he'd arrived with.

"Hendrik," Martin replied without making any gesture or

movement to include the man in the conversation. "He's doing some work for me."

The man nodded to Georgie but didn't say anything.

"When does today's practice end?" Martin asked, again looking at his watch.

"Six-thirty," Georgie replied, and turned to face the race car, being frantically worked on by the entire crew, including the driver. "We're about to try a big set-up change to see if we can go faster. The Ferraris have everyone scrambling for straight line speed."

"I hope you're not putting my chassis at undue risk," Martin commented, and Georgie frowned at the man.

"You weren't worried enough about what we did to show up in Germany, but now you're concerned?"

Martin ignored her dig.

Miles slid into the cockpit and began fastening his belts. The first thing he noticed was the vastly improved view in the mirrors, with no rear wing in the way. For the more experienced drivers, they could recall driving a Formula One car without wings just a few years back before Colin Chapman pioneered the new downforce trend which had made a dramatic increase in braking and cornering performance. Miles had only driven a formula car with wings, so he was about to have a very new experience.

"I see Martin has shown up out of the blue," Miles commented to Phil, who helped him secure the belts. "I hope the Italian police aren't after him too."

"Wouldn't be surprising," Phil muttered in reply. "Something about that bloke doesn't seem right."

"I hope he doesn't unravel what we have going on here," Miles said. "This team has so much potential."

Phil squeezed his driver's shoulder. "Shake all this rubbish outta yer head, lad. I shouldn't have said anything."

"I'm fine, Phil," Miles replied, pulling his fireproof balaclava up to cover his nose and his goggles down over his eyes.

"Good. Now be careful, lad. This will be a big change from what you've become used to."

Miles nodded as he flicked the ignition on, checked the car was in neutral, and hit the starter button. He didn't need a thermometer to know the day was still sweltering hot. He was sweating just sitting in the car under the scorching sun, but if he had to guess, it was cooler than earlier, and it wouldn't be long before the conditions would improve. Cooler air meant more horsepower.

Joining the circuit on the long front straight, Miles was careful through the first turn, Curva Grande, but ran wide open towards the corners known as Curve di Lesmo, which consisted of two similar right-hand turns. He could already sense the extra straight line speed, despite having cruised through Curva Grande. Braking hard, the car was reluctant to slow and Miles entered the corner faster than he'd intended. He urged the steering wheel towards the apex, but the Lotus didn't seem to respond, sliding in a four-wheel drift with no grip. The car rode all over the exit kerb and dropped the outside tyres in the dirt, twitching and bouncing until Miles tentatively guided it back onto the tarmac and eased off the throttle.

His heart was thumping in his chest. Phil had warned him and he'd taken his advice seriously, but he'd still almost crashed in only the second turn out of the pits. Slowing extremely early for the second Lesmo, he made sure he clipped the apex and conservatively accelerated away. The feeling in the car was so strange. Sure, the tyres weren't up to temperature yet, but he'd run much harder on cool tyres earlier in the weekend without an issue. He immediately realised the loss of downforce was no joke.

Two left-hand kinks led on to the back straight where the cars reached 180 mph before braking hard for Curva Parabolica, an iconic corner on the Grand Prix circuit. The turn made a full 180 degrees, but unlike a hairpin, it was fast, open, and seemingly went on forever. The first part was tightest, and it was crucial to make a perfect apex before the corner opened up in a decreasing radius, meeting the front straight.

Miles took Parabolica with great care, only pushing the car in the middle and later part of the corner to maximise his exit. Past the pits and down the front straight, the Lotus felt like someone had bolted a couple more cylinders on his DFV. His shift points were similar to before and by the time he approached Curva Grande, his rpm was about the same too, but he knew he was going faster. Then he remembered Phil had changed the gear ratios for the higher speeds without wings. The same revs as before meant he was going faster for the same engine rpm.

Miles braked early, downshifted to third with a solid blip on the throttle, and entered the turn well below the speed he'd run earlier in the day. Once again, the Lotus glided into a long slide, but this time the young driver was ready. He drifted through the apex and softly picked up the throttle, neatly riding the base of the exit kerb for a good exit. His rev counter showed he was 400 rpm down on his best from earlier, but he knew he'd made a decent corner for this set-up and the lap time would be the only way to tell if the extra straight line speed overcame the cornering loss.

After five more laps, Miles was becoming comfortable and beginning to enjoy himself. His lap times weren't going to move him farther up the grid, but they were close, and he hadn't had a good tow off another car yet. He pitted and rolled to a stop by Phil.

"Those times are some of the fastest being set at the moment, Miles," his mechanic told him. "Do you think we can improve the car in this configuration?"

Miles nodded. "You got it pretty good, I'd say, but I'm sure we can fine tune it a little. I'm not touching the ground anywhere, so we can lower the car more."

"How about the gear ratios?" Phil asked.

Miles laughed. "Threw me for a bit as all my references had changed, but I think we're fine. For running on my own, fifth is too tall, but it should be perfect in a slipstream."

"Balance?" Phil asked.

"I'd take a little bit more grip in the front, but don't make it too pointy. She's a handful in Parabolica with this lower downforce."

"I'll lower the front ride height an eighth of an inch more than the rear," Phil replied, and quickly huddled with Tina to instruct him on the changes.

Miles sensed another car pulling alongside him in the pit lane and looked over to see Jochen Rindt staring back at him. The Austrian pointed to the pit exit, and Miles answered him, holding his thumb and forefinger a little apart, telling him he wouldn't be long. Rindt nodded and used two fingers to signal Miles should look for him when he came out on track. Miles returned a thumbs-up and watched the red and gold Lotus spin its rear tyres as it streaked away.

Cloud nine didn't even come close to describing how the young driver felt. He was at the famed Monza Grand Prix, driving a Formula One car, and the championship-leading driver wanted Miles to help him get to the front of the grid. Rindt didn't just pull alongside either of his own teammates at Lotus. He chose Miles.

"Alright, mate," Phil shouted, a minute later. "Give that a try."

Miles wasted no time starting the DFV and setting off down the pit lane, merging onto the track and watching Ickx and Regazzoni fly by on his outside. Checking his mirror, he saw the next car several hundred yards back and Miles instantly knew it was Rindt. Eyes ahead, Miles ran as hard as he could through Curva Grande then down the straight, now confident in his reference points for the Lesmos corners. The factory Lotus was already picking up a tow, and by the time the two cars were on the long kinking back stretch, his timing looked perfect, gaining almost to Miles's gearbox before Parabolica. Miles moved right and braked, giving Rindt the ideal line to finish the lap, and the Austrian flew by on the outside, sliding the Lotus 72 through the apex and using every inch of road at the exit.

Miles hoped he'd timed his gap better than in Germany and chased Rindt down the front straight, well over one hundred yards back as they crossed the line. Initially, he thought he'd screwed up again, but in the opposite way as he didn't feel much of a slip-stream down the front straight. The two slid in almost identical four-wheel drifts through Curva Grande, and down the following straight Miles now felt his car picking up more speed.

In the first Lesmo, Rindt threw up a whiff of dirt from the outside edge of the exit kerb, but he made a perfect run through the second right-hander, and Miles cursed himself for being too conservative. The first kink on the back section was easily flat out, but the second one had been tricky to stay wide open with the lower downforce. By the time Miles reached the sweeping curve on this lap, he was going faster than he ever had, visually gaining the other car in the tow.

The barriers and trees of the city park which the circuit wound through flew by at an alarming rate, and Miles had a few milliseconds to make his decision. Holding the throttle pinned to the stop, he willed his hands to be gentle with the steering wheel, well aware he'd asked for more responsive turning from Phil. If the front tyres gripped too well at 180 mph and the rears couldn't keep up, they'd be picking up pieces of Lotus 72 and Miles Preston from all over the park.

His left front rumbled over the apex kerb and the Lotus began sliding. Miles locked his eyes down the road on the tailpipes of Rindt's car and held his breath. Before he could even blink, the Lotus rode the exit kerb, wiggled for a moment, then settled onto the straight with Miles's foot still all the way down on the throttle pedal. He breathed again and began thinking about his braking for Parabolica, which he was now flying towards, almost redlining the tachometer.

With Miles still six car lengths behind, as the corner approached, Rindt stayed on line and Miles smiled beneath his balaclava. The wily veteran had seen Miles wasn't close enough and he could still tow the privately entered Lotus from the exit to the line. This would be the best lap Miles could ever dream of, and the championship leader was sacrificing his next lap to give him this gift.

Just a few yards ahead, Jochen Rindt braked, and Miles watched the Austrian's car violently twitch, before turning hard left and slamming into the Armco barrier in an explosion of parts and pieces.

Georgie didn't realise it, but she was hanging on to Barney's sleeve as her team manager held the timing clipboard in his hands, poised over the lever. The entire team was lined up, standing on the low wall in front of the pit garage and gazing expectantly towards the exit of Parabolica, a quarter of a mile away. But no car appeared. Two Lotus 72s should have stormed off the corner already. Georgie looked at Barney.

"Where are they?"

Over the loudspeakers up and down the pit lane, a man spoke excitedly in Italian, which none of them could understand. A strange quiet fell over the circuit. A couple of cars trickled into the pits with their engines cut, rolling to a stop by their teams. One was François Cevert, the handsome, blue-eyed young Frenchman who was Jackie Stewart's teammate at Tyrrell. They were only three pit stalls away, so Phil jumped down from the wall and ran over to the car.

Georgie couldn't hear the conversation, but the driver was shaking his head as he slowly climbed from his cockpit. Jackie Stewart rested a hand on his teammate's shoulder, and Phil walked back at a much slower pace.

"What's happening?" Martin called out from behind Georgie, which irritated her, although it was the question on everyone's minds.

Phil said nothing until he reached Georgie, and the look on his face caused her heart to leap into her throat. Phil held up a hand, which she accepted to step down from the wall.

"He said it's really bad. At the end of the back straight," Phil managed to say, his voice wavering. "There are two Lotuses involved. Miles is one of them."

30

BONAIRE

On the ride out to the dive site, AJ and Reg spent the time rigging the extra 80-cubic-foot tanks to hang on the line. AJ also made sure she had a small lift bag with her in case they needed it for the mooring line. With the boat tethered to the rope, nothing was sinking, but if they wanted to leave the tanks hanging overnight, like they had been doing, she wanted to be sure the buoy was enough. Arriving after their rest day to discover the mooring line and bail-out tanks were sitting on the bottom – again – wouldn't be ideal.

"Did I mention some of the underside of the car is squidgy and some feels firm?" AJ said as she pulled on her wetsuit, the texture of the neoprene sparking her memory.

"What do you mean?" De Konig asked.

"I touched the underside near the front and it was soft, like the material was falling apart," she explained. "But farther back, I had to lean on it a bit, and I was surprised when it felt solid beneath the layer of sediment."

"Fibreglass," Reg said, squeezing his big frame into his own wetsuit. "At the front is the nose cone, which was made of fibre-glass. The bottom of the chassis would be aluminium."

"That's a good sign then, right?" AJ suggested. "If the aluminium hasn't decayed too badly."

"Would certainly be if we were bringing the whole thing up," Reg replied and raised an eyebrow at AJ.

She grinned and carried on getting ready. She also wanted to ask De Konig if he'd positively identified the race car from the radius arm they'd brought up, but he'd been so touchy about it before, she decided to leave the subject alone for now. Neither did she nor Reg bother discussing the additional tanks with De Konig or Laurens, figuring they'd only see it as a way for them to stay down longer instead of the additional safety measure that it was.

At least the older Dutchman seemed to be in a great mood, producing a more relaxed atmosphere on the boat than there had been, even though Laurens' sour disposition remained constant. After AJ moored the pontoon to the submerged buoy, she and Reg geared up and dropped into the water. Laurens made himself useful by handing them their deco tanks and the two extras, which he looked at with interest but didn't ask about. Resembling a pair of scuba tank trees, with bottles hanging from everywhere, the two descended swiftly to 60 feet, where they clipped the new 80s to a strap they affixed to the line. From there, they continued descending, reaching the wreck in just over three minutes, and depositing their deco tanks by the remaining sheet metal at the bow.

The trough had remained in good shape since that morning, with a minimal amount of sand having slid or wafted into the bottom. AJ hoped the visibility would be vastly improved inside, as they wouldn't be digging at the entry this time. She'd discussed the hose length with Reg beforehand and he had indeed moved her rig into the trough to give her more reach. He'd do the same again once she entered the wreck.

AJ hadn't been dwelling on her first experience underneath the barge, but now, facing the narrow gap she'd be voluntarily wriggling through without a back-up gas supply, Reg's words of caution hung in her mind. She uncoiled the long regulator hose then slipped off her fins and took off her rig, setting it in the sand by the trough. She looked over at Reg, tapped herself on the chest, then pointed at her eyes with two fingers, and then her Perdix dive computer, letting him know she'd be carefully watching her time inside. Reg held up an okay sign.

Dropping into the trough, AJ took the underwater reciprocating saw Reg handed her and placed it through the gap, followed by her torch she'd left in the trough. Dropping to her back this time, AJ shimmied herself under the gunwale of the barge, and into the darkness beyond.

Squeezing through the tight space stirred up the sediment once more, but once AJ was inside and had turned on her torch, she could already see more than at any time during the prior dive. Across the width of the barge, she could see the port-side gunwale, and beyond the race car was a pile of crates and various debris. She was feeling more settled when her light reflected off a mass of moving silver flecks and she jumped. A ball of silversides swirled in slow-moving circles. AJ wondered if they'd found their way in before she'd opened up the gap under the gunwale, or if by some miracle they'd shown up in the last day or two, instinctively knowing a new cavern had been created. They could have been there that morning and she never would have seen them through the scatter.

Staying close to the gunwale, AJ edged her way past the disintegrating wooden box she'd stuck her finger through earlier, taking the shortest path towards the second radius arm. The fine sand wafted from her knees, but the brown-coloured muck and sediment on top billowed up far worse and hung in the water like a muddy puddle. By moving slowly, at least the mess remained low to the sand so she could see ahead.

AJ paused where the air scoop, which Reg had told her over lunch was called a sidepod, jutted out from the chassis, knowing the radius arm would be behind it. She softly clawed through the sand, finding the rod buried deeper than the first side. Following her hand along the arm, she carefully leaned forward, hoping Reg had moved her rig to give her more reach with the hose, and found

244 | NICHOLAS HARVEY

the other end against the upright. It too was a few inches under the sand.

Brushing the sand aside, AJ exposed the rose joint, or at least it felt like she had by touch as she couldn't see it, and guided the blade of the saw to the thinnest part. Pulling the trigger made her shudder as the sediment and metal shavings flew and the sound reverberated off the interior of the metal barge. Just as she was sure the cut was almost through, the blade snagged and nearly ripped the saw from her hands. AJ released the trigger and wiggled the hefty saw until the blade finally came free. In the light from her torch, which she'd rested on the top of the rear tyre, she saw the blade was bent at an angle.

"Bugger," she muttered into her reg, and fished in her thigh pocket for the spare blade Reg had given her.

He'd also given her a thirty-second lesson on how to switch the blades, which had appeared relatively simple on the boat. Now, at 210 feet below the *Beste Leven* in a dark hole up against the clock, she couldn't instantly recall a word he'd said. Another thing she noticed with annoyance now her man-made cavern wasn't completely silted out, was that her exhalation bubbles were disturbing more fine particulate on the deck above her. Tiny specks of rust rained down on her head, settling in her hair and landing on her face, making her cheeks itch.

Checking her Perdix, she noted eighteen minutes of run time. She'd agreed with Reg that she would be out from under the barge no later than the twenty-five-minute mark, leaving them five minutes to get their gear together and leave. She had seven minutes to figure out the saw, finish the cuts, and scramble out. For a second, AJ contemplated crawling out to have Reg help change the blade, but she knew it would waste too much time. If they could hand De Konig the second radius arm he seemed so passionate about, maybe they wouldn't have to dive the wreck again at all. They certainly weren't going to be in Bonaire long enough to cut the whole car apart and take it up piece by piece. They both had businesses to return to, so the Dutchman would need to bring in other salvagers anyway. With renewed determination, AJ set about changing the blade, with Reg's instructions slowly coming back to her as she found the attached tool on the side of the housing.

Three minutes and one grazed knuckle later, the saw was ready to go, and a thin mist of blood wafted away into the dark beyond AJ's torch beam, which she relocated to point at the chassis end of the radius arm. Figuring she'd cut the second end before finishing the rose joint that had bent the blade, she once more cleared the sand and muck until she could see the rod. Her hand swiped it and she realised Reg had been right – it was smeared with a grease, presumably to protect the chrome-plated ferrous metal. No doubt whoever had done that was doing their best to prevent corrosion during the ocean crossing, but had likely helped save the parts from fifty-plus years of immersion in seawater. Its location beyond sunlight had also helped the cause, as no coral growth could eat away at the race car.

Resting the new blade against the second rose joint she'd now exposed, AJ pulled the trigger and leaned as best as she could on the saw. The sound of the motor echoed off the inside of the barge again and the usual shrapnel and mess spewed into the surrounding water, but this time the saw cut cleanly and quickly through the metal. Too quickly, AJ thought, falling forward when the rose joint surrendered far sooner than she'd expected. An excess of scatter billowed up as the saw punched into the sand, and she waited a moment, hoping it would quickly clear.

She was just about to check the run time on her computer when she felt something brush over her legs. Crouched on her knees, with her feet and calves outstretched behind her hidden beneath the dirty layer of water, she swung around, but her body blocked the torch beam. Looking beside her, the hazy brown layer wafted and swirled and she yelped into her regulator, with her heart rate leaping through the roof. AJ snatched up the torch and frantically searched all around for the culprit, but the more she moved, the worse the silt became and all she managed to do was whip the torch around in a frenzy and send the silversides into another corner, freaking her out all over again.

Knowing the clock was ticking and she should be leaving, AJ held her breath and reached into the muck and sand. Praying her companion had moved on, she wanted to feel the end of the radius arm she'd just cut. As she'd suspected, something was different. She could feel the stub of thread from the severed rose joint protruding from the end of the arm, but it was kinked at an angle. Instead of continuous tubing, her finger found a jagged hole in the radius arm where it bent slightly, and a piece of debris or broken metal fell away.

Blind through the murky, silted water just above the sand, AJ had no real idea what was going on, but suspected the arm on this side had succumbed to the seawater over time and rusted through. Maybe whoever greased the metal parts had missed this bit, or the coating had been wiped off somehow. She was about to pick up the saw and try to finish the upright end when Reg's voice nagged in her head. She was about to do the same thing she had done on the previous dive. The leave time was a hard number this time. She checked her Perdix. Twenty-four minutes of run time.

"Bugger," she cursed into her regulator, and picked up the saw.

But instead of finishing the cut, she shuffled around to leave. Remembering her torch she'd placed on the tyre, AJ turned back, grabbed it, and with a thought which sprang into her mind, she stuck a hand into the sand and felt for the end of the radius arm. Showing De Konig the state of the metal would be far better than telling him what she thought had happened to his precious part. Her fingers quickly found the piece of debris and she clutched it in her palm, turned back around, and shuffled alongside the race car.

At the opening, she watched the bottom of her Dive Rite rig and twin tanks disappear from view as Reg lifted them out of the trough to make way. AJ threw the saw and her torch out the gap and watched them both be scooped up by her dive buddy's beefy hand. She shoved the piece of debris under the cuff of her wetsuit, hoping it wasn't sharp enough to cut her wrist or the neoprene. AJ rolled to her back, checked her reg hose wasn't caught on anything, and shimmied under the gunwale into the trough. As her head appeared from under the barge, she looked up at Reg's masked face staring down at her. He nodded his approval, so she assumed she'd beaten the clock this time.

At a far more relaxed pace than earlier in the day, the two divers retrieved their deco tanks and finned to the line. Ascending, they actually reached 100 feet two minutes ahead of the plan, and AJ noted that the slightly shorter amount of time at 210 feet had knocked eight minutes off their decompression obligation. Her first thought was that she should have stayed inside and cut the other end. But Reg was right, as usual; they'd dived their plan and stayed on the conservative side because nothing went wrong. If she'd been held up exiting the barge in any way, they'd built themselves a two-minute margin to deal with the issue.

Reaching their two-minute stop at 90 feet, Reg flipped over his slate, cleaned whatever was written there – which AJ hoped was his silly bugger note – and wrote something new. He swung his arm out to show her.

"Did you see the moray eel?"

AJ shouted something incoherent into her regulator and thumped Reg on the arm, nodding furiously and making manic hand signals about things crawling over her legs. She could see his eyes crease in amusement behind his mask.

As they moved on to 80 feet and another two-minute stop, AJ remembered the piece of debris and carefully retrieved it from the sleeve of her wetsuit. Holding it up for them both to see, she initially frowned, as what she held between her fingers was not at all what she'd been expecting. Her eyes flicked up to meet Reg's stare. He looked mad as hell.

31

1970 – MONZA, ITALY

Georgie ran through the garage to the paddock with tears streaming down her cheeks. She almost bumped into Martin's friend, Hendrik, but he stepped aside in time. Spotting a pit bike belonging to a neighbouring team, she called back to the team.

"Phil! Take me out there!"

Phil ran after her, and she pointed to the pit bike. It was a squat, funky-looking thing with small, fat tyres and a double seat. Phil used the kick-starter and the little bike's two-stroke engine sparked to life. They both hopped on and Georgie put her arms around her mechanic and lifted her feet off the ground as he sped away. Dodging people, vehicles, and Italian officials who blew whistles and waved their arms around, Phil managed to find his way to the back straight and sneak through a gap in the Armco by a marshal's post.

Sirens now wailed, and down the track, towards Parabolica, a group of course workers gathered on the left-hand side of the circuit. Phil sped that way to a chorus of shrill whistles in his wake. The crowd packed against the fences behind the barriers on both sides, pushing and shoving each other to get a better view. Nearing the scene, Georgie could pick out pieces of wreckage scattered all over the grass around the remains of a red and gold car. Beyond Rindt's Lotus she caught glimpses of her blue Ashford Motor Racing Team entry.

"Oh God," she whispered into Phil's back, over and over.

Arriving alongside, she picked her head up to see the crumpled remnants of Jochen Rindt's car. The monocoque was shredded at the footwell and broken suspension pieces hung like sinews from what was left of the front bulkhead. The upper fibreglass bodywork was gone, broken into a million pieces, and the top section of monocoque, which should have covered the cockpit and housed the dash and steering, lay in a twisted mess to one side, revealing an empty seat. Miraculously, despite the carnage, there'd been no fire. Georgie's eyes quickly moved on from Chapman's car to her own.

Sitting in the grass, with his back against the sidepod, was Miles. His car appeared unscathed, although it sat parked on the grass, facing the wrong way. Phil bounced over the rough ground and stopped the bike near the race car, putting the kickstand down as he let Georgie jump off first.

"Oh my God, Miles. Are you okay?" she asked, rushing to his side and dropping to her knees beside him.

Her driver slowly picked his head up and looked at her. Tears rolled down the young man's grime and oil-stained face.

"It happened right in front of me," he croaked, barely able to speak. "One second we were on the straight, and the next... the car just turned left."

Georgie reached out and squeezed Miles's arm. "Are you hurt?" she asked again.

Miles shook his head. "I managed to get stopped and turned around out here on the grass to see if I could help."

Georgie swallowed and knew she needed to be strong for her driver and what he'd just been through, but then she noticed the blood on Miles's hands and knew it wasn't his.

"I couldn't help," Miles whispered, and she wrapped the young man in her arms.

The two sobbed into each other's embrace.

The paddock area was sombre, and although the session later resumed, no one had any enthusiasm to continue. A man from Lotus came by, asking for Lady Ashford, and explained to her that based on Miles's report and the circumstances of the accident, they suspected a front halfshaft had failed on Rindt's car. The factory team was withdrawing from the weekend, and they strongly advised anyone running a Lotus 72 to do the same. Georgie had no hesitation in agreeing.

"That moment," she explained to Barney once the Lotus man had left, "when I thought Miles was badly hurt or… you know. It was one of the worst moments of my life. Jarama was terrifying, Zandvoort devastating, but this was even worse. I absolutely adore racing, but I don't think I'm cut out for this business."

Barney nodded and was about to reply when Martin walked into the garage.

"I hear all the Lotus owners are pulling out," he said, looking at Georgie for her reaction.

She nodded. He was about the last person on the planet she wanted to deal with at that moment, which made her angry, as six weeks ago she would have sought comfort in his arms. Angry at herself. She'd allowed his good looks and charm to blind her to the man underneath. A man she didn't know at all.

"Can we speak for a moment?" he asked.

Georgie really didn't want to be alone to deal with him, but Barney politely stepped away. Short of making a fuss, she didn't have much choice, so she nodded.

"Maybe this is for the better," he said, and Georgie frowned at the man.

"How is the death of a driver better for anyone? I can't believe you just said that."

"That's not what I meant," Martin retorted defensively. "I wasn't talking about the accident."

"Then what were you talking about?" she demanded.

"You. Us. This team."

"You've suddenly found a whole lot of concern for this racing team which you've ignored for the past month, Martin," she scoffed. "When we get back to England, I'll have the lads take the engine out, and you can have your chassis back. Whatever I choose to do from here, it's not going to involve you."

Martin took a deep breath. "I'm sorry you feel that way, but in all honestly, that works for me too. Except for the part about taking the car to the UK. I'll take my chassis now, thank you."

"What?" Georgie responded, aghast. "What do you mean now?"

"Exactly that," he replied flatly. "And I'll keep the engine in payment for the wear and tear on my chassis."

"The hell you're taking my engine, you bloody swindler. No wonder the police are after you," she jabbed, losing her temper.

Martin nodded towards the back of the garage, and from just outside, his man, Hendrik, shoved Barney inside. The henchman lifted his untucked shirt to reveal a gun poking out from his waistband.

"What on earth do you think you're doing?" Georgie hissed.

Martin simply smiled.

"I'm sorry, ma'am," Barney said. "He just grabbed me."

"I'm getting a policeman, so you'd better be gone by the time I get back," Georgie ranted, and was starting towards the back door when she heard a dull thump and all the wind escaping Barney's lungs.

She whipped around to see her team manager on his knees, clutching his stomach, trying to catch his breath.

"You bloody animal!" Georgie gasped, but her mind was whirring, trying to come up with a way out of this.

"It's simple," Martin said, as though he had read her mind. "You're going to instruct your mechanics to help Hendrik load the car, as it is, into my lorry in the paddock. Barney will be with me. If you try to raise an alarm, warn your mechanics, or deviate in any way from my instructions, he will be the one to suffer. Is that clear, or should Hendrik show you what happens when you don't do what I say?"

Georgie looked at Barney on his knees and knew she had no choice. After the events of the afternoon, she wasn't about to risk anyone else's life over a race car. Besides, once they released Barney, she'd run to the police and let them chase after the two men.

"Where's this lorry?" she asked.

"Behind your transporter," Martin replied. "Have the car pushed around now. Hendrik will show you."

The henchman dragged Barney to his feet and shoved him towards Martin.

"Go with him," Martin ordered, nodding at Hendrik, who was already walking towards the pit lane.

Georgie gritted her teeth. "It'll be fine, Barney," she said, then glared at Martin. "You'd better not lay another finger on him."

Martin smiled again, and patted his lightweight jacket pocket, where she presumed he was hiding his own gun.

"Don't give me cause for concern," he added. "And just like you said, he'll be fine."

Georgie followed Hendrik from the garage and found her crew busy with the Lotus, which the marshals had towed back. She explained to Phil and Tina that the Lotus was to be loaded in a different lorry in the paddock. Phil began asking a series of questions about why, where, and when they'd get it back, but she asked him to please get it done right away and that she would explain everything afterwards. The two mechanics were clearly not happy, and likely concerned about what was happening, but they did as instructed, and thirty minutes later, the race car was loaded into the back of Martin's lorry.

"Please wait for me in the garage," she instructed once the ramps were stowed and the rear door closed. "And keep Miles with you," she added, seeing her driver walking towards them.

Hendrik led her around the front to the cab, where Martin sat with Barney next to him. Martin and Hendrik exchanged a few words in Dutch, which Georgie couldn't understand, and then Martin stepped out, letting his man take the driver's seat.

"Now we leave, and you take your team to the hotel," he said.

Georgie looked up at Barney, still sitting in the cab. "Now, you let him go as you said you would," she rebutted.

"That wouldn't work very well, would it?" Martin said. "You'd simply raise the alarm before we were out of the paddock. No, we'll take Barney for a little ride and once we're clear of the area, we'll drop him in a village and he'll call you at the hotel. You can contact the police then, but we'll be far enough away."

"I have no way of knowing you'll do that," Georgie complained. "You're a liar and a thief. Why would I believe you?"

Martin grinned. "Because you have no choice. Hendrik can quietly cut his throat right now and we'll take you instead if you'd prefer?"

Georgie's knees went weak. "Leave Barney alone and take me in his place. He can get everyone to the hotel and you can let me go in a village somewhere."

Martin shook his head. "Very brave of you, but your care for his life over your own is exactly why I'm taking him. You make too many decisions with your heart instead of your head, my dear."

Before she knew what she was doing or could stop herself, Georgie slapped Martin across the face. It must have stung him as her hand hurt and his cheek turned red. He glared back at her.

"If I as much as hear a siren in the distance, he's dead. Understand me?"

Georgie quickly nodded, terrified her outburst had made the situation worse.

"I'll be alright," Barney called to her, but she could hear the terror in his voice.

Martin didn't say another word. He walked around and climbed into the other side of the cab while Hendrik started the engine. The doors slammed closed, and Georgie watched helplessly as they pulled away, wondering if she'd ever see her team manager again.

32

1970 – SPAIN

It had been three days since they'd left the racetrack in Monza, and Hendrik had slept little. Before leaving Italy, they'd switched lorries, and the man who called himself Martin van der Meer had driven off in a car, leaving Hendrik with explicit instructions on how to cross France and enter Spain. The new lorry even had a Spanish furniture delivery sign on either side, which Hendrik was told to remove after entering Spain. It had all gone surprisingly smoothly. Better than Hendrik had believed it would, although he was glad to give the man his gun back. He'd never used a gun on a job before and found possessing one strangely and dangerously intoxicating, but far too risky in his opinion.

Martin – or whatever his name really was, as no one in their line of business seemed to use the name their parents had given them – must have greased the right palms at the borders, as Hendrik had been waved through with little more than a cursory glance at his licence. Not once was the door opened to the back of the lorry, where behind a few pieces of old furniture sat the race car.

Two things had kept him behind the wheel instead of parking the lorry in a small French town and taking a train north. Money was the obvious motivation, as he'd only received a third in Italy, the rest coming his way in two more payments. One when he arrived at the port in Barcelona, and the final third when the cargo was loaded for shipping. But the other incentive to complete the job was fear. Martin unnerved him. Hendrik had spent his life amongst thieves and dubious characters, but no one had terrified him the way this man did. Stone cold.

Hendrik had no way of actually knowing what fate had befallen the English fellow they'd taken with them from the racetrack. Martin had left with him in the car. Hendrik had a bad feeling that no one except Martin would ever know what truly happened to the man named Barney. Which begged the question, what would happen to him once he completed the job? At every small town with a railway station he drove through, Hendrik kept telling himself to abandon the lorry and run, but he never did. Fear had him paralysed to do anything other than what he'd been told. If the borders were anything to go by, Martin had reach all over Europe, so how hard would it be for him to track down a guy that screwed him over?

The port was huge, but Hendrik followed the directions and found the small warehouse at the end of a row where Martin stood waiting for him.

"Any problems?" he asked, his face as stern as always.

"None," Hendrik replied, bleary eyed and feeling like the man could see inside his head where all his fears, doubts, and thoughts of reneging lay open like a book.

"Good," he replied, handing him an envelope of cash. "We'll unload the car, and then you can sleep for a few hours or get a bite to eat. After that, I'll be ready to load everything into the shipping container."

Hendrik nodded and quickly scurried away to begin, glad to be getting on with the job so he could leave Martin behind for good. Why they couldn't load everything now, he had no idea, but he'd figured out questioning the man wasn't healthy. It took them less than an hour to unstrap the furniture, carry it to where a full-sized commercial container sat outside the opposite end of the warehouse, and unload the race car, rolling it inside the building. Hendrik didn't know the first thing about motor racing, and Monza had been the only circuit he'd ever been to, but the car impressed him. It was no frills and all business, clearly built to do one thing, and that was go fast.

Martin told him to make himself scarce for two hours, and Hendrik was happy to do so. More tired than hungry, he walked back to the lorry and climbed inside, lying across the full-width bench seat. He bundled a jacket under his head and his eyes were instantly ready to close, but a thought wandered into his mind. *Why did Martin make him leave? And why was the whole warehouse so oddly quiet, with no one else around?* The place wasn't huge, but he figured it would be too expensive to leave dormant while Martin was running around all over Europe. *Surely he had people working for him?* With no answers to his questions, his fatigue caught up with him, and he was soon fast asleep.

He had no idea how long he'd been out when a loud noise startled him awake. Hendrik sat up and saw another lorry outside the adjoining warehouse, the driver slipping off his gloves and walking to the cab after pulling down the rear door. Hendrik looked at his watch. It hadn't been two hours yet, but it wasn't worth trying to go back to sleep for the remaining twenty minutes. Besides, he needed to take a leak, and the thought of splashing water around his face held more appeal.

Slipping from the cab, he noticed the large roll-up door to the warehouse had been closed. He considered going next door and asking to use their loo, but he didn't speak Spanish, and he figured Martin wouldn't want him to be seen by any more people than absolutely necessary. Hendrik walked to the regular door and carefully tried the handle. It wasn't locked. He slowly opened the door enough to peek inside. The race car was where he'd left it, but parts and tools lay strewn about the concrete floor. A tub of grease with an open lid sat next to a rear tyre with several spray cans of WD-40.

A door from an office inside opened and Martin walked out, carrying a component Hendrik couldn't identify. He quickly but quietly pulled the outside door closed and stepped back. He had that bad feeling inside once more. Hendrik knew from what the lady had said at the track that Martin had stolen parts that belonged to her, but he sensed there was far more to this shipment than just a race car. He'd been involved in plenty of thefts and shady deals, but there was something about this gig which felt completely different. If Martin was moving guns, or drugs, which were fast becoming the most profitable illegal commodity, then that was well outside Hendrik's comfort zone. *Besides, Martin van der Meer was cleaning up all traces of his movements, so where did that leave him?* Probably in exactly the same boat, or shallow grave, that Barney found himself in.

On the spur of the moment, Hendrik decided the final payment wasn't worth the risk. Two out of the three would do. He'd rather stay alive and out of jail. On the verge of panic, he swiftly walked away from the warehouse and ducked behind a row of shipping containers. From there he ran until he reached the port entry, walking out as nonchalantly as he could manage in his sleep-deprived and frazzled state. From there, he used buses to get to trains and found his way back to Holland as quickly as he could, fretting over his decision and watching over his shoulder the entire way.

Hendrik's experience with Martin van der Meer had been both exhilarating and terrifying, but he was glad to move on. His biggest problem afterwards would be returning to the petty crimes and scams at home. They all felt underwhelming. He'd had a taste of something bigger. Crossing borders and switching vehicles like James Bond in the movies. He often found himself thinking about that moment when he watched Martin appear from the office. The moment he'd decided to bolt. The moment he'd question in his mind, over and over, and could never forget.

33

BONAIRE

In the hour of decompression time AJ and Reg spent ascending, AJ watched Reg's fury slowly subside into determined anger by the time they boarded the *Beste Leven*, and she decided it was best to let the big man take the lead.

"You didn't get the second radius arm?" De Konig quizzed as they dropped their gear.

"No," Reg replied, surprising AJ with the calm in his voice. "Much harder to get to. Next dive."

The Dutchman couldn't hide the frustration on his face, but he too maintained his composure.

"And there's no way you could make that dive tomorrow?" he asked. "Even if we limited the day to just the one dive?"

"I suppose that's possible," Reg replied as he dried his hair with a towel. "But I thought the main goal was getting this precious chassis plate? When you finally got around to telling us about the race car under the barge, all you talked about was the chassis plate. Now it's all about the radius arms."

De Konig stared at Reg for a moment and AJ could feel the tension instantly escalate on the boat. Laurens, who'd been sitting on a bench engrossed in his mobile phone, also looked over at Reg.

"Every piece is important," De Konig responded. "But you said the chassis plate would be a much bigger project. I figured I'd get what I could while you two were here. Unless you're now saying you can extend your trip?"

Reg shook his head. "No. I'm afraid we both have to get back. Businesses to run and what-have-you." He moved closer to the table in the middle of the boat, where De Konig leaned on the other side. "You reckon people will believe you've found this Lotus from the radius arms, then? Not a difficult part to fake, is it? Piece of steel tube with a welded bung in each end for the rose joints. Any fabrication shop could knock them out in an hour or so."

"As I explained," De Konig responded, forcing a smile. "The length and diameter are quite unique, and the example you brought up is clearly aged, so there's no chance it was recently manufactured."

Reg nodded. "I see. And there's nothing else special about these radius arms that you'd care to share with us?"

De Konig appeared puzzled. "What do you mean, Reg? I don't know what you're talking about."

Reg pulled the piece of debris from his pocket. He'd taken it from AJ and rubbed it clean on the deco stops. Placing it on the table, De Konig let out a sigh, then his lips curled slowly into a smile. The diamond sparkled up at them both like the morning sunshine on the ocean.

"The second radius arm is rusted through at one end," Reg said. "This fell out."

"I see," De Konig said, taking his time. "I don't suppose there's any way you two would agree to bring up the contents of the other arm without a fuss, would you? We could discuss a bonus on top of your fee."

AJ joined Reg at the table. "We told you. Nothing illegal."

"You're assuming what we're doing is illegal," De Konig replied. "Remember, I own the salvage rights."

Reg scoffed. "You're telling me we're finding diamonds hidden in race cars from the 1970s and it's all above board? You have to be kidding."

"Is this the Ashford Lotus?" AJ asked.

De Konig nodded. "It is."

"Were you the one who took it?" she asked. "In the article, it talked about a Dutch bloke who owned the chassis. He took it and disappeared after a Grand Prix. The police were after him."

"Was this your shipment on the barge?" Reg added, before the man could reply.

De Konig laughed. "No, no, no. Martin van der Meer is the man you speak of. At least, that was the name he used during his foray into Formula One. He put the Lotus, along with other possessions, on the barge."

"So, how do you know about this bloke?" AJ asked.

"Our paths crossed many years ago," De Konig confessed.

"You knew the radius arms had been covered in grease, didn't you?" AJ asked. "You almost let that slip earlier."

De Konig shrugged his shoulders. "I did, but no matter at this point. The question is what happens next."

"You take us ashore and we'll be on our way," Reg said firmly. "That's what happens."

De Konig turned and looked at Laurens. The younger Dutchman reached into the rucksack beside him and pulled out a handgun, aiming it at Reg.

AJ knew nothing about guns, but from the movies she recognised the extension on the end of the barrel as a silencer, or suppressor according to someone who once corrected her. She unintentionally flinched.

"Oh bugger," she muttered, holding up her hands, as she wasn't quite sure what else to do.

"Seriously?" Reg growled.

"Not really much choice at this stage," De Konig commented. "I must insist you head back down."

"And then?" AJ fumed. "We bring up your diamonds and what? You shoot us?"

De Konig held up his hands in a calming manner. "I really don't think it needs to come to that. We'll figure out a way for us to have a head start before you tell anyone."

"How about we get your stones, promise not to tell anyone, and you drop us ashore?" Reg suggested.

De Konig laughed. "I'm afraid your word is not good enough in this instance, Reg. But we'll tie you up in the condo and call someone to let them know you're there once we're well away from here."

"That sounds like BS," AJ countered.

De Konig shrugged his shoulders once more. "I'm sorry you don't trust me, but it really doesn't matter. Laurens here has the gun, so we make the rules."

"Fine," Reg conceded despondently. "But what do we do tonight? We can't dive again until tomorrow."

De Konig looked at Laurens once more.

"She's diving," Laurens said. "Now."

"We just came up!" AJ snapped.

"You know she can't go back down right away," Reg added. "Might as well shoot her as send her down."

"I won't shoot her," Laurens replied, waving the gun at Reg. "I'll shoot you if she doesn't. I'll also shoot you if she comes up empty handed."

AJ noticed the man's English had noticeably improved.

"At least let me run a dive through our planner and see what it gives me," AJ pleaded, hoping to buy some time. "But you realise it will be dark by the time I get down there," she added, pointing to the sun lowering in the sky.

"It's dark under the barge anyway," Laurens replied without a hint of concern in his voice. "Run your plan, but be quick about it."

AJ took her laptop from her rucksack and sat down on the bench, turning it on.

"Wait," De Konig said, beckoning AJ. "Bring it over here. We don't want you accidentally finding yourself online sending messages."

"It's not connected to anything," AJ argued. "I can't get online without Wi-Fi or a mobile."

De Konig tapped the table. "Work on it over here where I can see what you're doing."

AJ huffed, while quickly switching off the Wi-Fi so he wouldn't see she'd been in the process of connecting to her mobile in her rucksack. She placed the laptop on the table with the MultiDeco program already open, then took far longer than necessary, clicking around a variety of settings which didn't need changing to run the dive plan.

"Mobiles," Laurens said, looking at Reg. "Give me your phones."

AJ cursed to herself as Reg had no choice but to dig out their phones and hand them over. She continued clicking and typing, now trying different scenarios that wouldn't run her out of deco gas or give her central nervous system toxicity from the oxygen.

"If my surface interval is one hour," she announced. "I can get sixteen minutes of run time, but I'll deco on the 50 percent and then have to use the 80 percent nitrox we have hanging. The overall dive will be an hour and ten minutes."

"That's only thirteen minutes on the bottom," Reg pointed out. "And you'll be doing everything yourself. In the bloody dark."

"Well, two hours of surface interval improves things…" AJ began.

"We don't care," Laurens barked, getting to his feet from the bench. "You're getting back in no later than one hour and you're bringing up every diamond that's down there. If you don't, he dies," he reiterated, using the gun as a pointer. "Now switch tanks and get ready."

AJ now realised why they'd been sent on the errand to refill that morning's tanks. This scenario had been on their minds all along. With Reg's help, she switched out the doubles on her backplate.

"Once you get under, head straight for shore," he whispered. "Stay shallow, and with the current, you might make it in an hour or two."

AJ quickly ran the maths in her head. The swim, then getting to someone or somewhere with a phone, plus the response time of the police to get a boat out to the pontoon. Maybe that could all happen in two hours, but what would stop Laurens shooting Reg and tipping him over the side before the police boat reached them?

"No," she whispered back. "That won't work."

She heard the big man growl, but he couldn't argue with her without being overheard. AJ drank from a bottle of water and glanced at the horizon. The sun would set during her descent. She'd made hundreds of night dives over the years, and usually enjoyed them immensely. But she'd never been to 210 feet on her own in the dark, to then take off her diving gear and crawl under an inverted barge with nothing but a single regulator on a long hose. Where she now knew a moray eel liked to call home. AJ shivered despite the warm late afternoon air.

"So what happened to this Van der Meer bloke?" Reg asked, sitting on the bench.

"Nobody knows," De Konig replied. "I tracked him by the shipment from Spain to Aruba, which listed an unspecified car aboard. The manifest noted it was not for highway use and the paperwork was under a false company name. From there I found the mysterious barge which sank in a terrible storm on its way here, and the timing was so close, I figured it had to be the Lotus."

"Which you don't give a rat's arse about," AJ added.

"I wish I could, as the story is quite engaging, and the car is worth a lot of money, but incomparable to the stones."

"I still don't understand how you knew about the parts being greased," Reg said, scratching his beard, "if you didn't pick up the trail until recently."

"Van der Meer had to hire someone to drive the lorry with the race car out of Italy and sneak it across Southern France into Spain," De Konig explained with a grin.

"And that was you," AJ guessed, piecing the story together. "That's where your paths crossed all those years ago."

De Konig smiled more broadly. "Actually, a man named

Hendrik was my cell mate for several years. We were both inside for events unrelated to the diamonds, or the Lotus, but he liked to tell tales. My run in with Van der Meer happened two years before that. He tried to kill me by throwing me from a train."

De Konig rubbed his lower back as though even the mention of the event made the pain return.

"Enough talk," Laurens ordered, and De Konig held a hand up.

"Quite right, young man. I'm afraid I do get a kick out of telling the old stories. Spending most of my adult life in and out of jail not saying a word about the biggest jewellery heist in Antwerp's history will do that to a fellow."

"It's time to go," Laurens barked.

AJ checked her Perdix. She'd been up for fifty-one minutes. She could milk that into an hour. Taking her time, she geared up, being meticulous and careful with every detail. Her life had always relied on her gear every time she dived, but alone at 210 feet left her with no dive buddy to help if anything went wrong. She was truly on her own. Using Reg's shoulder for support, she waddled to the gap in the bow railing and took a giant stride into the water.

Reg handed AJ her single deco tank, as she couldn't use the 100 percent oxygen anymore, and De Konig rested a knee on the padded bench by the gap in the bow, watching them like a hawk.

"Be careful," Reg told her. "Don't worry about me. Understand?"

AJ knew what her mentor was really saying behind the few words he could get away with using in the moment. He wanted her to swim away and get herself to safety. By De Konig's willingness to share so many details, the man had made it pretty clear they had no plans for her or Reg to make it ashore alive. Once she returned with the diamonds, the two divers were nothing but baggage.

"I'll be back in a jiff," she replied and watched her friend softly shake his head.

What choice did she have? AJ wouldn't abandon Reg in the same way he wouldn't leave her for dead if the roles were reversed. Her only option was to bring up the rest of the diamonds and use her deco time to figure out some kind of plan to keep them both alive.

"Time to go," Laurens demanded. "But one last thing."

AJ finished clipping her tank to her harness and looked up.

"I think it's important you know how serious we are," he said. "I won't hesitate to shoot your friend if you come back empty handed."

"I believe you," AJ said, bobbing in the water, trying to settle her breathing before descending. "You seem like a real prick."

She watched a smile creep across Laurens' face, then looked down at her Perdix to triple-check her settings.

The noise from the suppressed gun was far louder than AJ would ever have imagined. She flinched in stunned surprise as something splattered across her face and mask, making her shudder as she looked up in horror to see De Konig's limp body fall into the water, just a few feet away.

34

BONAIRE

AJ descended in shock. She'd had the misfortune to witness death in the past, but nothing as unexpected and brutal as what had just happened. She frantically wiped away De Konig's blood and whatever other grisly particles had landed across her face and mask. Feeling sick to her stomach, she knew she had to calm her heart rate, but she couldn't catch her breath.

Most of the light had already vanished underwater, with late afternoon becoming evening as she dropped towards 200 feet. Leaving the line, AJ kept her deco tanks alongside her main rig instead of dropping them off the bow. It would be completely dark soon, so there'd be no point hunting in different locations with the limited time she already had. The other thing she quickly noticed was the current, which at the surface had switched to gently tugging the *Beste Leven* away from shore as the tide went out, but was still lightly running east at depth. The mooring line was almost vertical in the water column, placing the buoy closer to the surface and the bail-out tanks shallower than before.

Arriving at the trough, she unclipped her deco bottle and placed it just outside the shoring which kept the sand at bay. She took off her fins, placed the saw and torch by her feet, and unfurled the long regulator hose. She then ditched her rig and back tanks, making sure the first stage was as close to the entrance under the barge as possible. A few curious grunts swam around, already expecting activity which might provide them an evening snack before nightfall.

AJ was about to slither under the gunwale when movement caught her eye from the stern. Something large was dropping down towards the wreck, and in the dying light, she strained to make out what it was. It didn't move like any fish she'd ever seen. The profile was more like a diver. *Had Laurens followed her down? Or Reg?*

Her breath caught in her throat as she realised who was joining her at the wreck. De Konig's body, preceded by a weight belt wrapped around his ankles, disappeared behind the barge, throwing up a waft of sand as it hit the sea floor. She was sure it was exactly the fate that her future held, whether or not she returned to the surface with the diamonds. But she couldn't worry about that now. First of all, she had to retrieve the diamonds, and the clock was ticking.

Struggling to set aside thoughts of De Konig's murder and Reg's impossible position 210 feet above her, AJ slid under the gunwale and wriggled herself beneath the barge. Turning on her torch, she noticed something she'd all but forgotten about. Her GoPro lay next to the decaying crate. She grabbed it as she shuffled past on hands and knees; sand and sediment wafted, and her torch beam reflected off the ball of silversides circulating beyond the inverted race car.

Reaching the side pod, AJ considered her options. She'd been over it a hundred times in her head, but knew the final decision had to be made once she reached the car and made a better evaluation. *The question was how badly the radius arm was corroded.* If she could cover the damaged end and finish cutting the upright connection, the arm would be easy to carry out. But if most of the gems had already spilled into the sand, then it would take forever to gather them all.

She checked her run time. Seven minutes into the sixteen available. With so little surface interval between the incredibly deep dives, her margins were wafer thin. Shining the light at the sand in front of where she knelt revealed more of the grimy-looking layer of murky water from her disturbing the sediment. Her hand disappeared into the haze and found the arm in the furrow she'd made in the sand during the prior dive. Her fingers gently located the bent end and the rusted hole. Running her hand lightly along the arm, she tried to disturb as little as possible while she hunted for other holes and corrosion.

The surface of the radius arm had the now familiar texture of gooey grease mixed with sand, algae, and particulate, until her hand met another smooth rod of some sort, closer to the upright. AJ figured Reg would know exactly what part of the suspension it would be, but she had no idea. Whatever it was moved when she nudged it, so she carefully withdrew the part from the sand to set it aside. Raising the rod from the cloudy haze, it appeared in the torch beam and AJ yelped into her regulator, instantly dropping the object in a waft of silty brown water.

Terrified that she was hallucinating, and even more scared that she wasn't, AJ gingerly reached blindly to the sand and felt for what she'd dropped. Forcing her fingers to pick it up, she lifted it once more and confirmed she wasn't seeing things that weren't there. In her hand was a human femur, instantly recognisable by the hip joint. Shaking, AJ fought the urge to fling the bone away, and placed it carefully on top of the bulge she knew to be the rear tyre. Taking her GoPro, she turned on the camera, shone her light on the bone, and captured the image on film.

Time was slipping away at an alarming rate, and the only thought pulling AJ from the death that seemed to be all around her was Reg. She prayed he was still alive on the pontoon boat, and that she could formulate some way to negotiate their freedom before surfacing. But first she had to get the radius arm and diamonds out from under the barge. Knowing she was likely kneeling on or next to the rest of whoever must have gone down with the barge, AJ gritted her teeth and picked up the saw.

Fumbling for the cut she'd begun earlier, she laid the blade in place and pulled the trigger. The saw sounded even louder than it had before and it kicked, snagged for a moment, then cut through the remaining metal of the rose joint. Muck and silt billowed up from where AJ punched the saw into the sand below and she winced at the idea of hitting more skeletal parts. Setting the saw down, she carefully wrapped a hand around the corroded end of the radius arm and lifted it from the sand. Using her fingers, she wiped along the tube, accumulating more of the greasy mess around the holes, temporarily sealing them off.

AJ glanced at her Perdix. Thirteen minutes and four seconds of run time. She had less than three minutes to wrap things up and leave the sea floor. She turned to look for the faint glow of the opening, but all she could see was darkness. The sun must have finally set, robbing her of the dim beacon marking her exit. She thought of Jo's lantern on the steps at Weber's Joy and cursed herself for not setting an extra torch outside the barge. Plucking the torch from where she'd left it next to the bone on the tyre, she aimed the beam towards the bow. The crate lit up and blocked almost everything else. AJ flung the saw to the left of the crate and remembered to scoop up her GoPro, stuffing it in her thigh pocket.

With the torch in one hand and the radius arm in the other, she shuffled alongside the Lotus and made her way around the crate. It was hauntingly claustrophobic to shine her light through the freshly stirred up silty water and see nothing but blackness beyond the gunwale. She slid the saw and the torch under the gap, then lay on her back and pulled herself under the side of the barge. With the beam pointing into the side of the trough, AJ's eyes stared up at ink black all around. She knew her head had cleared the gunwale, but could tell little more. Her chest rubbed against the metal, indicating her position, so she moved her hands from the side of the boat to the sand on either side of her body, trying to shimmy the rest of the way out.

Something smooth and rounded rolled over her right hand and she gulped air from her regulator. The eel brushed over her shoulder and bumped against the back of her head as it exited the barge. AJ froze, praying the next thing she'd feel wouldn't be a chunk of her own flesh being ripped away. She had no way of knowing where the moray went, but it was no longer touching her and she wanted out of there in a hurry. Panting into her regulator, she frantically shuffled backwards in the trough until something suddenly plucked the reg once more from her mouth.

Her head hit the sheet metal along the back of the trough, and her shins banged the underside of the gunwale as she desperately tried to free her legs. She was now lying on top of her torch and awkwardly wedged in the trough, with a shitty choice to make: fumble for the reg she'd been using, or scramble upright and go for the back-up reg on her rig, just outside the trough. Either way, she needed breathing gas. And she needed it now.

Kicking herself to a seated position, AJ swept her right arm across the space before her, hoping she'd get lucky and find the hose. Nothing. Her legs were finally clear of the gunwale, so she shuffled to her knees and grabbed the torch, pointing back at the side of the boat. Silt and sand billowed everywhere from her rushed movements, and the gunwale, which couldn't be more than three feet away, was barely distinguishable from the sand or the wreck.

Something brushed her leg again, and she fought back the deadly urge to open her mouth and scream. A shadow curled in her torch beam, indistinct and barely visible through the hazy mess. AJ reached out and grabbed at the snaking object, feeling a moment of elation when, instead of being bitten, she hauled the regulator hose her way. It snagged again, but this time she had a firm hold on the line, leaned towards the barge, and shepherded the reg into her mouth.

She could almost hear Reg's voice yelling at her to watch her time, and she babbled into her regulator, telling him to shut up. Diving back under the gunwale, she shone the torch inside and through the scatter, could just make out the hose caught around the end of the rearward corrugated sheet. Stretching, she freed the hose and wriggled back out, standing up in the trough. Pulling on her rig was much harder without Reg holding it up for her, but she struggled into the harness and cinched the waist strap, ignoring the crotch strap for now.

Grabbing her 50 percent nitrox deco tank, she clipped it to the top D-ring on the harness, slipped on her fins, and was about to push off the bottom when she remembered the all-important radius arm. What a fatal error leaving it behind would be. AJ reached down with the deco tank awkwardly dangling from its single attachment and snatched up the arm. Next to it was the saw, and guilt made her take that too. It was useless to her now, but she simply felt bad leaving it behind. With a punch of gas into her wing, she pushed off the sand, launching out of the trough like a spaceman hopping around on the moon.

Stealing a glance at her Perdix, she noted sixteen minutes and ten seconds of run time. She'd run long and still had a further problem. The only way to find the mooring line in the dark was to trace it from the wreck itself. If she began ascending, she'd be looking for a dark brown rope in an ink-black ocean. With no way of knowing for sure which way the surface swells and currents had pulled the *Beste Leven*, she was more likely to miss the boat than find it, drifting at the mercy of the seas as she performed her decompression stops. Not to mention her second deco bottle hanging on the line. Without that, she'd be doubling her decompression time using trimix back gas, which she'd possibly run out of.

AJ finned hard towards the stern, playing the torchlight across the hull of the wreck to keep her bearings. She clutched the radius arm and torch together in one hand while she clipped the saw where the second deco bottle would have hung, and attached the second clip for the nitrox tank, tidying up her rig. The mooring line appeared ahead of her, and as she was about to angle upwards to join it, her light hit De Konig's body in the sand below. She almost jumped out of her skin.

Pausing for a moment she really couldn't afford, AJ fumbled in her thigh pocket for the GoPro, turned it back on, shone the torch at the corpse, and recorded a ten-second clip. The odds were against her coming out of this alive, but the odds were even slimmer that the Dutchman's body would still be where it fell by the time the authorities put a diver on the wreck. At least she had some evidence of his demise.

Shoving the camera away, AJ kicked as fast as she dared risk towards her first stop. When she paused at 90 feet for one minute, she checked her time to surface against her plan and calculated she'd be doing six more minutes of decompression obligation. That wasn't too bad, considering everything that had tried to kill her already on the dive. Yet now came the hard part. As she finned up the line to 80 feet, where she'd spend another minute, AJ began racking her brain, trying to come up with a scenario which didn't end with her and Reg each getting a bullet through their head.

35

BONAIRE

At 70 feet, AJ switched from her back gas trimix to her deco 50 percent nitrox. In the dark, she couldn't tell which way the mooring line was angling or where the boat was relative to her position. Usually on a night dive, the boat captain would hang some form of light by the ladder to help guide divers back aboard, but above her was nothing but endless ink black. The rope disappeared into the gloom. But thankfully, her torch illuminated the bottoms of three bottles, which she reached after moving up to 60 feet. Her stop at that depth was only one minute, which she used to free the 80 cubic foot 80 percent nitrox bottle from the line and attach it to her harness.

AJ felt a short-lived relief to be in possession of the deco gas she'd need shortly, but the feeling was quickly surpassed by an overwhelming panic. She hadn't the faintest idea what to do when she surfaced. Popping up and handing Laurens the radius arm felt like a sure way of getting herself and Reg shot as soon as the Dutchman confirmed he had the stones. But what did she have to bargain with?

At 30 feet, she switched to the 80 percent nitrox and settled in for a longer decompression stop of five minutes. The buoy was still above her and if she stared up long enough, the profile of the *Beste Leven* became a pitch-black blob surrounded by charcoal surroundings. Moving to 20 feet for nine minutes put her a few feet below the buoy, and she unclipped her 50 percent nitrox deco bottle and fixed it to the carabiner on the line. There didn't seem much point surfacing with more clutter than absolutely necessary.

The saw was an awkward lump hanging from her gear too, and AJ contemplated attaching it to the line as well. In theory, whoever came out to investigate the strange goings-on off Lighthouse Point ought to find the tanks and gear only 20 to 30 feet underwater. *But would they? Why would they even come out here?* Laurens wouldn't detach the line from the buoy. He'd untie it from the boat, or simply cut the rope. All anyone would see would be open ocean once the rope accumulated growth and sank. Unless authorities or curious divers took the time to scan the sea floor and find the wreck, nothing about the operation would be discovered, and their bodies would be lost to the ocean. Even their dive gear would be weighted and tossed over the side to follow their bodies to the bottom and join De Konig. She kept the saw, thinking that might at least make it back on the boat, but fished the GoPro from her pocket and attached that to the carabiner. If the submerged buoy was ever discovered, then so would a few pieces of evidence.

For once, her deco stops flew by when all AJ needed was more time to think. Her final stop at only ten feet was twenty-eight minutes long, the first few eaten up with carefully attaching the 80 percent nitrox tank she was breathing from to the line. This was more awkward as she was now on the more steeply angled rope between the submerged buoy and the pontoon. The soft swells were moving her far more now as the boat rose and fell, but she was careful to keep her average depth at ten feet to satisfy her computer.

After a while, a light shone down from the boat, but she doubted they could actually see her through the dark water. She'd long since turned her own torch off after completing her tasks. The light above extinguished, leaving her once more in complete darkness. Not one idea had come to mind that carried a decent chance of success, and with ten minutes left until she could surface, the time to make a final decision was fast approaching. Of course, she could stay under longer than her computer demanded, but already being behind the plan meant the two on the boat would be expecting her to pop up by now. Reg would be getting more concerned, and Laurens would be getting more agitated. Which likely made him more dangerous. It was better for him to think he was in complete control and everything was going to his plan.

AJ decided her only course of action now was to choose the least bad option. Making that choice was equally hard as picking from good ideas, as so much rode on the actions and reactions of other people. *What if Reg was restrained? What if Laurens had already shot him? How would Laurens expect her to exit the water?* Every scenario called for a different play on her part. But the time was almost upon her, so AJ nervously prepared herself for what she considered being a course of action with a lousy chance of success… but at least *a* chance.

Torchlight blinded her eyes as she surfaced.

"Point that away from me, would you?" she complained.

Laurens moved the focus of the light to the water between AJ and the ladder on the *Beste Leven*.

"Do you have them?" he demanded.

"Where's Reg?" she asked, ignoring his question.

"I'm here," Reg grunted. "Tied up, but I'm fine."

"I want to see him," AJ said, finning to keep herself six feet away from the boat.

"I don't give a shit what you want," Laurens snapped. "Did you get them?"

"Turn on the lights over the helm so I can see Reg," AJ persisted.

"How about I shoot you and drag you in with the diamonds?"

AJ turned on her torch and aimed it at the pontoon boat. Laurens, who was standing by the helm station, covered his eyes.

"Turn that off!"

She saw Reg on a bench with his hands tied together. He picked up one foot to show her his legs weren't bound. AJ turned off the torch and held her clenched fist in the air. "Go for it. Pretty sure I'll drop all these pretty stones when you shoot me. But all you'll need to do is dive down and pluck them out of the sand. Doubt they'd be *that* hard to find. Oh, but you just got bent, so you can't dive at the moment, can you?"

Laurens swore in Dutch.

"By the way," AJ continued. "I know your former partner, De Konig, said the two guys made it to shore from the barge, but someone else didn't. I found a body under the wreck."

"Van der Meer..." Laurens muttered, sounding surprised. "I'll tell my grandmother. She'll be pleased he died a long time ago. Like he deserved."

"Your grandmother?" Reg quizzed. "Wait, the bloke who stole the diamonds was your grandfather?"

Laurens muttered more unsavoury words in Dutch and flicked on one of the lights above the helm, setting down his torch. He held the gun in his other hand. After the darkness, the soft light from the 12-volt bulb over the helm illuminated everything AJ needed to see, and was easier on her eyes than the bright torch.

"We need to come to some arrangement," she announced. "If I simply hand you the diamonds, you'll shoot us both."

"I assure you I won't," Laurens replied. "But I will start shooting kneecaps if you don't get on the boat. Now."

The man pointed the gun towards Reg, aiming at his legs.

"Alright, alright," AJ yelled. "Keep your hair on. You start shooting and I swear I'm chucking these diamonds in the water. Just calm down and we'll figure it out."

"Hand them to me," Laurens demanded.

AJ held the radius arm aloft in her other hand. "Half of them are still in here. I smeared the grease around to bring them up, but wiped it off to get a bunch of them out," she explained, waving her clenched fist once more. "I'll give you the radius arm, so we both have half, alright? Then we'll figure out a way to get you the other half so you can leave us out here while you toddle off. Sound good? You'll have all night to get away. It'll take us until dawn to swim to shore."

Laurens waved the gun at Reg. "Come over and take the arm from her."

"Bugger," AJ groaned to herself.

So much for plan A, which involved pulling Laurens into the water, based on her hope he'd be reluctant to let go of the radius arm once he had hold of it.

Reg stepped to the gap in the railing, and Laurens pressed the gun to the side of his head.

"Slow movements," Laurens ordered. "Now take the arm from her."

AJ finned closer to the pontoon until she was next to the ladder, bobbing up and down with the boat as the gentle swells rolled underneath them. She lifted the radius arm up and Reg gripped the other end awkwardly in one hand, his wrists tightly restrained with zip ties. He tried taking it from her, but she didn't let go, catching his eye. Reg returned a subtle nod, and she prayed they were thinking along the same lines.

Releasing her end of the radius arm, Reg bobbled his end, fumbling to catch it again.

"You idiot!" Laurens yelled, shuffling forward, which moved the gun away from the big man's temple as they both watched the arm hang in the air while Reg tried to regain a hold of it.

The noise from the saw was even louder when unmuffled by the water, but was soon drowned out by the scream from Laurens. AJ dragged the saw back and forth across the instep of his left foot with pieces of fabric, flesh, and blood spraying in a line across the deck. Reg regained his grip on the radius arm and punched the jagged end into Laurens' chest as the Dutchman was bringing the gun around towards AJ in the water. The gun went off as Laurens fell backwards, crashing into the helm as the manic hiss of compressed air escaping erupted from the water.

Reg quickly followed through, swinging the radius arm like a bat, catching Laurens across the nose as he lay crumpled on the deck. The aged and corroded steel tube buckled across the bridge of the man's nose, crushing the bone, and opening up a gash across his cheek. In an instant, Reg tossed the bent radius arm aside, scooped up the gun in his bound hands, and pointed it at Laurens, who clutched his shredded foot.

"You alright?" Reg shouted over the racket of hissing gas. "AJ?" he bellowed again when she didn't respond.

Wrestling with the valve on the first stage of the manifold, AJ finally silenced the escaping gas and looked up at her friend.

"What's that now?" she asked. "I couldn't hear you over that awful noise."

Reg shook his head. "I thought he'd hit you."

AJ held up the extra-long hose that had kept her breathing for multiple trips underneath the barge. It was almost severed in two where the bullet had hit it after narrowly missing AJ's neck and shoulder. "Close," she replied. "But you'll need to call Lamar and get another extra-long hose made up."

Reg allowed himself a grin. "Did you drop the diamonds?"

AJ shook her head. "Nah. They were up my sleeve the whole time. But I think I dropped one or two when I was getting them out of the arm on my deco stop in the dark."

"That'll bring a bevy of treasure hunters to Lighthouse Point chasing that legend," Reg said, managing a brief laugh.

"They can have the bloody things," AJ scoffed, finally scaling the ladder. "Diamonds aren't this girl's best friend. I'm done with the bloody things."

Laurens groaned even louder from the bloodied deck of the pontoon boat.

"Did I make an awful mess of his foot?" AJ asked, glad she'd stopped the guy, but now concerned she'd caused a permanent injury.

Reg laughed. "I don't think you should put manicurist on your resume anytime soon."

AJ wrinkled her nose when she saw the bloody mess on the deck.

"And you're still a silly bugger," Reg added. "But well done."

AFTERWORD

As with all the novels in the AJ Bailey series, I enjoy using real people, local businesses, and quite often historical events in the stories. Lighthouse Point is full of the above. Bryan from TDS was my instructor in my tech diving course, Cheryl and I stayed at the Sand Dollar resort for four months, and Dick indeed owns and runs Breeze 'n Bites. The barge wreck is fictional, but the ostrocod dive is more amazing than my words could possibly do justice. Our friends Cris and Kristi Hall gave us our first experience of the special dive, which we excitedly paid forward when fellow author, diver, and good friend, Nick Sullivan stayed with us for a week. The lovely and very successful author Tricia O'Malley and her husband Alan live on Bonaire, and shared meals, dives, and many laughs with us during our stay.

On the racing side, Lady Ashford and her team are figments of my imagination, as is the young and talented Miles Preston. Everything else involving the 1970 Grand Prix season is as it happened, with my characters dropped into the scenes. In some instances, I swapped them for the real players – Carlos's accident in Jarama happened as described, but to Jackie Oliver – but in most cases I simply added Miles into the mix. Colin Chapman created, owned, and ran Lotus, and throughout the 60s and 70s was an iconic personality in motor racing.

Piers Courage, Bruce McLaren, and Jochen Rindt all lost their lives during the 1970 Formula One season, as described. Remarkably, Rindt had accumulated enough points by Monza to keep the championship lead through the final four races to be the only posthumous Formula One World Champion. An unenviable statistic. I turned five years old in 1970, and Jochen Rindt was the first F1 driver I can remember cheering for. I was devastated when he lost his life.

Motor racing is embedded in my DNA. My dad raced saloon and sports cars in the 60s, driving cars he tuned or built himself. He hung up his helmet to raise his family, and established a long career as a highly respected race mechanic, spending many years in Formula One. My brother Michael and I were raised in a household which revolved around the Grand Prix calendar. We still have our autograph books we'd take to every race we went to, with the signatures of many of the heroes from the era. I left my own career in racing in 2019 to pursue my writing passion. My brother continues his accomplished career as a motorsports management consultant.

When I decided to include a motor racing storyline in one of my books, it was memories of my childhood, my hero Jochen Rindt, and my dad, which drew me to 1970. It was an emotionally charged and tragic year which impacted everyone who followed or was involved in racing at that time. I knew that if I wrote about the sport which had been the backbone of my life, it would be a challenging and intense experience. I wanted to put the reader in the driving seat with Carlos and Miles, to feel the tactile sensations a race car driver uses to control the car at alarming speeds, and understand the precision and skill involved.

I'm sure it will come as no surprise for me to say that this story means a great deal to me personally, and I truly hope it was informative, emotional, and gratifying for you as the reader.

ACKNOWLEDGMENTS

My sincere thanks to:

My incredible wife Cheryl, for her unwavering support, love, and encouragement.

My family and friends for their patience and understanding.

These wonderful folks for their help with the story, technical details, and/or agreeing to be used in a fiction manner in the novel:
Bryan Skiba-Crafts and Technical Diving Services, Bonaire who patiently instructed me in my tech diving course!
Lamar and Lee Ann Hires, the wonderful owners of Dive Rite.
My author friend and Bonaire resident, Tricia O'Malley and her husband, Alan Burness.
Dick and Valorie (Vely) at Breeze 'n Bites. Cheryl and I spent plenty of time at the bar!
Devron Coday, who won the 'name in book' contest at the 2023 AJ Bailey Dive Adventure event and insisted his lovely friend Jo Buckiewicz Barendse be the name used!

My editor Andrew Chapman at Prepare to Publish. I really challenged him this time with all the tech diving and racing jargon.
My advanced reader copy (ARC) group, whose input and feedback is invaluable. They had their work cut out on this one too, and came through with great feedback as usual.

The Tropical Authors group for their magnificent support and collaboration. Check out the website for other great authors in the Sea Adventure genre.

Shearwater dive computers, whose products I proudly use. Reef Smart Guides whose maps and guidebooks I would be lost without – sometimes literally. My friends at Cayman Spirits for their amazing Seven Fathoms rum… which I'm convinced I could not live without!

Above all, I thank you, the readers: none of this happens without the choice you make to spend your precious time with AJ and her stories. I am truly in your debt.

LET'S STAY IN TOUCH!

To buy merchandise, find more info or join my Newsletter, visit my website at
www.HarveyBooks.com

Visit Amazon.com for more books in the
AJ Bailey Adventure Series,
Nora Sommer Caribbean Suspense Series,
and collaborative works;
The Greene Wolfe Thriller Series
Tropical Authors Adventure Series

If you enjoyed this novel I'd be incredibly grateful if you'd consider leaving a review on Amazon.com
Find eBook deals and follow me on BookBub.com

Catch my podcast, The Two Authors' Chat Show with co-host Douglas Pratt.

Find more great authors in the genre at TropicalAuthors.com

ABOUT THE AUTHOR

A *USA Today* Bestselling author, Nicholas Harvey's life has been anything but ordinary. Race car driver, adventurer, divemaster, and since 2020, a full-time novelist. Raised in England, Nick has dual US and British citizenship and now lives wherever he and his amazing wife, Cheryl, park their motorhome, or an aeroplane takes them. Warm oceans and tall mountains are their favourite places.

For more information, visit his website at HarveyBooks.com.

Made in United States
Orlando, FL
14 March 2024

44785409R00161